Heatherly Bell tackled her first book in 2004 and now the characters that occupy her mind refuse to leave until she writes them a book. She loves all music but confines singing to the shower these days. Heatherly lives in Northern California with her family, including two beagles—one who can say hello and the other a princess who can feel a pea through several pillows.

Books by Heatherly Bell

HARLEQUIN SUPERROMANCE

Heroes of Fortune Valley

Breaking Emily's Rules
Airman to the Rescue
This Baby Business

Other titles by Heatherly Bell are available in ebook format.

D0009291

For Aliyah

CHAPTER ONE

LEVI LAMBERT HAD piloted many birds during his service in the United States Air Force. He'd gone on missions he still regretted and some he never would. Made plenty of mistakes in his twenty-nine years. Some of them irreparable.

But this. Well. This might just kill him.

"Please. Please go to sleep." Levi gently rubbed his six-month-old daughter's back.

Moonlight spilled through the cracked blinds in Grace's bedroom. It was two o'clock in the morning, and she wasn't interested in sleeping. She didn't need her diaper changed, had just had a bottle of formula—warm…he'd checked—and he'd located her pacifier under the blanket and stuck it in her mouth. She spit it out with a face that said, "Nice try, sucker."

Levi was no stranger to zero dark thirty, but this was plain cruel. No sooner had he calmed her down and gently set her in her crib than she screamed bloody murder again. A few nights of that would have been fine, but after six straight weeks of it, he was beginning to feel the strain.

Strange, but the only thing that kept her quiet was being held. Held and walked around the house, as if it were the middle of the day.

Weren't babies supposed to sleep 24/7? What was wrong with his baby? She didn't seem to like him very much. Still, he'd known she was his the minute he'd seen her blue eyes, so much like his own. Just for kicks he'd asked for a DNA test. Yep. His. No doubt, even if he'd had the pleasure of being with Grace's mother, Sandy, only once. Only one night of mutual, temporary pleasure during a two-week leave in Atlanta, Georgia, he'd now officially never forget.

When he'd received the news of Sandy's accidental death, it had taken Levi a minute to remember her. Talk about life changing and re-arranging. He'd assumed he would die in the air force. His plan was to stay until he retired or was killed in action. It wasn't like he didn't have friends who'd left earlier than planned, among them his two best friends in the world, Stone and Matt. But Levi was a lifer. Supposed to be, anyway. He'd been raised for service. Until Grace had come along and changed all that. It would have been too much of a hardship as a single father piloting long missions. At the time he'd been located and informed of Grace, he'd been flying the U-2 spy plane and gone for months at a stretch.

She'd quieted down again with his swaying

and rocking, so Levi tried to lay her down in her crib. Grace scrunched up her little pixie face and wailed, as if the very idea that she would go to sleep was an insult to her intelligence. He picked her up again. Definitely not suited for this, although some people had thought it would happen to him eventually if he didn't settle down and stop sowing his wild oats.

The first thing his mother, Gemma Lambert, had said upon hearing that Levi had become a father was "Bless your heart. I told you so." His father, retired General Lambert, had decided to address the situation in his usual way: he ignored it. Easy to do, since both of his parents were on their latest mission trip to save the children of the world. Didn't matter, though, because Levi could do this on his own. Like he'd done so much else in his life.

Grace was now his responsibility, and he never shirked his duty. He'd followed the work, and one of his friends, Stone Mcallister, had a charter flight business and aviation school in Fortune, California. So he'd wound up in this little Podunk, bedroom community deep in the bowels of Silicon Valley. Everyone here gave him a patient look the minute he opened his mouth and out came the Texan drawl he'd grown up with.

Levi took a seat on the rocking chair he'd purchased from Buy, Baby, Buy—bye, wallet, bye, it should be called—and tried again. He'd been given most of Grace's baby stuff by Sandy's father, Frank, and stepmother, Irene, in a tearful exchange at the airport in Atlanta. It had helped, since he didn't actually know a stroller from a wheelbarrow. A rookie, he'd basically had a crash course in all things baby related for the past few weeks. He realized he'd never be father-of-the-year material, but still, this shouldn't be so hard.

"Is this personal?" he now asked Grace.

She had no response other than to blink twice and gurgle. Yeah, just his luck. She was wide-awake. At least it was better than all the screaming. Levi rocked because he didn't know what else to do. He'd never thought of himself as a daddy. When he'd first told Stone and Matt about his situation, you would have thought he'd dropped a missile on them for the absolute silence in the room.

Levi was grateful that Sandy had trusted him. Or maybe she'd just done the right thing. Either way, he'd been named the father on the birth certificate. He had a daughter, and he couldn't regret it. At least, not since the moment the social worker placed Grace in his arms, and she focused her wide, blue eyes on him. He was determined to raise her as a single father, even if Sandy's parents had other ideas.

He stifled a yawn. The rocking chair was damned well about to put *him* to sleep. He'd have to get up in a few hours and Grace looked no closer to closing her eyes than she had an hour ago.

"I'm just going to close my eyes for a minute." He snuggled Grace closer to his chest and leaned his head back.

LEVI WOKE WITH a start. It was morning, the first rays of early autumn sunlight flooding throughout Grace's bedroom. She was fast asleep. He'd fallen asleep with her in his arms and by some miracle she hadn't slipped out and landed on the floor.

"Are you a vampire?" he whispered, laying her in the crib. "Please don't be a baby vampire."

This time, of course, she stayed asleep. But Levi would still be late if he didn't kick it into high gear. He took an enlisted man's shower and dressed in the Mcallister Charters uniform of a white button-up and black cargoes within minutes. He hurried through his usual morning routine, prepping formula bottles like a pro and swallowing a Pop-Tart practically whole. He inhaled his morning coffee and glanced at the digital kitchen clock. Oh seven hundred and Annie wasn't here. He hated being late and people who were late. And Annie was perpetually late.

She was his third babysitter since he'd landed in Fortune a month ago. Bobbie Ann had left when Levi had turned her down, explaining he didn't date anyone under twenty. Ellen had left because of all the screaming, and Annie's only fault so far was her unreliability. Which, given the situation, was huge.

He looked out the window. Nothing. Dialed Annie's cell phone, hoping she'd be driving over and unable to answer it.

She answered. "Hey, Levi. I can't make it today."

"Why didn't you call me?"

He should have never hired one of the former baristas from the Drip. Even if she'd come highly recommended by Emily Parker as being a generally kind woman who wouldn't hurt a fly.

"I had a little trouble with the reception out here in Lake Tahoe."

"What the hell are you doing in Lake Tahoe?"

Levi heard a distinctly male voice in the background.

"Oh, sorry. I meant Reno. I'm all turned around." She giggled. "I'm getting married."

"Getting *married*? Since when?"

"Since Drew asked me last night. I'm sorry, but I forgot to call you."

Yep. Never should have hired her. "Great. Now what am I supposed to do about Grace?"

"I'm sorry. But hey, why don't you ask your next-door neighbor? I'm sure she would do it."

"You mean Cute Stuck-Up Girl?"

"Her name is Carly. I know her personally, so I'll vouch for her. We used to work together, and then her mother died and left her a business. I hardly see her anymore she's so busy, but I did see her last week when I was taking Grace for a walk. She came out to get a package and waved hello."

Levi glanced out the window, and there was Cute Stuck-Up Girl, bending down to pick up another UPS package. About the only times he'd seen her she was either signing for a package or hauling diapers into the house by the box. A couple weeks ago, she'd glanced in his direction. He'd smiled and nodded. She'd looked right through him. Hence the stuck-up part.

"You think she'd do it?" He glanced at his watch. If he didn't want to miss his flight this morning and risk looking like a damned fool who couldn't handle both work and being a father, he'd have to leave in fifteen minutes.

"Carly is supersweet. I'm sure she would help you out for the day."

"And after that?"

"Again, I'm sorry. But I'm getting married, and you really don't pay me enough anyway."

"Might have said something sooner."

He was going to have to get a handle on this sitter business. Next time hire someone highly qualified and serious about the job, not just someone between gigs. Levi hung up and glanced at his watch.

"Okay. Plan B."

A few minutes later, Levi had carefully and skillfully moved a sound-asleep Grace from her crib to her car seat. When the girl slept, she meant it. Too bad she couldn't mean it at two in the morning. He carried the car seat by the handle to Cute Stuck-Up Girl's front door. Probably should start calling her Carly from now on.

"Wish me luck," he said under his breath. "Just keep right on being adorable. And quiet."

Grace continued to snooze. He rang the doorbell. Once. Twice.

Levi was about to abort mission and launch into plan C when the door flew open. Cute—uh, Carly—stood behind it, blond hair sticking up in four different directions. She wore yoga pants, a pink-and-white Minnie Mouse T-shirt that fell past her hips and fuzzy slippers in the shape of the Tasmanian Devil. He tried not to laugh.

"You're not the UPS guy."

"No. Sorry." She was a lot prettier up close. Her eyes were amber, warm, with tiny flecks of green in them.

Those eyes took him in, doing fast work of assessing. When she fixated on the car seat, she did a double take. "What's that?"

Huh. Not too promising. He forced a grin and a wink and tried to relax, because he had approximately twelve minutes left to work his magic. "A baby. Ever seen one before?"

"I know what a baby is." Her eyes narrowed, and she pointed. "Is that *your* baby?"

He was beginning to resent the way no one believed he could be a father. "Yep. Mine."

She folded her arms over her chest. "Oh, I see. You must have heard about me, then. But all the advice is on my website. I'm thinking about adding Skype chats, but you're a little early for that."

"Excuse me?"

"Isn't that why you're here? You'd like some advice? Is she not sleeping through the night? Colic? Do you want to know the best diaper to use?"

He cleared his throat, because damned if he couldn't use all of that and then some.

"No. I'm fine. Okay, let's start over. I'm Levi Lambert, your next-door neighbor." He stuck out his hand and shook hers.

"Carly Gilmore."

"I'm in a bind this morning. My sitter, Annie, well, she ran off and got married yesterday and forgot to tell me about it. So…she's not coming."

"Annie. Yeah. That was not a wise choice."

"You're telling me. I'm new in town, and one of my friends recommended her."

"Yes, she's sweet but unreliable." She shook her head. "I'm not sure how I can help you."

A little worried that his cute neighbor might have been dropped on her head as a baby, and not encouraged by that possible fact, Levi took a deep breath. "Could you maybe just fill in for her today? I'm a pilot at Mcallister Charters, and I'm about to be late for a flight."

"Me? You want *me* to watch your baby?"

"Don't you hand out baby advice? So you have children, right?"

She had a ring on her finger, but that didn't mean she had children.

At this, she went a little pale, then gave him a tight smile. "I...I know a lot about babies, yes, of course. I'm what you would call an expert."

"Wow. This is my lucky day. If you could watch Grace just for a while, I'd be so grateful. I'll try to come home early, too, right after my flight, if I can arrange it."

"B-but where's her mother?"

Levi always hated this part, and the pity that flashed across people's faces. He didn't want or deserve their pity. "She passed away."

Cute Carly drew in a sharp breath, and sympathy flashed in her eyes right on cue. "I'm so sorry."

"Thank you. It's just the two of us."

She shifted from one leg to the other. "Well, okay. I can help you, since I'm a baby expert and all. Plus, I don't want you to think that I'm not neighborly, because I am. But just today!"

Levi let his shoulders unkink and carried Grace's car seat inside. He set it down on the hardwood floor of the entryway and handed her the diaper bag he'd packed.

"Thanks. I owe you one."

"Here." She handed him a scrap of paper and a pen. "Write down your phone number so I can reach you."

He gave her his cell phone number and also the number for Mcallister Charters and Magnum Aviation. And the local hospital. And poison control. He had all of them memorized. He also got Carly's phone number, then with one last kiss on Grace's sweet forehead, he headed out the door.

Levi climbed in his truck, where he studied his neighbor's house for a moment. Like his rental, it was a small tract home. Unlike his house, she had rows of colorful flowers lining the front yard and several others in pots hanging from the eaves. Fit right in with this older residential neighborhood. He made a mental note that he should probably buy some of them flowers at some point if he was going to stay in the rental. Grace should grow up in a home that reflected some kind of femininity. Not that she wouldn't play sports with the boys if that was what she wanted, and of course he prayed that she did, because he could help her with that.

Should he go back and get his baby and rethink this whole thing? He tended to reconsider every one of his decisions thanks to Sandy's parents. One false move on his part, one mistake, and he might give them ammunition. The last thing he wanted was a long, protracted legal battle he couldn't afford.

But the warmth in Carly's eyes when she'd heard about Grace's mother told him she was compassionate. Kind. Maybe he'd assumed too much and far too easily, but he had a good sense of people, and it hadn't failed him yet. No. This was good.

He started his truck and headed to the airport.

CHAPTER TWO

FROM A SHORT DISTANCE, Carly Gilmore had definitely *noticed* her new neighbor. Once when she'd had the day from hell. But up close and personal, the way he'd been on her doorstep this morning, he was a blend of tall and rugged, with a bad-boy charm that scrambled with her brain. He had deep and dark blue eyes that promised the fun kind of trouble, sun-kissed dark blond hair and a cleft in his chin that made him ridiculously gorgeous. She was grateful for a small scar through his left eyebrow that at least kept him from being prettier than her.

She'd done a double take on the baby because, really? Some woman had tamed this dude and made him a father. Which proved, as one of her best friends, Zoey, believed, that miracles happened every day. They just didn't happen for Carly.

But what kind of a father left his precious baby with a complete stranger?

Answer: one like her neighbor Levi Lambert, who had probably rarely heard the word *no* coming out of a woman's mouth. He'd so easily trusted her on the whole baby-expert thing. An exaggeration on her part, of course, but she was trying. That counted for something. His timing couldn't be better. She'd say that for him. Today, of all days, she could use his baby.

"You're a good sleeper." Carly carried the car seat and diaper bag into the kitchen.

The poor, motherless child.

Normally, hearing of such a sad situation, Carly would shed tears on a dime. But these days, she was all cried out. She bent down to get a better look at Grace. This must be the baby she'd seen Annie pushing last week in the newest Koolbaby stroller on the market. But until now she'd never had a good look at the baby. Her lashes were long and beautifully dark, and she had her father's dark blonde hair. Did she also have his beautiful dark blue eyes?

"Your daddy is quite the looker," Carly said quietly.

He had one of those rare and one hundred percent real Southern drawls that turned most women into limp noodles. Good thing Carly would not be one of them. She found the formula bottles he'd packed in the diaper bag and put them in the fridge. He owned some of the nicer baby bottles made by Just Like Mommy, the ones with the nipple that was supposed to most correctly re-semble a human one. She'd given it a high rating last month on the blog and pretty much guessed at the efficacy. Maybe she'd ask Levi later, if she could ever bring herself to ask a man like him whether his baby liked the nipple. She shook her head. Nope, not going to ask him. She'd see how Grace liked it when she gave her a bottle later.

This TotLuv diaper bag was also a good choice, one she'd given a five-star rating to, leading her to wonder if someone had chosen these items based on her blog's recommendations. It gave her a little dash of hope. Maybe, just maybe, her late mother's dream wasn't going to go down in flames with Carly at the helm.

A year ago, after Pearl had passed away, it seemed she would take her company with her. She'd built RockYourBaby.com from the ground up, a labor of love based on raising three children. Pearl had been the true baby expert. Her mother was the one who belonged at the helm of RockYourBaby.com, and Carly was merely the impostor.

Impostor or not, she now operated the company until they could sell it, because no one else wanted to run the company. Her father, who had retired from PG&E, had broken his hip and now lived in Maine with her oldest brother, Kirk, a civil engineer. The physical therapy bills were through the roof, Daddy wasn't getting any better, and among the many reasons to sell the company, one was to help pay for his treatment. Her other brother, Allen, was a lawyer in Tempe, Arizona, and since Carly was the only one with double X chromosomes, her brothers left it to her to salvage the business and restore it to what it had been before their mother died so they could sell it for a tidy profit.

Carly's laptop rang. *"Shh."*

She picked Grace up by the car seat handle and carried the seat closer to her office—otherwise known as the kitchen table. She settled Grace on the floor near the entrance of the kitchen and flew to the laptop to stop the ringing before it woke her up.

"Hello? Carly?" Jill, her other best friend, had taken to Skyping Carly from locations on the outskirts of town. The reception wasn't always the best.

Carly sat and turned to face the laptop camera. "I'm here."

"What's with your hair today?" Jill looked sideways through the screen.

Crap, was that what she looked like? And she'd answered the door to Mr. Hunk like this?

"I've had a rough morning." Carly smoothed her hair down into place and reached for her hair clip.

She hadn't even dressed. Last night she'd gone through the closet full of eBay fashion steals she'd accumulated over the years and set out her clothes for the next morning. She'd done that ritual every day for years. Her ribbed sweetheart-neck Urban Outfitters minidress paired with a cropped denim jacket and her Marc Jacobs Chelsea booties had been all ready for her this morning. But she'd taken one look at the supercute outfit and didn't have the energy. What for, when she would be sitting in front of a laptop most of the day?

Jill's face moved away from the screen and scanned her outdoor surroundings. "This could be the perfect location. It's even got a little boat dock by the lake. Sure, it needs a little work, but the owner is motivated."

A little work? Carly squinted. The boat *dock* seemed to be a wooden plank.

"Maybe you should keep looking."

"I'm meeting with the owner later today. It couldn't hurt. I hear they're desperate."

Sounded familiar.

Soon both of her best friends would be firmly entrenched in pursuing their lofty dreams. Jill with her long-held dream to restore an outdated inn, and Zoey as the owner and operator of Pimp Your Pet. They were both moving forward with their lives and dreams, while Carly was stuck. RockYourBaby.com was definitely *not* the best use of her fashion design degree.

She would never be able to move on to her own future if she didn't sell and get out from under RockYourBaby.com. But they kept losing sponsors, the real bread and butter of her mom's company. Carly feared she had a tiny authenticity problem. Namely, the entire RockYourBaby brand was now a bald-faced lie. She was at the helm of a company with a brand that was trusted and regarded for baby knowledge.

Ideally, she needed to create an image that would resonate with the RockYourBaby audience. Then they might be able to sell to a larger company. Carly had already decided she'd give most of her share of the money from the sale to Kirk, to help care for their father. Their dad, Jerry, needed almost constant care these days. Therapy and medications were not cheap, and health insurance helped with only a small part of it. The sooner she could get this company's value up and sold, the quicker her father could get adequate care.

No pressure.

"I say you keep looking."

Grace squirmed. She opened up wide blue eyes and blinked a couple of times. Uh-oh. The thing was awake now.

Jill's face appeared on the monitor again. "And how are you doing? What did your mom's accountant suggest?"

Carly didn't want to talk about it. Patsy had suggested it was all a matter of perception and it occurred at every major firm when there was a change at the helm. RockYourBaby.com was simply no longer relevant.

Ouch.

Still, the suggestion was that though they'd lost some footing in the market, recovery was feasible. Her mother had created a solid brand. In other words, all was not lost. Yet.

Grace let out a piercing wail, and Carly stood and walked out of the camera's view to unbuckle the baby from her seat. She picked her up carefully, like she was fine china, and carried her to the table slowly so neither one of them would fall.

"What was that?" Jill was saying. "Did you get a cat?"

"Sorry." Carly propped Grace on her lap and resumed the Skype chat.

Jill stared, jaw dropped. "Um? Care to explain? What are you doing with a *baby*?"

"Oh, this is my neighbor's baby. Grace. His sitter cancelled last minute, so he came over and begged me to watch her for a day. Can you believe it? He doesn't even *know* me. Rookie dad."

"What are you thinking, offering to babysit? Like you don't have enough to do."

"First, I didn't offer. He asked. And I'll be able to finish my blog post with some real honest research and not just the Watch-Me-Tinkle baby doll."

"This is not your brightest idea. You should stick with the dolls."

"That's not real research. I need to own this baby-expert thing."

"Well, I hate to be the one to tell you this, but that baby is about to blow. She's puckering up for a good, loud scream."

Carly turned Grace so she could see her face. Sure enough, she had a stiff bottom lip and her tiny, angelic sleeping face had turned a frightening shade of mauve. She took one look at Carly and out came an earsplitting wail.

"Oh, no!" Carly stood up with her. "How did you know?"

"I worked as an au pair the year I lived abroad," Jill shouted. "I don't remember much, but I know that look."

"What do I do now? Help me!"

"In order to really help, I'd have to rewind to the minute you agreed to help Hot Dad out!"

"How do you know he's hot?" Carly swayed and rocked with Grace on her hip. She didn't know if that would help, but it felt like the right thing to do.

"Just a guess."

Grace continued to screech, a wild and guttural sound that scared Carly. Grace's mouth was wide-open, so Carly could see down to her tonsils, and she was sure they were vibrating. Was that even normal? What if she was hurt? She'd never forgive herself!

"Okay. I've got to go. I'll call you later."

"No! Wait." Carly danced back to her monitor. "Are vibrating tonsils a thing?"

"I can't hear you." And then Jill, Carly's one connection to the outside world, was gone.

Gah!

Carly searched through Levi's diaper bag one-handed, silently praying he wasn't one of those parents that thought pacifiers were the devil. She found one, thank God, and stuck it in Grace's mouth. She promptly spit it out.

Why did Grace have to be one of the babies who didn't like pacifiers?

"Please stop crying, little baby. Oh, please." Carly danced around the kitchen, but that did absolutely nothing except perhaps burn a few extra calories. "Maybe you're hungry. Yes! Why didn't I think of that?"

How could such a little thing let out a scream worthy of the lead singer in a hard-core metal band? How could her lungs be big enough?

Carly reached for a baby bottle from the fridge. Let's see. She remembered reading about this in her mother's baby bible before she'd done a blog post on "Bottle or Breast? Which Way Is Best?" Of course, in a million years she hadn't implied that a mother should do it one way or another. No idiot, just like Mom, Carly vowed to stay clear of titty politics. She'd simply listed options. The bottle way was to warm one in a pan of hot water. No microwaves!

Time slowed to a snail's pace as she filled a pan of water and waited for it to simmer, then stuck the bottle in, while simultaneously holding a baby who was screaming so loudly Carly wondered if she'd ever regain her hearing in the left ear. She did all of this while dancing and swaying and begging. But Grace seemed immune to all the begging.

"You looked so sweet and innocent when you were asleep," Carly said, near tears herself. "Your daddy fooled me."

Carly tested the baby bottle on her wrist. At this point she'd settle for anything between arctic cold and the fires of hell and damnation. Good enough. She settled on a kitchen chair and offered Grace the bottle. She latched on to it like Carly would the last dress on clearance at Saks Fifth Avenue. Carly threw her head back in relief and sighed. Finally, blessed silence, other than the sucking sounds of Grace and her bottle. Amazing how much Carly had taken silence for granted. She never would again.

"Yes, that's all it was. You were hungry. Sorry, I shouldn't have been so slow, but I was lying about being a baby expert."

Lying had started to come so easily these days, but that was what happened when you were pretending to be someone else.

Or maybe it was what happened when you'd forgotten who you were.

Boy, Grace was sucking down this bottle of milk in a New York minute. Carly tensed, worried the silence would be over soon. And sure enough, Grace was eyeing Carly as she drank her milk, no doubt making plans to unleash the hounds of hell on Carly when she finished the important business of eating.

"Listen, this isn't my fault. Your daddy was in a bind. Please don't hate me."

Grace got to the end of the bottle, first sucking down the last dregs and then just air. Carly didn't know much, but that couldn't be good. She gently pulled the bottle away from Grace. She reacted by sticking out her bottom lip, scrunching up her pixie face and letting go a wail worthy of a wounded animal.

And Carly was back to swaying, rocking and begging.

Mostly begging.

CHAPTER THREE

"THANK YOU FOR flying with Mcallister Charters," Levi said to the businessmen he'd picked up in Las Vegas and transported to Fortune.

He glanced at his phone. No messages or missed calls, and no news would always be good news in his book. Still, he wanted to check in with Cute Girl and make sure everything was cool with Grace. It was true that she slept on and off most of the day, but her crying had been enough to drive one nanny away. He stayed seated in the plane as his passengers walked across the tarmac toward the hangar.

Carly answered on the fourth or fifth ring. "Hello?"

"Hey. How's it going? How's my baby girl?"

"Okay. She's very sweet, but, um, she cries a lot. Does she do that with you?"

"Yeah. What's she doing right now?"

"She's taking a nap."

She did some of that during the day in between all the screaming. "Good. I had hoped she wouldn't be too much trouble for you."

"Well…no, she's fine. So cute."

Was that hesitancy in her voice? "Is it okay, then, if I stay until my shift is over?"

"Of course. You take your time. I'll be here."

Levi hung up, pretty proud of his baby girl converting Cute Stuck-Up Girl into a fan, and strode inside the hangar. He checked email from his phone.

Another message from Sandy's father, Frank, saying that, no, they couldn't come to see Grace in California. Did he have any idea how expensive plane tickets were to people who were not pilots? Why didn't he just fly himself to Atlanta and stay with them for a few weeks? They wanted to see Grace. He fired off another email explaining that he was a working man and couldn't take that much time off.

One thing appeared to be certain—they'd never be happy until he handed Grace over to them.

He headed toward Magnum Aviation's offices to check in with Cassie. The older woman pretty much ran the show around here, even if she kept threatening to retire. She'd worked for Stone's late father and had stayed on the past few months to ease the transition. Levi guessed it was a consequence of this being a small, south county airport, but it did seem as though there were an awful lot of relatives working it.

Emily Parker was Stone's fiancée and one of their regular pilots. Sarah, Stone's sister and part

owner of the business, was a local artist who occasionally worked at the Short Stop Snack Shack.
She also happened to be engaged to Matt Conner, one of Levi's best buddies from the air force
and also a pilot on staff. So if it seemed that there
were about two degrees of separation from Stone
and half of the people who worked for him, Levi
would not be wrong. Basically, he, Jedd Taylor,
the mechanic, and Cassie were the odd ones out.
They should form a club.

"Hello, darlin'," Levi said as he approached
Cassie.

"Hi, cowboy," Cassie said with a wink. "How's
that precious baby girl this morning?"

He rested a hip against her desk. "It's not the
mornin' that's the problem. It's the middle of the
night."

"Ah, she's still not sleeping through the night?"

"Any advice for me?"

"Well, it's like that advice they give to parents
about sibling rivalry. You know the best way to
avoid it?"

This was not his problem, and the way things
were going with his love life, Grace would never
have a chance at a sibling. "Tell me."

"Have one kid. So if you'd like your baby
to sleep through the night? Fast-forward a few
years."

"Aw, hell's bells. Not helpful. And I'm going
to need me a new sitter, too."

"What happened?" Emily asked as she walked out of Stone's office.

"Annie got married. She called me from Reno this morning."

Emily slapped a file on Cassie's desk. "What? No heads-up or anything?"

"What did you do with Grace?" Cassie asked, a little squeak in her voice.

He stuffed his hands in his pockets. "I left her with my next-door neighbor."

"Carly, I hope." Cassie nodded.

"Yeah. How'd you know?"

"I know everything," Cassie said.

It didn't surprise Levi much, since Cassie was pretty much the senior-citizen oracle of Fortune, California.

"I was in a bind. Annie quit on me, no notice." Levi relaxed and took a seat near Cassie's desk. "I have a good sense about people. She's obviously got a few rug rats of her own running around. Said she's an expert."

"Um, not exactly," Emily said, coming around to her desk.

"What's that supposed to mean? She *lied* to me?" His spine stiffened. If she'd lied, he'd have to get out of here now and go pick up Grace. He did not deal with liars. Period.

"I doubt she *lied* to you. Her mother died last year and left the family a baby company, and

Carly's running the show now. So that's probably what she meant by she's an expert," Cassie said.

She'd never said she had children of her own. He'd just assumed, and she hadn't corrected him. Not quite the same as lying, but he still didn't like it. Maybe sleep deprivation had his senses off-kilter. Wouldn't surprise him any.

"This time I suggest you take a little more time finding a sitter." Cassie frowned in his direction. "You need someone who has the time to do it. Someone like Carly, reliable and dependable, but with the extra time to give attention to a baby."

He shrugged. "Annie said I didn't pay her enough, but I was paying all I could afford."

When the landlord had told him how much he wanted for rent, Levi had thought the man was kidding. Levi had made a joke about the Kardashians, which the landlord hadn't found funny. Levi hadn't thought it funny, either, once he'd realized the rent figure was actually considered a deal for the area. Back home in Lubbock, he'd have land at those prices. But he had steady work and benefits as a pilot in Fortune, and Stone had promised him a raise as soon as possible.

"Sandy's parents still want me to bring Grace back to Atlanta. I don't want to give them any reason to think I can't handle raising her and working."

"Millions of women and men do it every day. Why can't you?" Emily said.

"Exactly."

While he'd like to believe he had nothing to worry about with the Lanes, nothing in life was one hundred percent certain. Least of all when it involved people and their emotions. Not everyone had mastered mind over matter. Sandy's parents, for one. They were somewhat hysterical people who were still operating from raw emotion. He'd tried to be understanding, given that they'd lost their daughter. But while he was sure they understood that Sandy's death had nothing to do with him, he'd become a convenient scapegoat for their pain. He got an email from Frank Lane every day, and they were never kind.

As far as Levi was concerned, he would raise Grace on his own. It didn't matter where. At the moment it happened to be in the small town of Fortune, where he had a good job and a community of friends. But he'd go where he had to go in order to make ends meet. To create a life that worked. No need to get sentimental and emotional about one particular place when there were so many all over the country. If there was one thing he'd learned in the summers he'd spent with his grandfather on his ranch while his parents were traipsing all over the world, it was to rely on himself.

For now, he'd stay in Fortune. It was what he told himself every time his boots got too itchy about the idea of settling down in one place for too long. The stability of a small town would be good for Grace. With the Sierra Nevada Mountains and snow just hours away, the beach a forty-five-minute drive and San Francisco only an hour away, both location and weather were near perfect. And despite being south of the larger Silicon Valley, he'd found a small community of like-minded people here, in a place where he could see himself raising Grace.

A few hours and flights later, Levi headed home to Grace. This had already become his routine, and it had become comfortable. On some mornings, he smelled garlic wafting from the closest town, the garlic capital of the world. He drove down Monterey Road toward his residential development on the other end of Fortune. When he'd landed here weeks ago, he'd discovered a three-stoplight town. A bedroom community just south of San Jose. Even so, here in Fortune, Levi had immediately noticed a strong sense of community, reminiscent of a small town.

It was no Lubbock, even though there were still a few small mushroom farms hanging on for dear life. This was the mushroom capital of the world, after all. The smell of fertilizer didn't faze him at all. Instead, it was the high cost of living. The price of gasoline. The heart attack–inducing price tag on ownership of a single family home. He could go on, but why depress himself?

He definitely felt squeezed like an orange, but it wasn't as if he wasn't familiar with sacrifice. One way or another, he'd find a way to make it work.

CHAPTER FOUR

A THOUSAND OR so years later, Carly had changed Grace's diaper about five hundred times, give or take, and fed her all three bottles. Levi had better get his cute ass here on time, or someone was going to blow a gasket. At this point she really couldn't say whether it would be her or Grace. Possibly both.

Oh, yes, because Carly had cried at times right along with Grace. Turned out to be kind of cathartic. It had been a while since Carly had had a good cry. She'd always been guided and driven by her emotions, despite her attempts to think with her head and not her heart. She was a full-grown, twenty-six-year-old woman who'd always struggled in school, seen her career go up in flames, lost her mother from a sudden heart attack and had her father nearly confined to a wheelchair due to a hip injury. Carly considered herself a survivor. But today she'd been reduced to sobs because of a helpless baby.

As it turned out, Grace did sleep. Occasionally, that was, and only when the spirit moved her. It seemed to move her every half hour for about forty-five minutes, give or take. Carly had tried to get work done during that time, but she was so tense and exhausted that all she could do was sit and stare at the blank screen. Where to begin? *Practice safe sex. Don't have a baby until you're ready to be tortured by a fifteen-pound human with a set of lungs that should belong to a six-foot-three male.* But probably her audience wouldn't appreciate that. All of her readers were already stuck—correction, *blessed*—with babies.

Regardless, Carly had made it through the day, and she couldn't help believing she deserved an award for that. A badge or a trophy. Something. She'd certainly received an education. This baby business was so much harder than it appeared from a distance. Right now her living room looked as if someone had stood in the middle of the room and thrown everything she owned up in the air. She hadn't had a shower yet. She'd barely eaten any breakfast, much less lunch. In fact, she hadn't even managed to change out of the clothes she had on since this morning.

"When your daddy gets here, if he so much as thinks about judging me…I'll—I don't know what, but it won't be nice."

The good news was she'd narrowed down her favorite brand of diaper with Grace's help. The bad news? She still had to write the blog post, because they didn't write themselves. The fact that she'd struggled all her life with the written word, fighting and working around her dyslexia, meant that it would take her twice as long as it had ever taken her mom to write a simple blog post.

Interesting. Carly had dared to set Grace down on the activity blanket that a brand-new baby start-up had sent her for a review. She hadn't made a noise in about five seconds. Might be a record. She kept blinking as if she couldn't quite trust her eyes. She seemed fascinated by the plastic mirrors sewn to the blanket, as if she'd just found a friend she wasn't sure she liked or hated.

"I guess that makes two of us."

Carly wasn't sure that she liked Grace. She was way too loud, for one thing, and had the manners of a chimpanzee. Once today, she'd looked Carly straight in the eye and spit up all over her shirt. Carly thought for sure Grace had been aiming for her eye and missed. She'd been changed twice and now wore a red velvet dress that a new baby fashion company had sent Carly.

But Carly had learned something significant today when she'd pulled out Mom's baby bible during one of Grace's power naps and tried to get through some of the entries in it. Crying wouldn't hurt a baby. Grace would still be in one piece when her daddy came to pick her up.

And because Carly wasn't actually Grace's mother, just the babysitter, in a few minutes, her clueless dad would pick her up. Carly would be able to give her back. She'd take a shower, clean up her house, write her blog post and go to bed, where she would sleep without interruptions. She had an end in sight.

Maybe, just maybe, Grace could help her a little bit longer. Just until she got Mom's company in the black. Because Grace could go a long way toward solving her authenticity issue. She could turn Carly into a serious baby expert.

She wasn't sure Levi would be interested in her proposition, but why couldn't Carly just fill in until he found a new babysitter? She was right next door. Easy. And good grief, if Levi even went through half of what she'd been through today, he *needed* her help. She would suggest— no, demand—that he allow her, a bona fide baby expert (in training), to help him.

Incredible. It had to have been four whole minutes and Grace was still on her belly, blinking into the mirrors. She gurgled, reached out with her chubby hand and tried to grab it.

"You like that, don't you? It's something new. I think I'll give it a five-star review, since it's kept *you* quiet."

The doorbell rang.

Levi. Right on time. Great. Carly shot up from her chair, but she didn't know if she should take Grace with her to answer the door. What if something happened to her in the two seconds Carly would be out of the room? And what would Levi think? But if she picked Grace up now, she risked opening the door with her crying again. That also wouldn't look too good.

The doorbell rang again. Impatient man!

Carly picked Grace up off the blanket again like a delicate china plate, taking the blanket along.

"Please don't cry, baby. I need to make a good impression. You don't know this, but you and I could be partners. I know you don't like me, but to be fair, the feeling is mutual. You threw up on me and I know you were aiming for my eye. Don't even try to deny it."

So far not a peep from Grace, who had a piece of the blanket in her mouth and seemed to be gumming it. She was going to write a glowing review for this blanket and title it Lifesaver.

Carly opened the door to Levi, as suspected, and watched as his gaze went immediately to Grace. The way those blue eyes lit up gave Carly a little smackdown right in the chest, but then he noticed the dress.

"You changed her?"

"Do you like it?" When he didn't answer, she waved him inside. "It's a new dress and my gift to you both. And also, she spit up on two other outfits."

"Uh, thanks. And sorry. Welcome to my world."

Grace's little legs kicked and pumped double

time with some serious action at seeing Levi, and Carly handed her over.

"Hey, baby girl." His love-struck smile was quite a sight.

Carly cleared her throat and got ready to tell a big fat lie. "She was perfect today."

"Yeah?" Levi checked Grace out from head to toe as if to make sure she wasn't missing any parts.

Carly tried not to feel insulted. "Do you like the dress?"

"Sure, it's…nice."

"But?"

"Not too practical."

This was interesting information she could use, so she walked to the kitchen to get a pad of paper and pen from the counter. "So how would you rate it, say, on a scale of one to ten? If you were going to judge the dress, for instance?"

His eyes narrowed slightly. "I appreciate the dress. I'm not judging it."

"No, of course not. I…didn't mean to imply that."

She made a note on the pad of paper. *Appearance: ten out of ten. Practical use?* She needed Levi for that, because at the moment he had more experience with babies than Carly did. When it came to her own clothes and sense of fashion, Carly always erred on the side of appearance versus practicality. She'd once lost the feeling in her feet for a day because of a gorgeous pair of paisley-patterned five-inch-heeled Louis Vuitton boots, but it had been worth the agony.

She could see it would be different with a baby.

"It's just that she looks uncomfortable." He shifted her from one hip to the other.

"You're so right. There was something bothering me about the dress, but I couldn't quite put my finger on it."

Liar. She was completely useless. *Practical use: five out of ten. Six out of ten?* She didn't want to be unfair. "No one makes cute, stylish *and* comfortable clothes for babies, do they?"

"But…she really seems to like this blanket." He removed a corner of it from Grace's mouth and handed it to Carly.

If this all worked out, she would need the miracle worker again tomorrow.

Levi picked up the car seat and diaper bag from the foyer. "Thanks again. We should get going."

"Wait!"

She'd pretty much shouted the word, but rather than appear startled, he seemed slightly amused by her, his mouth twitching in a half smile. "Right. Sorry, I forgot to pay you." He set the car seat down and, impressively juggling Grace, pulled a wallet from his back pocket.

"No." She put out her hand to stop him. "Today was a freebie."

Slow down, you don't need to scare the man off. Take your time and do this right.

"Freebie?"

"How about… How about a drink of water before you go?"

"I'm just next door." Levi tucked his wallet away.

"This will only take a minute. How about a beer?" She led the way to the kitchen, hoping with any luck he'd follow.

He did. And stood in the framed opening of the kitchen entryway, holding Grace with an easy assurance she envied. Like a real pro. "Actually, do you know any babysitters you could recommend?"

Sometimes, when opportunity knocks, you shouldn't just open the door. Open the door, go make a pot of coffee and bake some cookies. Maybe it will stay awhile.

She swallowed and gave him what she hoped was her best, most dependable babysitter smile. "Me." She twisted off the top, then handed the beer to him.

He accepted it. "But you said just for today."

She waved a hand in the air, in a pay-no-attention-to-me-before-noon move. "That was before. Okay, here's the thing. I can help you, and let's be honest here, you *need* me."

He studied Carly, took a swig of his beer, but didn't say a word. Maybe Rookie Daddy had finally wised up and decided he shouldn't leave his baby with a complete stranger. He got points for that.

Carly chose her next words carefully. "I kind of have this baby advice website."

"I heard."

Of course. If he worked at the airport, he worked with Cassie. And Cassie was an old friend of the family. Carly let out a breath. "I'm running the baby website RockYourBaby, but I don't have any kids of my own."

"Heard that, too." He quirked an eyebrow, and in that single move Carly realized he was less than thrilled with the fact that she hadn't come out with the whole truth this morning.

But she hadn't exactly lied. What did her mom's accountant say? Emphasize the positive, ignore the negative. Sell it! "But I'm still a baby expert."

"Uh-huh." He didn't sound too convinced.

"Look, all I'm saying is that I can watch Grace until you find a new sitter. If you're not sure about me, I'd be happy to give you references. I've lived here in Fortune all my life, and I'm extremely reliable. I'm always home. Besides, I'm right next door."

"And how will you watch her and run your company?"

This suddenly felt like an interview, and she wished she'd prepared better. She'd done too much assuming that Levi would immediately

take her up on this idea. But she'd become better at selling in the past few months, out of sheer
necessity. If she told a little white lie every now
and again, no one was the wiser.

Balance. It was all about balance. She'd do it as
mothers all over the country did. Like the readers
of her blog did. Like her mother had.

"I can handle her. I'm great at time manage-
ment." Boy, the lies kept coming, didn't they?
Getting easier, too. "And also, Grace— and babies
everywhere, in fact—happens to be a big part
of my career. Because babies are my business."

She did a chin lift on that one, as she'd noticed
Jill do on a number of occasions when she wanted
to make the point that she was hot shit.

Levi seemed to notice and maybe even appreciate the new confidence. His shoulders lowered,
and he gave her another one of those slow, sexy
smiles. "It would be a big help to me. I'm out of
the air force recently. Originally from Texas."

Hence the drawl. She pictured hot and humid
plains, oil, ranches and cowboys. Levi didn't look
like a cowboy, even if he sort of sounded like one.
And something told her that it was just a matter
of time before Levi knew a lot of people in the
area—mainly those of the female persuasion.

"I know a lot of people in Fortune," Carly said.
"I'm practically a fixture here. And I can try to
find you the perfect babysitter."

"A grandma type?"

"Sure, if that's what you want."

"I want someone who really likes kids. Someone who will stick around for a while. I don't need a whole lot of help, except for when I'm at work. But maybe she needs a woman's touch."

When he threw another one of those protective glances at Grace, and this time rubbed his jaw against her little semibald head, Carly's knees went weak. "Yes," she managed to squeak out. "Good idea."

"There's another problem." Levi shifted Grace in his arms. "I can't pay you much right now. That seemed to be an issue for Annie."

"No worries. Pay me what you can, when you can." In fact, any money at all would be welcome.

Maybe she should pay him.

"Are there any grandparents nearby?" she asked conversationally and got herself a beer.

"No one nearby. My parents are out of the country right now, working with the World Health Organization."

"Impressive. How long have they been doing that?"

"All my life, really, but there's more time for it now that they're retired."

"If I can ask, how did you lose your wife?"

He cleared his throat. "You must mean Grace's mother. Car accident. And we were never married."

"Oh. I guess I...misunderstood." Not a sad widower, then.

"No more than most people do. I guess I should wear a sign or something."

She laughed and brought her hands together. Mentally cracked her knuckles. Maybe she'd asked enough questions, and it was time to move in for the pitch. "So here's my offer to you. I'll watch her for you during the week and a few nights, too, if you'd like."

"Really?" His eyebrows went up on that one.

"Sure. Why not?" She set her beer down. "I just want most of the nights free so I can catch up on any work I can't get done during the day. But maybe you want to go out sometime with the guys. Or your girlfriend."

He smiled. "Are you sure? She's kind of a... handful."

"She's adorable." She threw what she hoped was a loving look in Grace's direction. At least she seemed to be happier in her father's arms. He didn't even have to walk around the house and pace and jiggle to keep her quiet.

"What about your husband? Will he be cool with a baby around some of the time?"

She caught Levi staring at her lucky ring. Oh, damn. She'd nearly forgotten. She'd had the ring all through high school and design school and wore it as much as a week before a major test for the extra good juju. It wasn't anything fancy, a

simple gold ring that she liked rubbing and twist-
ing around her finger like a worry stone. But
these days it fit on only the ring finger of her
left hand.

"I'm not married. This is just my lucky ring."
And lately, she needed the extra luck.

He set his half-finished beer on the counter.
"I'll tell you what. Why don't we both take the
weekend to think about it?"

Seriously? He didn't want to jump on this opportunity to have the owner of RockYourBaby
babysit his daughter? How had she failed to sell
this to a desperate man?

*You have to apply yourself, Carly. Try a little
harder. I know you're not stupid.*

The words of every teacher she'd ever had
growing up reverberated in her mind. This was
a challenge, like RockYourBaby was a challenge.
Like reading and writing had been for so many
years when it felt like no one understood how
hard she did try. All she had to do was work
harder. Smarter. It might take her twice as long
as someone else, but she'd get it done.

"Sure, sure. I understand. Why don't you check
out my website over the weekend and tell me what
you think?"

"It's a deal." Levi smiled one last time, then he
and Grace were out the door.

CHAPTER FIVE

THAT EVENING LEVI fed Grace dinner, cleaned up her mashed potatoes and high chair mess, bathed and powder-puffed her, dressed her in one of those so-called sleepers with a bazillion snaps, then laid her on a baby blanket in the living room. It was eight o'clock and he had no delusions Grace would be ready for bedtime, but at least she wasn't wailing.

He took a seat on the floor near Grace and pulled out his laptop. He was about eighty percent sure he would take Carly up on her offer to babysit, because he had no other choice. She seemed determined to look after Grace until they could find someone else and it made sense. But this time he hadn't wanted to jump as quickly, because he'd been in reactive mode since he arrived in Fortune. And frankly, he'd been a little too intrigued by Carly to just accept outright. More curious and drawn to her than felt comfortable despite her being single.

If she ever got it in her head that she wanted a date with him, it wouldn't be as easy to turn *her* away. And it probably wasn't a good idea to date his babysitter, anyway, whether under twenty or someone like Carly, who definitely appeared to be his age. While he couldn't put his finger on what it was about her, she drew him in with those soulful hazel eyes. And they had something in common, too.

They were both desperate.

He did a Google search for Carly Gilmore and came up with a Facebook profile, mostly filled with photos of her with friends. She was linked to a business page and the RockYourBaby website. He clicked on the link and a busy website came up with the slogan The Place Where Babies Come First. A buddy of his had started a paddleboard business a while back, and Levi had firsthand knowledge of the cost of a professional-looking website. Carly's looked like a top tier–priced website, and he noticed several popular baby product companies advertised prominently on the landing page. There were several photos of Pearl Gilmore, obviously the image behind the company. A grandma type if there ever was one, she had short salt-and-pepper hair, a wide and toothy smile, and a regal and distinguished air about her that said, "You can trust me with your baby."

And he *would* trust this grandma type. Carly, he wasn't so sure about. She had the baby company, so he didn't understand why she'd take on Grace, too. He wanted to believe she was simply being kind and neighborly, but that didn't ring true on some level. She wanted something from him.

There were a few photos of Carly on the website, and a clear indication that she had taken over in Pearl's place. What would it feel like to be called a baby expert and have no children of your own? His guess was that she might feel like a bit of a fraud.

It takes one to know one.

He'd been the only child of parents who were overachievers and had instilled the same values in him. Study hard, work hard and give back. He'd spent summers at his grandfather's ranch in Texas because Levi's own parents didn't seem to have time for him if it didn't involve quizzing him on his studies. He'd had to make the honor roll every semester or suffer a long sermon about wasted opportunities. Pop's ranch had been the only place Levi could be himself and unwind. Have fun for a change.

He'd gone straight to the Air Force Academy after high school and received his degree, going into the service as an officer. His good friends, his AF brothers, were the only ones who understood Levi Lambert could be impulsive at times. Wild. He'd carefully compartmentalized his life to be two people: the officer and the playboy. A bit of a cliché, but hey, he'd paid his dues.

Then Grace had come along. She had brought

out the very best in him, but he'd had such a wild past that anyone who could see him now would be stunned. Spending nights alone with his daughter, looking forward to nothing more than a full night's sleep. If he got lucky. There again, *getting lucky* had taken on a whole new meaning. It used to mean a night of uninhibited, balls-to-the-wall sex with a woman who didn't want much in return other than a couple of orgasms. He could give her that but not a whole lot more. The whole love, marriage and kid thing had never been on the agenda.

Grace rolled over, squealed and kicked her legs out, reminding him that a kid was now on his agenda, like it or not. Then she went knees up and elbows out again and did her rocking thing. She squealed her delight at having managed to roll over to her back again, bringing an end of the blanket with her in her chubby little fist. The corner of the blanket was now in her mouth.

Levi pulled the blanket closer to him, taking the edge of it out of her mouth. He handed her a pair of plastic keys to chew on. He'd try keeping her up late tonight, then maybe she'd be too tired to wake up much during the night. Logically, it should work.

It was the way he liked to tackle any problem in his life. Logic always won over emotion, hands down. He'd been taught to never make knee-jerk decisions. Emotions tended to cloud good decision making. Contrary to what some of his friends believed, he hadn't chosen to raise Grace out of emotion. Out of overwhelming love and devotion. No, that had come a little later. His had been a logical decision, based on responsibility and doing the right thing. Not abandoning his child, the way his parents had abandoned him. Sure, they'd done it for the greater good. But it had still left him feeling unwanted. Expendable. They could go ahead and save the world's children. He would start with his child.

Of course, it was always better to make life-changing decisions on your own. He hadn't had that luxury.

Still, Sandy's parents clearly didn't see Levi as a shining example of a father, saying they'd never even heard of him. At first they'd tried to claim that Grace's father was Sandy's boyfriend, a man who had died in the same car accident. But thankfully the birth certificate stated Levi Lambert as the father. The DNA test had confirmed it.

He assumed Frank and Irene were grieving, and he got that. He understood the grieving process. But he wasn't the enemy. If they had been logical about it, he would have agreed that, of course, they could be involved in Grace's life. Instead, they'd come out guns blazing and demanded that he give her back to them. Even tried to file a motion in family court to bar him from leaving the state of Georgia. Hadn't worked. They continued to insist that Sandy had meant to leave them in charge, but she'd died suddenly and without a will. Frank, who loved to hurl insults via email, had once referred to him as "the sperm donor."

Levi could take a lot of shit and not blink, but when they insulted him, they were insulting Grace's father, too, so he got a little more sensitive. To his mind, how she'd been conceived was nobody's business. The way he raised his daughter would be his business and his alone. He'd be there for her—present, not absent like his own parents had been, although the distance his parents had created wasn't one he or anyone else could blame them for. They'd been concerned for the poverty-stricken people of the world, and Levi wasn't one of them. As a child, he'd had the added weight of guilt for missing his parents. They were off saving the world. And him? At least he'd had his grandfather.

But something had gone right for him today when he'd knocked on Carly's door. He'd found himself an expert. If nothing else, maybe her heart was in the right place. Not to mention her legs. Her ass. Okay, he was going to try not to notice that again.

She'd offered to babysit nights, which meant he could have a social life again.

He hadn't seriously dated anyone in years. Grace had reformed him overnight, but the stiff boots still didn't quite fit. He'd need to stretch them out, wear them in. Carly was just the kind of girl he never would have approached in the past. Nice girl. Good girl. Pretty and sweet, but wouldn't want to get too dirty or anything.

LEVI WOKE WITH a start. The midafternoon Saturday sun slid through the cracked blinds of his bedroom, almost blinding him. It was official. Grace had turned him into a vampire. He'd fallen asleep with the baby monitor in his hands when he'd only meant to close his eyes for a second.

Since he was off the clock, he'd fallen asleep when Grace went down for her nap. And dreamed of sweet Carly, which made no sense when he could dream about a *Playboy* centerfold, Katy Perry or anyone else in his wild fantasy life. But the girl next door was kind of smoking hot up close. Unapologetically curvy, with legs that went on for a country mile. Sensual, full lips. He'd been dreaming about licking those kissable lips of hers and more. Much more.

The doorbell rang and Levi groaned, rolling out of bed. He rubbed his eyes and quickly looked in on Grace to see that she was still sleeping in her crib—it was daytime, after all, what else would she be doing—then went to open the front door.

Carly stood there smiling until her eyes locked in somewhere around his pecs. As if she could see right through him again. She wasn't smiling any longer but seemed something more like transfixed. He checked to see if Grace had spit up on him again, and that was when he realized he wasn't wearing a shirt.

"Crap. Come on in."

Levi dipped into his bedroom to grab a T-shirt and pulled it over his head, meeting Carly in the foyer. "Sorry about that. I fell asleep."

A smile had become frozen on her face. "Am I interrupting…anything?"

It took him a minute, because sue him if he was beginning to forget what a sex life resembled. Lately when he took off his shirt in the middle of the day, it was because there was regurgitated baby food on it. But Carly had just reminded him of how much he missed sex. This was not helpful.

He rubbed his prickly chin. Hadn't bothered to shave this morning, when the only girl he had to impress didn't have any of her own teeth. "Nah, I was sleeping when Grace sleeps."

Smile back full force. "That's smart."

"You doing okay?" He felt a smile coming on. She seemed so…enthusiastic.

"I could use some help if you have a little time. No worries if you don't."

"What's up?"

"A manufacturer sent me a crib to review that's supposed to be the easiest to assemble, and I thought I'd put it together and test that out." Her hands were in the air, as if trying to reenact the process. "And then if you decide I can babysit her, she can take naps at my place, instead of in the car seat. But—"

"Too many moving parts?"

She sank her teeth into her lower lip. "The diagram makes no sense to me."

"That's okay. I put together Grace's crib in a few minutes. It's not a problem." He went to his bedroom to grab the baby monitor handset, then followed Carly to her house.

Carly led him to the spare bedroom, where he set the handset on a nearby dresser. The room had a sewing machine in one corner, piles of fabric on the chair and a dummy wearing half a dress. In the middle of the room stood random parts to the crib. The rails, headboard, baseboard and screws and nuts were scattered all over the floor. A screwdriver lay near the diagram and instructions wrinkled enough to appear as though they'd been through someone's fist. So it looked like she'd tried, really tried, to understand the instructions. Made him smile. She was winging it. In many ways, he could relate. Oh, hell, who was he kidding? Lately, in all ways.

And for someone who had gone through his life with a plan set in stone, sue him if he felt like the ground underneath him was constantly shifting these days. But this, assembling a crib, he could do. It was mechanical. The parts fit together and made sense. What's more, they'd stay together after he was done.

He went to his knees and took a quick look at the instructions. Simple. But when he grabbed the screwdriver, Carly stopped him.

"You should teach me how. Let me do it."

"Seriously?"

"Sure. I mean, if I'm going to rate how easy or how *not* easy it is to assemble for moms, I think I should be the one to do it." Her amber eyes fixated on his, hand held out for the screwdriver. Waiting.

He handed it over after a beat. Reluctantly. It was her house and her crib. Next door, he had a tool kit with power tools, including a screwdriver. But hey, this could be a lot more fun.

He did, in fact, enjoy working side by side with her for the next few minutes and surely could be excused for taking a whiff of her hair when she leaned close to grab a screw. Smelled like coconut.

"Here," he said, handing her another screw and nut. "You'll need this next."

She took it from him, her hand bumping into his briefly. Her skin was silky soft. Smooth. And all this talk of screws and nuts had made him as horny as a bear after a long damn winter. It had been a while since he'd felt this attracted to or this pulled in by any woman. But why did it have to be this woman?

After a few more minutes, Carly successfully

attached one side rail—while he held it up for her—and smiled at him with such obvious pride that his heart pinched.

"Hey, you're pretty good at this," he lied. He'd have been done with this crib twenty minutes ago, but maybe that part didn't matter as much as the look on Carly's face.

"Well, I don't want to brag, but I know my way around a sewing machine. Mine breaks down a lot." She nodded in the direction of the machine in the corner.

She leaned forward to reach in front of him and her low-riding jeans slid down just enough to reveal a beautifully curvy patch of smooth skin rounding out to a perfect ass. He swallowed hard, his mouth suddenly parched. If she kept this up, he would soon tease himself into oblivion.

Finally, after what seemed like an hour of torture, she'd put together the crib. She then checked the sturdiness by tugging on the rails several times, making him smile again.

"Hey, look, I did it."

"You did."

"With your help."

She left the room and came back a few minutes later, a pad of paper and a pen in hand. "I need to write some thoughts down."

"Is this for your blog? Because if it is, I agree with you that this diagram looks like someone on crack drew it."

She laughed at that, scribbling something down. "So glad it's not just me. Sorry, Cribs for Mommies, I'm going to say it's a two-person job."

"So does it work?" He stood up to stretch his legs. "Do they take your advice when they read your blog?"

"I don't really know. They used to take my mom's advice."

"But not yours?"

She lifted a shoulder. "My mother was the real baby whisperer."

"Baby whisperer. I could use me one of those."

"I do have her baby bible. But it's incredibly disorganized, and sometimes it's hard for me to understand. Of course you need to put a baby on a schedule, but it doesn't say what to do when your baby is too tired to stay awake because they've been up all night."

"Exactly." Finally, someone got it. "I have it on good authority she'll sleep through the night. When she's a teenager."

He wasn't going to be one of those parents who wouldn't let their teenager sleep till noon. Figured she'd have a lot of catching up to do.

Carly jotted something down on her pad while he checked the baby monitor. Grace slept peacefully. Still, he should get out of Carly's house right now before he had any more random thoughts about kissing her. Because at the moment, it would be nice to find out if the rest of her was as soft as her rosy pink skin. Like her lips. For starters.

Carly met his gaze and caught him staring at her lips. He didn't bother trying to hide it. She smiled and looked away first. Back to her notes.

He understood. That was a lot safer than dealing with…whatever *this* was. There was a definite pull between them, and he didn't know what to do about that. Acting on it would probably be stupid. But face it, stupid was pretty much his calling card when it came to women. Still, the appeal didn't make sense to him. She'd normally not be his type at all, but he felt a magnetism that had to do with a lot more than her looks. Even though she *was* incredibly pretty. Naturally beautiful. Yeah, that was the thing about it. She didn't *try* very hard. It was just…there.

He took a step closer, telling himself he wanted to see what she'd written down about the crib. "What are you writing?"

Her eyes narrowed. "Why?"

But his height gave him an advantage. "Because from here it looks like a doodle."

A floor-length dress, which had pretty much nothing to do with the efficacy of the directions to this crib. Unless he was missing something.

"It's a sketch." She pulled it away from him.

"Cool," he said. "You don't have to be shy about it."

She blushed again and gnawed at her lower lip. "I'm not *shy* about it. It's just not… Never mind."

"Already forgot all about it."

She folded up the piece of paper. "Let's talk about you. Have you decided if you're going to retain my services yet?"

He quirked an eyebrow. "Your *services*?"

"My baby help." She put her hands on her hips. "I don't offer any other…services."

Shame. "You've got the job. You didn't realize it, but this was your interview. And you passed."

"I did?" She smiled, clutching the folded paper against her chest.

"I like to make sure that my nannies can put together a crib. Just because. I'm weird that way."

"That *is* weird."

"Yeah. You'll do just fine."

"You won't be sorry." She traced the edge of the crib rail with one finger. "I've got a lot of baby knowledge."

He took a step closer, just to make sure he'd chosen the correct three-point level for the mattress rise, he told himself. "When they're infants, you use the highest level. This adjusts for later, you know."

She came up beside him. "Good to know."

It occurred to him that he possibly stood a little closer than he should. Somehow that didn't bother him at all as his eyes met hers. He was close enough to see every tiny speck of green.

When his gaze slipped to her lickable lips, he knew he was in trouble here. She was sexy and pretty. Real. Not at all stuck-up as he'd previously assumed. And she was one hell of a complication in his already chaotic life.

But he'd be lying if he didn't admit he wanted her.

He reached out to tug on a lock of her hair. Silky soft, too. Her eyes were shadowed with lust, making him feel like a superhero for the first time in a long while. He couldn't actually remember the last time he'd seen a woman look at him that way. This was good, because damned if he didn't want to be alone in this...whatever this was. With his hand on the nape of her neck, he pulled her close enough that they shared oxygen. Her eyes were warm and fluid, showing him all the things he wanted to see. An invitation. A welcome.

He kissed her, deep, long and lingering. When her tongue met his, soft and tentative, he tugged her closer still. Took the kiss deeper and wilder.

She pulled back, a bit out of breath. "What was that?"

"I kissed you. And I think you liked it."

As if to acknowledge that, yes, she liked it, she kissed *him* this time. Her hands were on him, clutching his T-shirt, hanging on. He clung, too, one hand dropping to her hip, where he pulled her closer. The other he used to grab a handful of her wild hair in his fist.

From the monitor, Grace wailed. And every good part of him froze.

Carly tensed under his fingertips and he lowered his forehead to hers. "I should go."

"Yeah. Y-you should." She stepped away, an unreadable gaze in her eyes.

Relief?

Disappointment?

He didn't know which one of them was more frustrated, but he'd lay bets in Vegas on himself.

CHAPTER SIX

WHEN THE PAPER airplane hit Levi's forehead on Monday, he was awake, though definitely not firing on all cylinders. So what else was new?

He crumpled the paper in his fist. "Which one of you ladies did this?"

His bet was on Matt, who sat a few feet away from him in Stone's office, making no effort to conceal his smile. "Wouldn't need to ask if you were paying attention."

Levi would grin like that, too, were he engaged to Sarah Mcallister, spending nights wrapped in those mile-long legs.

Damn, he was horny. It had been so long. He wouldn't mind a sweet woman lying under him or on top of him. Just…not Carly.

This morning when he'd dropped Grace off at Carly's, she'd been wearing a short dress that showed off a pair of wickedly curvy legs he couldn't have even imagined. Her hair wasn't pointed in different directions like it had been the first day she'd watched Grace. She'd put some effort into her appearance this morning, maybe to reassure him that he'd made the right choice.

So he had a new nanny, and he wouldn't kiss her again. Levi didn't need someone like Carly in his life. She had the power to draw him in and suck him dry when he had so little left to give these days. Right now he needed easy, casual and definitely no more life-altering situations.

The three of them, Stone, Matt and Levi, were having one of many meetings to work toward the achingly slow progress of turning a small county airport into a regional one. Even if all his synapses were optimal, he had nothing. He was a pilot, not an administrator. But when Stone needed help, a friend didn't say no and live to tell about it. So Levi had come to the meeting and nodded in what he hoped were all the appropriate places. A regional airport would mean the pain of TSA but also more traffic, more flights and, most important of all, more money. He sure as shit could use more money. He could also use at least one decent night's sleep. Just one, please.

Levi squashed a yawn.

"Hey, I can't have you up there if you're not on track," Stone said. "Fresh as a daisy."

"No worries, boss." Levi saluted. "I've got this. I was with the air force. You may have heard of it?"

"You've got to fix it, bro." Matt leaned back in his chair and studied Levi.

"What am I supposed to do? Order her to go to sleep? It doesn't work that way."

"Hell if I know," Matt said with a shrug. "But you can't do this on your own. You know that, right?"

"Why the hell can't I?" There again, he resented the fact that no one seemed to have the slightest bit of faith in him as a father.

While he told himself that they were all trying to help, when Matt and Sarah or Emily and Stone showed up on the occasional weekend and shoved him out the door for some R & R, he fought it every time. Grace was his deal, his responsibility, and not theirs. And he did not fall down on his responsibilities. Plus, he could handle it, lack of sleep included. He already had enough of the lack of confidence in him from Sandy's parents and didn't need his buddies questioning him, too.

"You're a *guy*." Stone slid him a look as if those three little words explained everything.

"Wake up to the twenty-first century. There are single dads doing this every day, and doing it well." He tore off a piece of paper from the airplane and wadded it up between his fingers.

"Maybe so, but it wouldn't hurt *you* to think about settling down now. With a good woman." This was from Matt. "And I don't mean the beach babes you normally hang with."

"What the hell? That's my favorite kind."

Matt quirked an eyebrow. "You need a woman with an IQ bigger than her tits."

Levi scoffed. "This is about what I expected from you whipped fools. Never would have thought I'd see both of you settled down like a couple grandpas."

"Hey, life is good." Matt crossed his arms behind his head, his I-got-laid grin full throttle.

Stone gave Matt a censuring look, and Levi took that time to wet his spitball.

"You going to see Lily again?" Matt said.

"Who knows. Maybe this could be the one."

Lily did seem nice, so too bad he didn't believe in *the one*. She worked events at the ranch Emily's family owned, and they'd been introduced a week ago. They'd had coffee at the Drip, talked for a couple hours. Levi was supposed to call her next week to set up dinner. He didn't expect much. In fact, he'd had more chemistry with Carly while bonding over a baby crib, which said something.

"I'm never getting married. It's the single life for me." Levi scoped out his aim and best shot. It was looking like Matt for the win, which was perfect.

Most of his friends wanted him to slow down. And he understood the reputation he had, though much of it had been greatly exaggerated. For instance, it wasn't true that he'd taken two women home after a bar fight in Yonkers, New York, two years ago. The bar fight part was true, since some jackass had been slapping a girl around. But the rest of it? Levi had never found out how that particular rumor started.

Matt opened his mouth as if to add something when the spitball Levi aimed hit him square in the nose and fell to his lap. "Well, shit."

The conversation went downhill from there.

A few minutes later, Emily opened the door and caught all three of them in the middle of Spitball War Z.

"Not again." She shook her head. "You're cleaning that up."

"Enough." When Emily shut the door, Stone threw his last volley, which Levi caught in midair.

After the meeting in which they'd discussed the planes that most needed work, picking up more plane inventory and how they might best accomplish that with little or no money, Levi had a flight lesson scheduled with a retired software CEO from the valley who'd recently purchased his own plane. Before that, he grabbed his phone to check in with Carly.

When he heard Grace crying in the background, it was all he could do not to run out like a jet at Mach speed. "Something wrong?"

"She's okay. Okay, that's okay, baby," Carly said, sounding a little frantic herself.

He got that. Grace's wailing could even make him break out in a trickle of sweat when she carried on for hours.

"I'll get her down for a nap now," Carly said. "Don't worry. She's fine."

He hung up and found a desk to check his email. As anticipated, another one from Frank Lane. God forbid he should pick up his phone even one of the many times Levi had tried to call him. This one suggested that Levi retain a lawyer, because Frank would sue for custody if it came to that. To pile on the guilt, he mentioned that Grace's grandmother cried for her daily. He hoped Levi felt good about that.

Levi felt like a pile of dog shit.

Of course, he couldn't afford a lawyer. Levi fired off a response, inviting both of them to visit him in Fortune yet again, but clearly stating that he would never give up his daughter.

Maybe this time the message would get through.

So far, all was not going according to plan for Carly.

Why was Grace *always* crying? That couldn't be normal. Carly consulted the baby bible section on teething. Grace had gone through no fewer than five cold rags she gnawed until they were no longer cold. They entertained her but did nothing to stop the crying.

She had growing sympathy for Hot Dad. If he had to deal with Grace all night, he had to be working on fumes. A girl wouldn't know that, though, if she went by the way he kissed. That kiss had scared her a little bit, given that she'd been hot and bothered within seconds. Not the reaction she'd expected. Loneliness and desperation had weakened her. That, and the way Levi had checked her out, his heated gaze sliding over her as if he'd seen a cookie he wanted. As if he'd die without a bite.

But she needed to stay away. After months of juggling nothing but responsibilities and heavy commitments, she would sell this baby business and pursue her own dreams. Her life. Besides, she and Levi both had people who depended on them and who needed to be put first. She had her father, and Levi had Grace.

They'd settled into a bit of a routine after that hot kiss, one that didn't include any more of those kisses. Every afternoon Levi picked Grace up right on time, threw her up in the air, then caught her. Grace would squeal and laugh for the first time that day. Carly would pretend it didn't scare her to see Grace airborne. They'd talk a little bit about his search for a permanent babysitter—which, frankly, was not going well—and about Grace's day, then go to their respective corners. He and Grace to his house. Carly to her sewing machine, where she had a little fun before hitting her business chores after dinner.

Interestingly, he'd not taken her up on her offer to babysit evenings. She supposed that meant he wasn't dating anyone yet. Thank God for that, because she'd offered in a moment of over-the-top selling of her idea. She didn't want to facilitate his getting laid. Carly was the one who needed to get out more. She missed her clothes. Marc Jacobs, Kate Spade, Louis Vuitton and all their cool friends were sitting in her closet collecting dust.

Carly sat at her laptop to do what she did best. Also known as stalling. In the background, an old but favorite episode of *Never Wear This* played. On one hand, she wasn't sure why she bothered with the blogging. The posts took forever to compose, and her post on the best diaper for babies' skin had a whopping one comment. It was from someone who claimed to know the secret to making a million dollars, tax-free. Not one comment from a weary parent looking for advice. Or hope.

As usual, she squeezed the words out one by one. She'd put a sentence together, living by spellcheck, and hoping her grammar was decent. It was never simple, not for her, and felt like being in high school again. Insecure. Inadequate. This wasn't what she should be doing with her life anyway. She'd always wanted to pursue graphic arts or fashion design. That was in her blood and, though hard work, was something she could do well. She'd gone away to school to the Fashion Institute of Technology in New York City. Everything had been going so well there, too, but then even that had blown up in her face. Something she didn't want to think about right now.

Giving up on the words after a few minutes, she padded into the spare bedroom and her sewing corner—the place where dreams went to die. The half-dressed mannequin wore part of the design she'd been working on before Pearl passed away. Despite her failure, she'd kept at it, the pleasure at creating never completely leaving her. Only her confidence had been shattered. And unfortunately, her fashion prowess, should she manage to get it back, would not be of much help when it came to the world of baby products. But frankly, if she had to choose between an empty screen and playing on her sewing machine, the choice was a no-brainer.

It had been far too long since she'd torn something apart and put it back together again. Levi had been right in that the red baby dress was beautiful but impractical. She'd seen a lot of that in the months since she'd taken over RockYourBaby. Carly held up another one of the baby dresses from the lot that had been shipped to her.

She cut into the dress, ripping seams and removing sleeves. Found a piece of a soft white cotton with a flowery print that she'd bought at the fabric shop in town the last time she'd been in there. Seemed like ages ago. She could replace a velvet sleeve with a cotton one. Carly went to work cutting out pieces and holding them up.

Okay, weird. But somehow it worked. She held it up and admired the juxtaposition of solid red velvet and flowery cotton print. It still needed… something. Maybe ribbon or lace.

She'd always loved this part of fashion. Seeing something in a brand-new light. Satin and denim…leather and lace. She had no doubt it was what she'd be doing right now if she had a choice. She could do it all right here from her sewing machine. One thing for sure—she didn't want to run RockYourBaby.com. That was her mother's dream, and Carly couldn't hang on much longer.

Finally, Carly finished and forced herself away from her sewing machine to trudge to the computer screen. She leafed through the baby bible for almost an hour but found nothing inspiring to give to her readers. Nothing to turn their boring, mundane lives into something interesting, or even to remind them that what they were doing was important. She imagined that when it came down to it, raising a baby was all about routine and not much about fun.

What was that saying about a picture being worth a thousand words? A thousand words were really all she needed for this post. Grabbing her high-resolution camera, Carly took photos of the baby outfit she'd just sewn together. Not bad. She downloaded them to her laptop and uploaded them to her blog. It looked okay, frankly, even without any words. She hit Publish.

Grace wailed, awake from her nap. When Carly reached the crib, Grace had rolled over onto her stomach from her back. What's more, she looked immensely pleased with herself, her chubby little legs kicking.

"Daahh…dah," Grace said, then blew a raspberry. "Bff."

At least Carly had the diaper changing routine down. It hadn't taken long to figure out as it wasn't exactly rocket science. She'd done her share of babysitting younger cousins years ago. And some baby care, she had come to realize, was so routine that it could be a little mind-numbing at times.

Maybe they needed a change of scenery. She could take Grace for a walk. Not exciting, but at least it got her outside the house after months of nearly hibernating. Jill and Zoey, her two best friends, had tried to get her to go out more, but Carly hadn't much wanted to go out and celebrate being young and alive when she'd still been grieving.

But today, she needed a diversion. Carly rummaged through her closet and pulled out her distressed short overalls. She rolled them farther up at the hem and paired them with a white T-shirt and her broken-in flat brown leather boots. A long-brimmed black fedora completed the look.

"There." She felt like a new woman, or more like her old self.

Carly then spent the next two hours taking Grace for a stroll around the neighborhood and to the nearby park in the lightweight umbrella stroller rated as the most portable and functional by *Baby Today*. They were the standard in the industry, and Carly hoped they would consider buying RockYourBaby for top dollar. Time was running out.

Last night, she'd checked in with Kirk and asked to speak with Dad.

"He's having a bad day," Kirk had warned.

That was always code for "He's not talking to anyone and being a pain in the ass. He won't do his exercises."

"I'll try back tomorrow."

Mom's death had hit them all hard, sure, but none harder than their father. He regularly fought with the therapists who were trying to get him to rehabilitate his hip and wasn't the man Carly remembered anymore. He'd always been her biggest supporter. Her protector. When Carly had wanted to go to New York City and study design, instead of something far more practical as her mother had suggested, it was Daddy who had supported Carly's decision. He'd smoothed things out with Pearl. And he'd smoothed again, double time, when Carly had returned from the Big Apple a big fat failure.

Grace squealed. She seemed happiest outside, distracted by the outdoors. Entranced by flowers, trees, dogs and children playing. Carly stopped to pull out her phone and take several photos of her. She was a cute baby. Long dark lashes and blue-gray eyes. Toothless smile. Maybe Carly could ask Levi for permission to use Grace as a baby model for the website. Holy cow, she was totally rocking the great ideas today. She could dress Grace up in cute outfits she created and post photos of her on the blog. Another way to avoid actual words.

Grace fell asleep on the way home, and she was still asleep when five thirty rolled around and Levi pulled up outside. A person could set a clock by the guy.

She met him at the door. "She's still sleeping. Want to come in and wait?"

"Yeah." He stepped inside. "Might as well let her sleep."

How exactly did he manage to look like sex on a stick at the end of a long day? He had this whole badass look going on, late-afternoon scruffiness over his jawline, making her want to rub against him like a cat.

Bad, bad Carly. "I wanted to talk to you about something anyway."

"Oh, yeah. I haven't had a whole lot of luck finding another sitter. I'll make a few calls to-night." He followed her into the family room.

"That's not it. I need a favor."

"Done."

"You don't even know what it is yet."

He gave her an easy smile. "Doesn't matter."

"Be careful, Levi Lambert. You never know what I might ask."

"Bring it on." His eyes filled with obvious male appreciation.

She was reminded of her bare legs. The look he slid her was so full of heat that she thought her panties might spontaneously burst into flames. *Focus, Carly, focus.*

"I want to put photos of Grace on my website. I took some cute ones today." She took her phone out and showed them to him. Shots of Grace staring with delight at a tree as if she'd just discovered them. Smiling as she watched a child playing ball, staring wide-eyed at a woman walking her poodle down the street.

"You took her to the park. She loves it there." Levi didn't take the phone from her but instead held her wrist and brought the phone up closer.

Her stupid wrist tingled as if it thought it might be about to have a good time. She cleared her throat. "I know. Just look at this one. I think she noticed a cloud for the first time."

He grinned, still holding her wrist. "Nah, she saw one last week."

"Right. So…is it okay if I put her photos up? She's an adorable baby."

"Fine with me."

"Don't worry. I'll never share her real name

with my readers. And no one has any idea that the company is based in Fortune. My mother took great precautions to protect our privacy."

"I trust you." His big, rough hand slid from her wrist to her elbow, and the tingle traveled.

"Thank you." She stared at his lips, willing him to kiss her. "The trust is…important."

"Extremely."

That talented hand now settled on her waist and pulled her closer. And somehow her hands were squeezing his biceps and she went up on the balls of her feet to get closer still. He kissed her long and deep, his hot, wet tongue insistent. It got wild and crazy as her hands fisted his shirt and his hands palmed her ass.

"Levi." She broke off from the kiss, breathless. "We probably shouldn't do this. It's not…a good idea."

He pressed his forehead to hers. "You're right."

Great. He agreed with her. "It's stupid."

"Yeah." He tugged her in tighter and kissed her again. And again.

She threaded her fingers through his hair and moaned into his mouth.

And they continued to be crazy stupid for the next hour.

CHAPTER SEVEN

A FEW DAYS LATER, the blog post with the photos of the outfit Carly had created went viral.

It had been reblogged over a thousand times. Someone, possibly one of her readers, had created a Pinterest board named Fashionista Baby. The hashtag #fashionistababy was trending on Twitter, with mothers posting photos of their own favorite baby outfits. All wanted to know where they might find similar clothes to the one Carly had made.

Patsy, her mother's accountant, phoned to tell Carly that whatever she'd been doing, she should keep it up. They'd received renewed interest from some of their lost sponsors. Companies were calling and asking questions. She didn't think it would be long now. They'd get an offer, Carly would sell the company and Daddy would have the money he needed for the extensive physical therapy ahead of him. And Carly would finally find...something to do with the rest of her life.

Definitely not this baby business.

While Grace took a nap, Carly finished her

latest blog post—"How to Handle a Teething Baby"—then dialed her father to give him the good news. This time Kirk gladly handed him the phone.

"Hi, Daddy. How's the hip?"

"Still hurts like hell, honey. But that's hardly your problem. These physical therapists out here don't know shit."

"Are you doing your exercises?"

"Yeah, yeah. It's like I told my PT guy—I spent half my life on my feet. Climbing, lifting. Never had a fall or a broken bone. Not one. Come out east to visit with Kirk, and a piece of ice does me in. But now that I have a new hip, those people won't let me take it easy for a minute. I tell them to let me rest the hip, but no one listens to me. I'm just an old man, so what the hell do I know?"

Dad was a retired PG&E lineman and had worked physically hard all his life. At sixty-five, he didn't like anyone telling him how to spend his time. When he'd once been asked what he'd planned to do in his retirement, Daddy said he had plans to surf. From his couch.

"Well, I'm glad I called, because I've got great news," Carly said.

"Could always use some of that."

"RockYourBaby is doing *much* better. I had a blog post go viral, and now we're getting all of our sponsors back."

"What's viral? That's a good thing? Let me

get Kirk back on the phone. I don't want to talk about that company."

Daddy still sounded bitter, even if "that company" could be a part of his retirement if they played their cards right. If Carly could get any real help from her family, it would be so much better, but she had long ago realized she was in this alone.

"No, that's okay. We don't have to talk about the company. Just know that soon I'll be able to sell it and send you and Kirk some money to help with the physical therapy bills."

Too late, Carly forgot it had been the wrong thing to say to Dad.

"No, I don't want any of that money coming to me. I told you and your brothers. Your mother meant that to be for our children. Not me. I'm an old man."

"But Da—"

"I want you to take your part of the money and go back to New York City, honey. Finish school. I know your mother could have been more supportive, but she was worried about you. She liked having you nearby, you know that."

But if she hadn't been home, she would have missed out on the last year of Mom's life. It had all worked out for the best. "I sometimes think I'd like to go back."

"Maybe the timing was off. You can't give up."

"Okay, Dad, you're right. I'll think about it."

It was the only way she'd get him off the subject. Agree. It wasn't like she didn't think about it every single day. It would be nice to get a second shot at her dream of life in the Garment District. But that wasn't likely to happen until she grew a little more confidence in herself. In her own abilities. They'd taken a hit, and even if she was pissed that she'd let one person derail her dreams, she couldn't go back until she felt sure he was dead wrong.

LEVI WOKE IN a good mood. To put a real stamp of approval on the morning, Grace had gone to bed at ten o'clock the previous night and had woken him up only once. A record.

While he waited for his coffee to brew and Grace to wake up, he checked email on his phone. There was a new email from Sandy's father stating that he'd asked for an emergency child custody screening in California family court because he now feared for Grace's safety.

Feared for her safety.

Levi was her father and would sooner light himself on fire than hurt a single hair on her head. Not much fazed him anymore, but that lone email managed to piss him off royally. Sandy's parents were methodically chipping away at him. It took everything in him not to throw his cell phone across the room. They were never going to give up—he should have realized. Should have dealt with the situation early on and maybe he wouldn't be in this mess.

He woke Grace, changed her diaper and put her into one of the many outfits Carly had given him. No sooner had he turned his back to lob the diaper in the trash can than Grace spit up all over and he had to change her again.

Monday went FUBAR fast after that.

He'd dropped Grace off at Carly's, where even seeing her open the door in her Tasmanian Devil slippers didn't manage to cheer him up.

Later in the day, two delayed and entitled Silicon Valley VIP passengers did not help his piss-poor mood. He was still exhausted. Hell, he'd been tired for weeks. Now, seeing Carly day in and day out—and playing tonsil hockey with her—had him horny as all get-out, too. If anyone so much as looked at him the wrong way today, he might have to kill them. Matt and Stone were avoiding him, because they were the only two people who would sense he was on the edge and ready to snap. They were both smart enough to know he could kick their collective asses with one hand tied behind his back. If the past was any indication, they were going to avoid him for a while and let him simmer. Then they'd stage a sneak attack.

If they could find him.

The fact was he couldn't risk losing Grace. Ever. He'd been taught to make decisions first with his brain, not his heart. This one required little thought. She was his daughter, not theirs. All he wanted was to be left alone to raise his daughter in peace, but that clearly wasn't going to happen. Another serious talk with Sandy's parents would be his next logical move. Actually, it was long overdue. It would be even better to meet face-to-face, and since he figured they'd be in California to attend the sham hearing, maybe he could meet with them first. He couldn't afford a lawyer, so he guessed he'd represent himself.

An emergency screening. This had to stop. Worse, they almost had him doubting himself.

Was he being selfish in raising Grace on his own? Maybe she'd be better off with a grandmother to raise her and a female influence in her life. It was logical, his left brain said. A woman's touch for a little girl. But in this one instance, his brain wouldn't cooperate. The idea couldn't take root. Because even if he'd never had much of a sense of family other than summers with his grandfather, he wanted that kind of stability for Grace. His friends had become a sort of family for him—getting up in his business all the time for one thing—but he wasn't sure that would be enough. They would soon have their own children to raise. Their own families.

He finished two flying lessons and a chartered flight to LAX, then in the afternoon he walked into the Magnum Aviation hangar, where he found Cassie waiting for him. Her face was dialed to Angry Mama.

"You've got Emily hiding in Stone's office. I know everyone's afraid of you today, but I'm an old lady and I don't scare easily."

He loved Cassie like a second, far less distant mom, but he kept walking without saying a word. He'd done his best to mask his anger, but apparently it had seeped out. The problems he had weren't anything that his friends could help him with. No point in bothering them.

Cassie followed him as he strode across the hangar. Sarah Mcallister, who still occasionally worked at the Short Stop Snack Shack, was working today.

He sat on an empty stool. "Give me a coffee. Black."

"Like your mood?" Sarah poured coffee into a mug.

He fixed her with a look he hoped choreographed that even beautiful and sweet brunette fiancées of best friends weren't safe today.

"Hand it to me and I'll pour it all over his head." Cassie had finally caught up to him.

"Uh-oh," Sarah said, holding the mug out as if unsure of whom to hand the coffee to. "What did he do?"

"He's being ornery." Cassie took a seat on a stool next to him.

"I don't want to talk about it." He grabbed the coffee from Sarah and took a long gulp.

"Oh, boy," Sarah said and exchanged a look with Cassie.

"What?" Levi said.

"It's a woman," they both said at once.

But they were wrong. Carly wasn't the problem. She was his happy place right now. A happy place he didn't want to share with anyone. She was driving him crazy, but in all the good ways. Who would have known a good girl could kiss him like his hottest wet dream? When she'd had her tongue halfway down his throat, his favorite organ had wanted to RSVP to the party. He didn't know if it was the somewhat forbidden nature of their nanny/boss relationship, but he couldn't stop thinking about her. She was right, though. The whole idea was stupid, and this confrontation with Cassie and Sarah was only one reason why. He didn't need to drag all this drama into Carly's life when she was still dealing with her own. And he could clearly see it in those lost eyes of hers. She was still hurting. Still reeling from her mother's death and the business mess she'd left in her wake.

"Said I'm not talking about it."

"That means yes," Sarah said, then, possibly at the glower he gave her, went back to wiping the countertop.

"Wrong," he said with his scary calm. "It's nothing you can help me with."

"It's the grandparents again, isn't it?" Cassie scowled.

He shook his head. "Doesn't matter. Point is they're not giving up. I see that now."

"Listen, Levi," Sarah said. "If you need money to hire a lawyer, Matt and I can—"

"No." His friends had done enough, and Sarah and Matt were getting married next year. Saving money was their goal, not bailing him out. "I'm not taking your money. This is my problem."

Cassie patted his shoulder. "You'll figure it out."

"It's crazy." Levi took another swig of coffee, then set it down. "But sometimes I catch myself thinking that maybe Grace *would* be better off with Sandy's parents."

He didn't voice that thought often, but what did he know about raising a little girl? The only thing he knew about parenting was what *not* to do. Don't leave your kids every summer. Don't make them feel that the only way you'll love them is if they're on the principal's honor roll. A parent's love should never be conditional. And beyond everything else, don't abandon them, whatever the reasons.

Cassie picked up the newspaper Sarah kept on the counter for customers, rolled it up and swatted him over the head with it.

"How could you possibly think that little baby girl would be better off without you?"

"They have more resources than I do. And Sandy's stepmother already raised two other daughters."

Besides, what the hell would Grace learn from him, other than stats for the Dallas Cowboys or how to keep her emotional distance from the people who loved her?

"All I know is that this isn't the first time in my life I've had to face that the right thing to do isn't always the easiest one."

Cassie pointed at him. "Do not try that with me, young man. I know that better than anyone. So now I have to ask you a question. What makes you think it's going to be *easy* to raise her?"

"I didn't say—"

"Exactly. It's the hardest thing you'll ever do. Believe me."

"No. The hardest thing would be losing her when she's older and she realizes what's happening."

After she gets used to me, and I can't live without her.

He'd never had that in his life. Never had anyone he couldn't easily walk away from. He had his parents to thank for that. They'd raised him so that he would depend on himself, and not on them.

But he couldn't deny there were times he longed to get away. To be free to go back to the air force and let that be his entire life again. It was comfortable. Routine. A life he understood. As soon as that errant thought would cross his mind, though, he'd be consumed by guilt. He'd picture Grace's angelic face as she slept, tiny mouth suckling in her sleep. He couldn't leave her behind. She was his, and the truth was he could no sooner give her up than he could stop flying.

"Levi, please don't say you're doing this." Sarah had tears in her eyes. "A baby is such a wonderful gift."

"Look at what you've done! You made Sarah cry," Cassie said.

"I'm okay." But she threw her head back, presumably to keep the tears from rolling out.

Cassie sighed. "It can't go on forever. Sooner or later they'll give up and regain their senses. Figure out that they're too old to start over and raise a baby. Then maybe you can just let them see Grace every once in a while. Just to be a part of her life."

They'd gone so far now he wasn't sure he could ever trust them with Grace. But he wanted to. She needed an extended family. He still wondered if his own parents ever intended to come back stateside to meet their only granddaughter. Of course, they'd said they would, but they said a lot of things.

"You're wrong. They requested an emergency

screening. Claimed they fear for Grace's safety in my care."

Cassie slapped the counter with her newspaper. "What do you need from us? Character witnesses? Whatever you need."

"Me, too," Sarah said. "And you know Matt is there when you need him. Anything."

When he'd held Grace in his arms for the first time, he'd had no idea how much his life would change. And continue to change. The hits just kept coming. When would they stop? By the time all was said and done, he might not recognize his life at all.

Matt came out of nowhere, let himself behind the counter of the Snack Shack and wrapped his arms around Sarah's waist. "Hey, babe. What are we talking about?"

"Levi has some trouble."

"Oh, yeah?" Matt smirked. "Women, right? That's his usual trouble."

Sarah turned in the circle of Matt's arms and smiled at him. "Tell him. Tell him how easy it is to say, 'I was wrong, and you were right.'"

The idiot man didn't even blink. He simply appeared to have been hit with the silly stick. "Sure. I was wrong. You were right."

"See?" Sarah turned briefly to smile at Levi, then to Matt to give him a hug. "Easy."

Matt took that opportunity to grin over Sarah's

shoulder and mouth to Levi, *"I am so getting laid tonight."*

"I told you to listen to her," Cassie said.

But Levi had already mentally checked out of the ridiculous display. He knew exactly what he had to do. Never one to back down, he'd take action and treat this like any other problem. Deal with it. Head-on. Just slice all the pesky emotions right out of the deal. It was surprising it had taken him this long to do it, which he'd blame on lack of sleep. Not being at the top of his game. He whipped out his phone, and while Matt and Sarah were making out, he fired off an email to Sandy's stepmother, Irene, bypassing Frank altogether. Short. Sweet. Simple.

Let's talk.

CHAPTER EIGHT

CARLY SPENT MOST of the day begging Grace to stop crying, taking her for three walks in the stroller because that seemed to be the only thing that worked and giving her a sponge bath after Grace took the pear-flavored gourmet baby food Carly spoon-fed her and put it in her hair, in her ears and up her nose. How she managed to do that Carly would never know, but once those chubby hands started flailing, it was like a mystery wrapped in an enigma. The UPS guy had delivered three packages—one of them she'd had to sign for when Grace was in the middle of testing out the great set of lungs she'd inherited.

She'd worked at the sewing machine during one of Grace's power naps and pulled apart the little baby jeans she'd bought on a whim. They hadn't fit right—just not well designed, in her humble opinion. And way too...plain. But Carly saw possibility. She added ribbon and lace and a cute hem. Then took several more photos of Grace wearing lacy hipster jeans and uploaded them to the blog, continuing to bank on the theory that a picture could take the place of words. Because the writing…it felt like bleeding sometimes.

Fortunately none of the readers had asked about the baby in her photos. They probably simply assumed she had the kind of money to hire a baby model. She was fine with that. She certainly didn't want her readers to know that she, Carly Gilmore, was the baby's *nanny*. How would that look?

While Grace took another nap, Carly filled out several interviews for a publicist Kirk had hired to help: why, yes, she looked forward to heading up RockYourBaby. Moms everywhere should eagerly anticipate what they'd have going on in the next few months.

Fear pressed down again, creating a solid lump in Carly's throat. She was getting much closer to making a decision about *her* life. This was both wonderful and terrifying. Dad thought she should finish school in New York City. It was true that she shouldn't have allowed one setback to determine the rest of her life. She'd been young and made a stupid mistake she wouldn't make again. It was time to take another chance on the life she wanted.

She would finally be able to do that soon enough, and she couldn't afford for anything to go wrong now. Not now that she'd regained the confidence of all of Mom's loyal readers.

Carly heard Levi's truck pull into the driveway

next door and glanced at the baby monitor on the coffee table. In her spare room, Grace was still quietly asleep in the crib.

Levi walked in the front door as he had become accustomed to when she expected him. He stood in the doorway, framed by the late-afternoon sun, aviator shades still covering his eyes. Then he took them off, propped them on his head and let her see his expression.

She frequently had trouble reading him, but the drawn-together eyebrows and tight jaw told her one thing: he was not happy.

"Hey." He shut the door and took a few steps toward where she stood in the middle of the great room.

"Grace is still taking her nap. Is something wrong?"

"Yeah."

His voice, low, deep and gravelly with just a touch of a Southern accent, caused a pull to start low in her belly and move south.

She followed him into the living room, where he plopped onto her couch. His hands hung between his long, spread-out legs. "Sandy's parents asked for an emergency custody screening. They fear for Grace's safety with me."

He made this rather painful comment with little emotion, even while her heart plunged to her stomach.

Determination was set in his square jaw.

Clearly, Levi was a man who rolled with the punches. Who didn't waste time being too bitter about things he couldn't very well change. And damn, whatever else she felt right now, she admired that about him. While she'd been caught up in Levi's blue eyes and boyish grin, while her ovaries had done cartwheels for him, he'd been going through a rough time.

At the first meeting with her brothers and father about RockYourBaby, it had been decided within minutes that she would take over. They'd all been sucker-punched, grieving over Mom's sudden death from a heart attack. Her father had been inconsolable, rendering him incapable of making the big decisions. Her brothers had families and careers of their own. Carly had worked at the Drip, and so it was left to her to manage and sell the business. Ironically enough, she'd felt as though she'd been handed a baby she didn't want. Her life had switched directions in one swift moment, because she needed to be the one to step up.

So yeah, she could relate. But in her case, her brothers clearly had more faith in her than they should have. Sounded just the opposite of Levi's problem.

"Why? Th-that's ridiculous. She's perfectly safe."

"They don't see me as the brightest example of fatherhood. Maybe I'm not, you know, but I'm trying. I've already done a lot that's been asked of me. I left the air force and settled down in Fortune. I have ties to the community. I've got a job. A house. But to Sandy's parents, it's all done for show."

"What are you going to do?"

He opened his mouth, then shut it again. "Whatever it takes."

"Good."

"I sent Sandy's stepmother an email earlier today. She emailed me back to say that they're flying out here on Wednesday. So we're going to meet at the park the next day, and I'm bringing Grace. She wants to see her, make sure she's okay. She seems reasonable. Maybe we can talk this out and come to a logical conclusion."

He acted as though he were talking about the weather. The last time she couldn't find Double Stuf Oreos at the store, she'd been more upset than he seemed at the moment.

"I think you're smart to let her see Grace. Once she sees how well Grace is doing, she'll back off."

"Maybe."

"I'll do anything you need. Be a character witness for you. Tell them how much you love her. How she follows your voice and she knows you. She wouldn't do well without you." She got teary just talking about this. "And I won't mention all the crying she does."

Just the thought of Grace and Levi being ripped apart, and she was near tears. What a sap. But simply put, poor Grace couldn't also lose her father. She'd already lost her mother so young.

"Sometimes you're the only thing that keeps me grounded," Levi said, shoving a hand through his hair.

It was left mussed, sticking up slightly, and her pulse kicked up at seeing him look so... defenseless.

"Me?"

The thought that she could do that for him meant more to her than it probably should.

"Babe, you have to know that you drive me crazy." He gave her an easy smile. "In a good way."

She sucked in a breath but didn't speak. It seemed they'd just crossed some kind of invisible line. *Babe.* No point in ignoring the obvious. They liked kissing each other. And maybe they'd like a few other things, too.

He crooked his finger.

She went to him like a cat to catnip and allowed him to pull her onto his lap. Her short floral skater skirt rose to indecent heights as she straddled him. He took full advantage, hands skimming up her bare thighs.

"So soft," he said in a low and throaty tone.

His voice, deep and gravelly, had her nipples hard. Carly nipped at his lower lip, earning a very male groan from him.

His gaze heated. "That's hot."

Levi kissed her, his wicked tongue warm and wet. His hand dived under her T-shirt, sliding up and down her spine, settling at the small of her back. She lost her head and rocked her hips against the bulge in his pants. That pulled an even rougher, more erotic sound out of him, and his hands lowered to tighten on her hips.

"Mmm," she whispered into his warm neck. He smelled so good. "You know, this is still not a good idea."

"Agreed. Because of the nanny/boss thing. So predictable." He gently pushed her to her back and covered her with his warm, big body.

She wrapped her legs around him. "If there's one thing I hate, it's being predictable."

"You and me both."

He continued to kiss her and drive her out of her mind, the bulge in his pants rock hard and pressing into her belly. She really wanted to take care of that for him, but there was a baby in the next room. His baby. Then Levi's hand was under her skirt and between her thighs, fingers pushing aside her panties, and she forgot all about Grace.

"Levi," she moaned, clinging to him, undulating her hips as his fingers slid in and out of her folds, creating a rapidly building and delicious friction.

"Shh." He brushed a kiss across her lips.

"I'm going to stop talking now," she gasped.

"Thank you."

He gave her a slow smile while his fingers continued their magic. He whispered hot and dirty words in her ear of what he'd like to do to her, urging her closer to the edge of the precipice. She came shockingly fast, shuddering and moaning his name, climaxing harder than she ever had before.

"Now you," she said, reaching between them.

"No. This was about you."

"But—"

"There's no time," he said, pressing a kiss to her temple. "I'm going to need a few uninterrupted hours."

"A few...hours?"

He rose from the couch. "You didn't think once would be enough for me, did you?"

As if on cue, Grace wailed from her crib, which led Carly to believe that perhaps Levi was not just gorgeous, smart and a great kisser with magic hands.

He might also be a little bit psychic.

WHEN THE PLANE landed at San Francisco International, Irene Lane reached for her husband Frank's hand and squeezed it.

"Maybe while we're here we can check out one of those cute little B and Bs in wine country I'm always reading about in *Travel* magazine."

"Yeah, sure," Frank grunted.

But after more than twenty years of marriage,

Irene could interpret Frank's grunts like an expert. That grunt meant "Are you crazy, woman? We're here to get Grace back, not to have a good time."

She let go of his hand. "Can we stop here in San Francisco and visit the wharf?"

They hadn't had a real vacation in years. Sue her if she wanted to take advantage of this trip to California. Of course, it helped that, unlike Frank, she had a strong sense of Levi Lambert. And he was no deadbeat dad. The email she'd received, which she'd kept secret from Frank, told the story. Levi wanted to work something out. She knew better than to tell Frank, because, with his usual flair, he'd make a federal case out of it. Accuse Levi of trying to play them against each other. Insist he had a plan to come between them.

"The airport is *south* of San Francisco," Frank said with his mock patience. "Going to San Francisco is out of our way."

She supposed that was a dig at her fantastic sense of direction. "But the emergency screening isn't until Monday."

"We need to check in at the hotel and get situated. I have to work on my strategy. You don't expect me to give up when I'm this close to getting her back? Just watch. Once we've got him surrounded from all sides, Levi is going to fold like a cheap umbrella."

Frank made it sound like he was planning an attack at daylight.

And then what? she wanted to ask him. They'd have Grace, but she wouldn't have her father *or* her mother in her life. Irene loved her granddaughter, but she wasn't exactly in the position to start over again at the age of sixty-two. These were supposed to be their so-called golden years as Frank neared retirement. They'd planned to travel and visit the children and grandchildren scattered all over the United States.

Not this.

She hadn't wanted a legal battle, because she'd already seen how dirty they could be, but she had one now. Having been through one divorce, Irene knew how ugly this could get if they allowed it. But Frank wouldn't listen to her. She wanted to believe that all she needed to change his mind was one good argument and he'd bend. Proof that Grace would be safe. He'd go back to being the same solid and strong man she'd fallen for all those years ago. A man raising his daughter, Sandy, on his own. Surely he could understand why Levi might want to do the same.

Reminding herself that Frank was still grieving, she put a metaphorical sock in it. Time to pull up her big-girl pants. Despite the fact that his grief seemed a solid wedge between them, the way they were drifting further and further apart might be her fault. She had to be more pa-

tient with Frank. More compassionate. Caring.
Her therapist told her that men dealt with grief
differently. They needed to fix it. Put things back
in order. And having that goal gave them a way
to handle the overwhelming pain. Unfortunately,
Frank's single-minded goal since discovering that
Sandy had lied to them about Grace's father had
been to punish the man who'd actually fathered
their granddaughter. As if it was his fault. Irene
figured that was easier than having to face the
fact that Sandy had let them both down one last
time.

THE DRIVE TO Fortune took longer than she had
anticipated—it was an hour or more before they
pulled into the bedroom community. Considering all the wealth and privilege gathered in Silicon Valley, she figured Frank had booked them
the kind of hotel where she'd be almost regretful
to go back home.

But Frank pulled into the Budget Inn, a place
that looked like a home to the traveling business-
man. "Here we are."

"This is it?" Not her idea of an inn. She tried to
keep the dismay out of her tone. The least Frank
could do was find a decent place for them to stay
in this beautiful town.

"You said you wanted to stay in an inn, and
this one was a good deal. Don't worry, everything
here must be nice." He patted her hand. "Besides,

we have to save our pennies if we're going to move here. You've seen the price of real estate."

"Don't start with that again. We can't afford to live here."

"You never know." Frank popped the trunk latch. "But the main idea is for Levi to *think* we're moving here. That will rattle him good."

Frank didn't seem to see that his logic was circular and didn't make much sense to someone not deep into the mind of Frank Lane.

Later, after they'd checked in and hauled up all their luggage, and Frank was situated in front of the TV, losing himself in another action thriller, Irene stared at her reflection in the bathroom mirror. At sixty-two years of age the laugh lines around her mouth and the crow's-feet were deeper. Proof that she'd lived a busy and happy life. Two marriages, four children. One between them, two of her own and Sandy, her stepdaughter.

She'd taken pains to take care of herself over the years by meticulously watching her diet and exercising. Yoga was her saving grace these days, not only building her muscles, but also soothing her grief and pain and giving her a simple peace.

She couldn't change the past. But she wasn't done living. She still craved Frank's attention and affection. Loved him even if he wasn't lovable these days. When she met with Levi and

Grace at the local park, her love and allegiance to Frank would cause her to do everything in her power to heal this situation. Levi, who seemed a reasonable—if rather cold—man, would listen to her words. And Frank would be overjoyed that she'd taken this step for him and see how much she loved him. Understand he still had so much to live for.

With that in mind, Irene dressed in a classy black one-piece swimsuit. It emphasized the fact that she'd been gifted with good genes and maintained an impressive yoga regimen. She walked out of the bathroom and stood by the TV screen in the muted light. Arnold Schwarzenegger had just indicated that he'd be back.

"I saw that there's a hot tub downstairs. That will be so good for your aching back and tired muscles. Want to join me?" She gave him a wink and a wiggle.

He barely looked at her. "Nah, I just need to rest my back by being horizontal."

And don't forget sleeping all day.

"Well…that works for me, too, you know." Funny, they used to spend much of their time horizontal and together.

He seemed to ignore that. "Have fun."

Apparently the cheerful and optimistic message of *The Terminator* was more appealing to Frank than his own wife.

ON THURSDAY MORNING, Carly checked email on her laptop. She'd fallen into a pattern of getting up earlier and taking care of most of her work before Levi and Grace arrived. She filtered through all the emails from readers—more and more each day—and found a message from one of her old classmates at the Fashion Institute, Jenny Martinez, asking for a good time to call. The message was short and sweet.

I've been following your career at RockYourBaby, and I'm interested in what you're doing. Let's catch up. Send me some good times to call you.

Carly wondered if the Cutting Edge, a design company always at the forefront of all new fashion and product trends, might possibly be interested in a baby blog. But her *career* at RockYourBaby? More than likely, Jenny had heard about the viral post, because she was a lot of things, and one of them was a social media guru. Jenny had been on the fast track at the FIT, so it didn't surprise Carly that she was emailing from the headquarters of the Cutting Edge in New York City. It had been three years now since those in her class would have graduated and gone on to internships and jobs. Three years since Carly had come home. And she couldn't blame it all on Alec. The pressure, all the competition, had gotten to her, but her *thing* with Alec hadn't helped.

Smart and gorgeous Alec Higgins, who thought she was beautiful and unique. Who told her that dyslexia would never stop her from achieving her dreams. He'd been the first teacher to believe in her. The first person other than family and friends to give her encouragement.

Carly rubbed her lucky ring and wrote back with her cell phone number and good times to reach her. She spell-checked three times before hitting Send.

Imagine that. She'd been working at this for months, but one little viral blog post and suddenly she'd arrived. If Jenny had been following RockYourBaby and was interested in what Carly had been doing, maybe there was a way she could pitch the website to Jenny. The Cutting Edge had the kind of powerful presence that would keep RockYourBaby relevant, continuing to help and inspire new mothers everywhere, as Mom would have wanted. Dad could have money for his PT. Carly could move on, back to New York City. Win-win-win.

If the Cutting Edge was interested.

But if they were, this could be all she needed to sell RockYourBaby. Even a small amount of interest from the Cutting Edge, announced in a thinly veiled press release, might mean other companies would sit up and take notice. Nothing could go wrong now. They were so close she could taste her looming freedom.

Later, Carly fed Grace lunch. Peas, which Grace chewed, spit out, then found were much more fun to throw at Carly. After cleaning up the mess, Carly decided that stay-at-home mothers deserved gold medals. Maybe she'd write a blog post about that. "Ode to the Unsung Heroes." She bathed Grace close to the time Levi would pick her up so she'd be exceptionally clean for the meeting with her grandmother. Dressed her in a pair of cute blue baby leggings and a matching top she'd sewn one night when she couldn't sleep. This cute outfit should impress the grandmother if nothing else. If only all fashion could be as simple as sewing cute baby clothes. With her own clothes and style, Carly knew what she liked, but it was hard to re-create it in a new and unique way.

For once, Levi was late to pick up Grace. If there was one thing you could say about Levi Lambert, it was that he was always on time unless he was early. She texted him.

She's ready to go. Are you on your way?

No response, but there wouldn't be one if he was in a plane. Of course, he shouldn't be in a plane. He should be on his way home now so he could get to the meeting at the park on time. Unless his flight was delayed and he had no control over it. She thought of dialing the airport but didn't want to overreact. Zoey and Jill were forever telling her that she got too emotional too fast. Time to stop that.

Levi would get here any minute. Sure he would.

And a few minutes later, Levi was officially late. This had never happened in the nearly two weeks since she'd known him. A text message buzzed.

Just landed. Flight delayed. On my way. Meet me at the park?

She texted that of course she would. Carly changed from her casual leggings and top and searched for the most conservative outfit she could find in her closet. She settled on a black peplum skirt and high-necked sheer blue blouse and was out the door with Grace within minutes.

Carly pulled into the parking lot a few minutes later. The park was mostly deserted other than a middle-aged woman sitting at a picnic table a few feet away. She had shoulder-length dark hair, carried a cute Coach bag—looked like a knockoff from here—and wore beige slacks and a scoop-neck T-shirt. It was possible she wasn't Grace's grandmother, because she looked young to be a grandmother.

Sitting in her car, Carly tried to relax, knowing she was on borrowed time with Grace. The baby had been lulled to sleep by the car ride, but as soon as she caught wind of the fact that she was no longer moving, she'd start fussing. The fussing would become crying, and then she might not look as adorable as she had a few minutes ago.

Grace fussed. Carly leaned back to check, and yes, she was now officially awake.

Grace's grandmother scanned the park twice and glanced at her watch.

"Executive decision time." Carly hopped out of her car and went to get Grace out of her car seat.

She hadn't started crying yet and stopped completely when Carly pulled her out of the car and she got a look at a tree. Possibly one of her favorite things in the world. Grace cooed and held her little arms out as if she had a prayer of reaching the limbs. Then she turned her head in the direction of children kicking a ball nearby.

"You're about to see Grandma, little one."

Carly would just calmly explain that Levi had sent her over because of a flight delay. She had plenty to talk about. As the nanny, she could tell her exactly how healthy Grace seemed to be. Mom's baby bible implied Grace had hit every one of those so-called baby milestones on time or early. Carly would talk about what a great dad Levi was. She'd explain he just couldn't be without his little girl.

It would be okay.

Carrying Grace in her arms, Carly approached the woman, who smiled when she saw Grace.

"It's you," the woman said.

But something about the way her gaze stayed on Carly while talking to Grace was a little strange. "Hi, I'm Carly, the na—"

"Yes, I know exactly who you are!" She was staring from Grace to Carly with wide eyes.

Carly had no idea why she looked so thrilled and surprised, but she wasn't going to argue. She smiled. "Do I know you?"

"Oh, I'm sorry." She stood. "I'm Irene Lane. Sandy's stepmother. Grace's grandmother."

"I know."

She covered her mouth with one hand, then lowered it. She shook both hands, fanning herself. "Forgive me. I'm just so surprised to see you here, with my granddaughter."

And she'd been worried that the grandmother might be judgmental! She seemed like a perfectly delightful woman. "Well, it's no problem."

"I'm a huge fan of RockYourBaby. So are my daughters, and Sandy was, too. When she signed up for her baby shower, she chose every one of the brands you recommended."

That certainly explained how Levi had all the brands.

"We loved your mother so much. I was very sorry to hear about her passing."

"Thank you."

"Honestly, I thought that was Grace in the

photos on the website, but I kept telling myself I had to be wrong. But it *is* her, isn't it?"

Carly swallowed hard. This felt suddenly so awkward. She hadn't expected to meet a fan today. "Um…"

"She's a beauty, isn't she? So much like her mother."

Actually, Carly thought Grace favored Levi, but she kept her mouth shut, simply nodding.

"Can I hold her?" Irene moved closer.

Carly handed Grace over, who took her attention away from the children playing and the trees long enough to glance at her grandmother with muted interest. She wasn't green, after all. But Irene didn't seem to mind the lack of recognition as she cuddled Grace close. She squirmed and tried to turn back to the children.

"She loves being outside," Carly said, trying to explain.

"You must be so busy with all that you do for mothers and their babies. How did you meet Levi and Grace?"

"He's my neighbor. And Levi wanted me to tell you that he is running late because his flight was delayed."

Irene shook her head, clucking over Grace. "A pilot. I can't imagine a much more dangerous profession. But look who I'm talking to. You believe in putting babies first. Always."

"Yes, over at RockYourBaby, we definitely do."

Why did she sound like a commercial?

"Levi will be here any minute now." Carly glanced at the parking lot. Still no Levi.

Irene sat on the bench and, as Carly had suspected she would, began to inspect Grace from head to toe. She seemed satisfied and looked up to Carly. "I didn't know what to think about Levi. I had hoped that he'd be a good father, but this is unacceptable. Not that it's your fault, mind you. But his letting you use her as a model for your website. A baby shouldn't have a job."

"Oh, no! You've misunderstood."

I'm the nanny, and I take photos of her for my website because I can't afford a model. Also, she's my guinea...research baby. None of it sounded right. She didn't want one of her mom's fans to know that it had come to this—Carly working as a nanny.

I can't afford for anything to go wrong. Not now. We're so close.

She didn't want Irene to know that RockYour-Baby hung by the thinnest of threads. Irene stared at her expectantly.

"See, Levi and I…"

What to do? What to say?

"We, um…" Carly stared at her fingernails.

I've been following your career.

Irene was waiting. "You what?"

I'm really interested in what you're doing.

"We're…together." Oh, boy. She rubbed her

ring. Open mouth, tell a lie. It had become like breathing. "So that's why I post photos of her on the blog. I…obviously spend a lot of time with her."

Irene stared at Carly's ring and gave such a huge smile she looked happy enough to levitate. Carly sucked in a breath. *Oh, god. No.* She rubbed the ring harder, like maybe it could stop this from happening.

"You and Levi are engaged? Oh my goodness! This is incredible news. And I thought my little granddaughter was being raised by a playboy pilot. Sandy never talked about him to us, you know. I kind of think he was a—" she lowered her voice to a whisper "—one-night stand."

Carly didn't speak, since she'd done enough damage the last time she opened her mouth. But Irene seemed so pleased with the misunderstanding that suddenly Carly began to think maybe this wasn't *such* a horrible idea. She'd just take what she had and use it. To help Levi and Grace, too. And really, was there any harm in it? Irene would go back home and never be the wiser.

A little white lie that made them all look good.

But Levi, on the other hand… Most men would probably want to be given a heads-up on their impending marriage. Fake or otherwise. Just a guess.

Irene bounced a standing Grace on her lap. "I can't tell you what a relief this is. I won't worry anymore, knowing you're going to be her step-mother. You're Pearl Gilmore's daughter. The baby whisperer. Oh, baby girl, it's going to be all right. I couldn't have picked anyone better myself. Wait until I tell my husband. He keeps saying we have to move here."

"M-move here?" This could put a bit of a crimp in her plan. "Why?"

"He thinks if we're closer, then we can better know whether Levi is raising her properly. Maybe even get some visitation rights. That's what this visit is about. But we have other children and grandchildren, and I hate to be so far away."

"Oh, well, you can just rest assured that I will take good care of Grace. No worries there. You can go back home and know all is well."

Please. Please go back home. Now would be good.

"It's far too expensive to live here." Irene shook her head.

"Yes, yes. Last week someone sold a shack in Palo Alto for a million dollars." Okay, another lie. But hey, it wasn't far from the truth.

Irene's lip curled in disgust.

Just then Levi's green truck pulled into the parking lot. He climbed out and rushed toward them, a man on a mission. A man about to find out he'd become engaged in the past five minutes.

The question remained: Would he kill her now, or wait until he got home?

CHAPTER NINE

IT HAD BEEN a long time since Levi had been fifteen minutes late to anything, and he couldn't even remember a time when it had mattered this much. Certainly not as much as it did today.

His morning began with two flight lessons, one with a sixtysomething-year-old former AF man who'd never been a pilot but still thought he could tell Levi how he should fly a plane. Then he'd had three flight hops, two of them delayed because his passengers weren't ready. Chartered flights didn't run on a tight schedule because the customers with deep pockets paid for the delays. He wanted to talk to Stone about better scheduling—higher fees for this kind of shit, or some way to discourage it from happening.

Now this, to top off his craptastic day.

He rushed to the two women seated at the picnic table.

"Hi, babe." Carly sat across the table from Irene, who held Grace in her lap.

"Hey, guys, sorry I'm late."

"No worries. I explained everything to Irene." Carly smiled but didn't meet his eyes.

"Congratulations! I just heard the big news," Irene said.

"Big news?"

She winked at Carly. "Just like a man. What *big news*? he says. Look, I'm sorry about this emergency custody screening. I'll tell Frank to back off. The whole thing was his idea, anyway."

"Thank you," he mouthed to Carly, who still wouldn't meet his eyes. Odd.

"I appreciate that," he said to Irene. "I've wanted you guys to come out and visit for a while. I'm sorry this had to be the reason."

"You'll have to forgive my husband. He's had a hard time with all this. We all have." Irene kissed Grace's plump cheek. "But weddings are wonderful beginnings, and maybe that's what we all need now. I just want you kids to be sure and invite us. We definitely want to be there."

Levi was sleep deprived, granted, but that still didn't make any sense. "I'm sorry, how do *you* know Emily and Stone?"

"Who are Emily and Stone?" Irene wrinkled her nose.

Carly rose from the table and came to his side, took his hand and squeezed it hard. "She's talking about *our* wedding."

"Wedding?" He froze. "Our wedding."

Carly laughed. "Sometimes he still gets a little tongue-tied about it."

"Frank was the same way. He asked me to marry him, then on our wedding day acted like someone was about to cut off his leg. Honestly, you men. But this is going to be so good for Grace. I can't tell you how much better I feel about everything."

Stunned. That was the only word that fit. *Confused* was a good runner-up. It was true that the stress had been getting to him lately, the worry and concern over Grace, but this didn't make much sense. Carly had put him in a difficult spot. What could he do? Tell the truth and admit he'd hired a nanny who would lie about being engaged to him? That would only make things worse. Frank and Irene would never trust him again. He was here to build trust, not destroy it. With great effort, he stopped himself from glaring in Carly's direction.

"Irene is a huge fan of my website, RockYour-Baby. She recognized me right away."

So, apparently Carly had chosen to use that connection and reach out to Irene. But while he understood that, he seemed to be missing something.

He gave her a smile, but it felt tight. "Right."

Carly squeezed his hand again, twice, like trying to communicate in Morse code. "I better go and let you guys talk some more."

Oh, hell no, she was not leaving him here alone. "Wait, babe. You sure you want to go? I mean, we'll be *married*, so we should probably both stay and talk."

If she'd wrangled him into this mess, she would help him swim in the muck.

Irene smiled. "No need to rush off, Carly."

He led her to the picnic table by the small of her back. *Oh, she will pay for this.*

"I'll stay if you both insist."

He sat on the other side of the bench and pulled Carly down next to him.

"Have you two set a date yet?" Irene asked.

Levi was going to go ahead and let Carly take that one. He turned to her. "What was the date again?"

Carly whipped out her phone. "Let me check, because Reverend Parnookie was going to try to squeeze us in next, um, when was it?"

Reverend *Parnookie*? Was that even a name, or had she just made it up on the spot?

"No idea," he said through gritted teeth. "Men. We're hopeless."

Irene laughed. "You sure are."

While Carly kept playing with her phone, Levi changed the subject. He talked to Irene about Grace, making a great case for how well she was doing. He shared how much weight she'd gained, and how she was trying to crawl. She was eating solid food and starting to babble more and more.

Irene listened with genuine interest, for which he felt immensely grateful. This reminded him that he already had a grandma type right in front of him. Grace's grandmother. And if it wasn't for the fact that he'd just become engaged without his knowledge, he'd wish that they lived closer. Although he still wasn't sure about Frank.

"What about the emergency screening?" Levi finally asked.

Irene waved her hand dismissively. "I'll tell Frank to cancel it. Don't worry, he listens to me. Although lately, not so much, but I think I'll get him to listen to me on this."

"Is it that simple?" He didn't think once you started the ball rolling in family court you could just stop the forward momentum. Frank had accused Levi of being a danger to Grace.

"I don't know. That's all Frank's doing. God knows what he does late at night on that computer. He researches California custody law and whatnot. I'm sorry about all this trouble."

Levi suspected as much. He'd been worried that Frank had spoken for both of them. Grace, who had been on Irene's lap while staring up at the trees and some children playing nearby with their dog, finally noticed him. She squealed and held out her arms to him from across the table.

"She wants you, Levi." Irene scooted Grace over to him across the table. "Isn't that sweet."

Carly was still staring at her phone, obviously

a real pro at stalling in addition to lying. Either that, or maybe it would take forever to find a date that didn't exist.

"I heard about how you two met. Frank and I met at work, a few years after he lost his first wife. Frank is a good man, really, once you get to know him. We'll be here for a month. Plenty of time to get together."

"A *month*?" Carly dropped her phone.

Levi coughed and hit his chest.

"Frank had some time off, and he decided we'd come here and spend a little quality time together. I'd like to drive up the coast, see San Francisco, and some of the B and Bs in the area. And of course, get to visit with our little Grace. Just to make sure you two are doing well. Maybe we can all have dinner sometime."

A month. A month in a small town where he and Carly would have to keep up this pretense or risk looking like complete idiots. Right now, he wanted to wring his pretty little neighbor's cute neck. She might have solved one problem but had given him another.

Grace, who was cuddled in his arms but still fidgeting, reached out to Carly and touched her face.

"She's not sure which one of you she wants more," Irene said. "This is adorable. Let me take a picture."

She pulled a phone out of her purse. "I want a

photo of the happy couple. Believe me, this will help Frank. I think if he sees you three so happy together, he'll stop being so angry all the time."

Levi doubted that very much, but if a simple photo would make a difference in fixing this mess so he could go on and live his life with his daughter in peace, he was all over it.

"And I also want my friends back home to see the real Carly Gilmore." Irene backed up a few steps, presumably to get a panoramic shot. "Wait until they hear the authority on babies is going to raise my granddaughter. I still can't believe it. Scoot in closer, you two. Act like you love each other."

He pulled Carly in tighter. "You have a lot of explaining to do," Levi whispered near her earlobe, then gave it a slight tug.

She sucked in a breath. "I know."

CHAPTER TEN

CARLY TOOK A detour on the way home, choosing not to follow Levi and Grace. She wasn't ready to face Levi and explain. Not yet. Or ever.

Realistically, considering she lived next door and happened to be his nanny, the avoiding couldn't last long. But for now, she would stay away from one Levi Lambert. He of the magic tongue and fingers. Because this was embarrassing. And anyway, what she needed more than anything right now was ice cream. Or coffee from the Drip. No. Ice cream *in* coffee. With cookies. And also her two best friends so they could tell her that she hadn't been crazy stupid to come up with this lie. Or, that even if she'd been crazy stupid, they would still love her. Especially when she wasn't sure she could even love herself right now.

Did you go along with the lie for Levi or for RockYourBaby?

How about both?

When Irene had noticed Carly's ring and made a huge leap, Carly could only think of how that scenario played a hell of a lot better for her than being Levi's *nanny*. It made a difference, of course, that Irene had been such a fan. Otherwise, she would have probably corrected Irene.

But she'd never done anything this crazy in her life, unless you counted taking off to New York City to study fashion design. And look how well that had worked out.

As she drove down Main Street, she tried to wrap her mind around the past two hours. How could she have possibly known that the Lanes would spend a month in Fortune? Who did that? She didn't see how she could be blamed when that seemed so random.

Sorry, Levi, but the sale of RockYourBaby is more important than your peace of mind. I can't afford to lose even one customer right now. And certainly not a true-blue fan.

Anyway, Levi should simply be grateful that the emergency screening would be cancelled and he would no longer have that stress hanging over him. Of course, now he had a different kind of stress and worry. And, hello? So did she. If news somehow managed to get back to Daddy that she was engaged, fake or not, he'd probably break his other hip.

She hadn't wanted Irene to know that she was the nanny, because how would that look for the owner of RockYourBaby? Besides, was it *such* a crazy idea for her and Levi to be a *thing*? They certainly connected on a physical level. Oh, how they *connected.* And also, she had *helped* him! Irene had been so happy. She absolutely loved the idea of Carly being Grace's stepmother. Another win-win.

Definitely the angle she was going to use with Levi.

She blamed this latest disaster on the past few months of being in constant sale mode, presenting the very best side of everything, whether it was one hundred percent true or not. Maybe she'd been a little desperate, too. She'd already seen how fast a viral post could change things. It wouldn't surprise her if her popularity could drop as quickly as it had risen. Fame and popularity were fickle beasts, or so she'd heard.

She glanced at her phone. One message from Levi:

Why?

She blew out a breath. Fine, she was going to ignore that one because it wasn't safe to text while driving. She would explain everything to him. Soon. But for now, she needed a few minutes to regroup. Sometimes, even with the best of intentions, she screwed things up. Hopefully not in this case.

Carly pulled into the small parking lot of Pimp Your Pet, which was adjacent to The Bushwacker Salon. Both were housed in a large split Victorian that had been renovated a few years ago by the city of Fortune.

Zoey Caballero was one of Carly's best friends and the owner of Pimp Your Pet. They'd practically grown up together after Zoey moved to Fortune to live with her aunt Rosario and uncle Pedro. Carly and Zoey had attended high school together, where they'd often challenged the teachers. Carly did so with her inability to please a teacher, no matter how hard she'd tried, year after year. Zoey had challenged them with her fondness for stray animals. She'd once gotten into a heap of trouble with the biology teacher when she'd rescued a filthy pigeon with a lame wing.

They'd both met Jill later, while working at the Drip, but since then the three of them had been inseparable. And it had been some time since they'd hung out together, because Zoey spent long hours working at Pimp Your Pet and Jill had been scouting cheap land on her days off. Carly, of course, had spent most of her time indoors and behind a computer screen.

Carly opened the door to Pimp Your Pet, and the door meowed.

"Be right with you," Zoey's sweet voice rang out.

Carly scanned the pet shop that Zoey had worked in since she was a teenager. It used to smell like a litter box, but since the renovation and Zoey taking over, the shop smelled like fresh wood, pine and, somehow, lavender. The name was new, too, and Zoey's idea. In keeping with the pimp theme, there were colorful sweaters and collars for dogs and cats with plenty of sparkly bling. Other items that went further than Carly would have imagined one would go with a beloved pet. Birthday cards for your dog with a treat included inside. Dog diapers. A type of brush one could put in their mouth and act like a mama cat licking her kittens. Too far.

Zoey's head appeared around the corner, her long, dark brown hair, as usual, pinned to the top where it would stay out of her way. Mostly.

"Hey, you! What's up? I saw more of the fashionista baby Tweets today. I retweeted from Pimp Your Pet and my personal account. Then I hit up Instagram and started up a Pinterest board for you."

"That was you? Thanks! I'm taking a break and figured you could use one, too."

She frowned. "Everything okay?"

"No." Carly shook her head.

"Uh-oh. I thought going viral would be a good thing."

"It is. Actually, we've gained more sponsors. But that's not my problem." She took a breath. "I kind of told someone a big lie and now I'm in trouble."

"Here." Zoey handed Carly a box of dog treats. "Help me put these in the dispensers."

Zoey had an array of dog treats in a large dispenser toward the front of the store. All manner of flavors, shapes and colors. Organic. Grain-free. Carly followed Zoey, placing a few of the different treats in every opening.

"I mean, as always I only wanted to help," Carly said.

"Sure. I know."

"It's very exciting. Things have been going so much better, and I guess I just lost my head for a minute." Carly twisted the ring on her finger. Might as well keep it on now.

"That's normal." Zoey looked up, studying Carly with her chocolate-brown eyes. "So did you overinflate the numbers? Exaggerate about how well you're doing?"

Sort of the normal way business owners tended to inflate the truth. Not her. She went big. Stellar. "Not exactly."

After Carly explained the entire situation, and how she'd inadvertently become engaged to Levi without his knowledge or consent, Zoey whistled low. "Dude, that's bad."

"Yeah." Carly eyed the dog treat in her hand. It was shaped like a dog bone, but the box said "yogurt covered" and it looked like a real cookie.

Oh, man, she needed a cookie. *This cookie.*

"Don't even think about it." Zoey took it out of her hands. "You need a people cookie. Come with me."

She grabbed Carly's hand and tugged her toward the cash register, where she grabbed her purse. A few minutes later, Zoey left her part-time helper Reggie in charge of the shop and Carly drove them both over to the Drip. Jill was already there, pulling a shift. They grabbed a booth, and Jill brought over their usual array of biscotti, lemon cake, scones and people-sanctioned cookies.

Carly hadn't hung out with her friends in too long. After she'd spilled her guts once more for Jill's benefit, there was nothing but silence from them, highlighted by the comforting whooshing sound of the espresso machine. That, plus the wafting scent of fresh-brewed coffee, brought back fond memories. Carly felt safe here. Cozy. Sure, it hadn't been the best use of her almost-completed fashion design degree, but she'd been happy here for a while.

New York City and the fashion industry hadn't been what Carly pictured at all. The pace was too fast, the people too cold. She was shy and insecure, far too nice, and kept getting passed over. Her designs weren't horrible, but they also weren't good enough. She'd done her usual struggling with anything regarding the written word. And then Alec had done his damage.

She'd returned to Fortune and her family feeling spit out like a piece of chewed gum.

So Carly had found work as a barista, and she, Zoey and Jill had worked together at the Drip.

Concocting café lattes, frappés and mochas, Carly frequently misspelling names on takeaway cups (Stephanie, Stefanie or Stephane?), and let's not forget their four o'clock dance-offs. All three had wanted to go into business together at one time, but then Zoey had taken over the storefront and lease for Pimp Your Pet when Rosario became ill and wound up in a long-term care home.

Then Pearl had died and Carly was tasked with selling RockYourBaby.

"I will say this," Jill said. "When you tell a lie, you don't fool around."

Carly couldn't argue with that, but she'd call it inexperience more than anything else.

"So you're engaged," Jill said with a laugh. "Congrats!"

"Shh. I don't want anyone to know." Carly lowered her voice and glanced around to see if anyone had heard.

"How's that going to work? A secret engagement?" Zoey said.

"I see issues straight ahead." Jill leaned in. "So how did he take it? Does he seem like the type to go along with it?"

No, he seemed like the type who couldn't be pushed around. Who wouldn't do much of anything unless it was his idea first. She was in a lot of trouble with him, in other words.

"I...haven't talked to him yet," Carly confessed, taking a bite of biscotti. "Not since I—"

"You dropped a bomb like that on the guy, then ran away?" Jill said.

Carly covered her face with her hands. She looked down at her cell phone as it buzzed. Another text from Levi.

I know where you live.

Carly groaned. "I'll explain everything. He's the type who will listen."

This was her hope, anyway.

"He's nice, I think. I saw him last week when I had a meeting with Emily about the pet wash on Saturday," Zoey said.

"What's so nice about him?" Jill said.

"He said hello and smiled."

It didn't take much for Zoey.

"I haven't met the guy yet. Does he fall anywhere on the Chris Scale?" Jill asked.

The Chris Scale was a complicated rating system based on all of the significant ones: Hemsworth, Pine, Evans, Pratt. Jill had created the scale and made frequent updates to it.

"He is the high end," Zoey said, holding her arms out about a foot apart.

"Really?" Jill cocked her head at Carly. "He rates on the scale and you didn't *tell* me?"

"I would have, but I almost didn't notice." Carly shrugged and took another sip of her mocha.

Both Jill and Zoey fixed her with dumbfounded

stares. They were not buying it. Anyone who came close to the scale usually meant a phone call with all the details. The last significant Chris Scale sighting had been a guy Jill had spotted in San Francisco. Three years ago. Chris sightings didn't come around every day. Hence the stares.

"I'm sure once you explain everything, he'll understand you weren't thinking straight," Zoey said with her positive attitude.

Yeah, right.

"And I bet he appreciates the fact that you were thinking outside the box," Jill added helpfully.

"That's the thing. I didn't think. I just went along with her mistake because it seemed easiest. Just like in New York, I always had the small ideas. Nothing wild and innovative. Just…derivative stuff." The big fail in the Big Apple.

Carly couldn't take the stress. All the posturing and illusion. As soon as she sold RockYourBaby she would never exaggerate again.

She still didn't know what she'd do after selling her mother's company, and held no small amount of envy that both Jill and Zoey knew exactly what they wanted out of their lives. What's more, they were both firmly entrenched in pursuing their dreams. Reaching for it. But what did one do when plan A had been a bust? Where was plan B and how could she find it?

"My break's over." Jill, her Rise and Shine and

Have a Drip apron now tied on, walked toward the counter, hips swinging.

"Obviously, I shouldn't have been put in charge of RockYourBaby. But now that the blog post went viral, and the others are doing so well, we have our best chance to sell. What if I blow it before we can?"

"You won't blow it. Believe in yourself."

"You're right. I've got this. It's practically a done deal."

"That's right. How's your dad doing?"

"Oh, you know. Not good."

"That's okay. He'll get better." Zoey patted Carly's hand.

Yeah, and unicorns would fly.

"What are you going to do after you sell the company?"

Travel? Join the Peace Corps? Or go back to New York City the way her dad thought she should? Maybe it wasn't too late to try again.

"I don't know. I'll figure it out, just as soon as I sell RockYourBaby. It's got me a little…stuck."

Even if she had a willing audience, she didn't want to talk about all the humiliation she'd experienced, thanks to Alec. Reality had coldcocked her. Maybe she'd never fit into that world. A world in which a designer needed tough skin, because there were plenty of Alecs out there.

But she wasn't sure she belonged here in Fortune, either. Maybe it was copping out to stick close to home where everything seemed easier. Manageable.

"You ever hear from that dude again?" Zoey asked, eyes narrowed.

"You mean my teacher? Alec?"

"Don't know if you can still call him your teacher." Zoey made air quotes.

Probably not, since she'd made the colossal mistake of sleeping with him. Once. Because she'd been lonely, and he'd been kind. Encouraging. He'd loved her designs, really liked *her*. She thought she'd liked him, too. He was tall, dark-haired and incredibly charismatic, if not classically handsome. Full of the energy of the city. And for a while, he'd convinced her she had something special to offer the world. Her dyslexia had forced her to tap into her creative side. Surrounded by brothers who were academic overachievers for most of her life, it had finally been her time to shine. Be unique.

Zoey grabbed both of Carly's hands. "What happened wasn't your fault."

"I know."

Carly couldn't blame herself for being young and making a mistake. But she'd never completed the program, and that was her doing, not Alec's. She shouldn't have let him change her plans. Or allow his hurtful words to decide her future.

"What do you want to do? Go back and finish your degree?" Zoey asked.

"Maybe."

Finishing now would be one of the toughest things she'd ever had to do. Not doing so meant she'd let Alec have the final say. Sooner or later, maybe she'd be ready.

But not today.

CHAPTER ELEVEN

LEVI WAS IN a hurry dropping off Grace the next morning, so he simply locked gazes with Carly. "We need to talk. Later."

She blushed, took Grace from him, nodded, then shut the door.

His morning was spent with Jedd, helping him with diagnostics on a plane they'd recently sidelined. Later, Levi strolled inside the hangar to meet a client for a flying lesson. He topped off his morning by taking a couple daredevils skydiving over Napa Valley. To each their own. He'd never jump out of a perfectly good plane.

Grabbing a quick lunch from the roach coach that dropped by every day, his thoughts turned to Carly again. Her cheeks had been flushed when they'd left the park after meeting Irene. She'd clearly been embarrassed and so he'd let it go, while reminding her frequently, via text, that they still had to talk about this situation. She wasn't getting away from him. They were going to have to find a way out of this lie and save face with the Lanes. He didn't want to pretend at anything, least of all a relationship. Besides, hadn't she been the one to remind him that the two of them together was a stupid idea? Given the way she kissed him—like she wanted to inhale him— he didn't necessarily agree, but he understood. He didn't need to sign on to a serious relationship right now. He hated lies and wasn't about to go along with this one.

Levi caffeinated for the fourth time when he got back from lunch. He'd been awake at two in the morning again, but not because of a woman. There were good reasons to lose sleep, and then there was Grace. At the moment he was thinking about the very best reason to lose sleep— with Carly writhing under him or on top of him, crying out his name. She'd shift her hips to take him deeper, and his eyes would roll to the back of his head with the intense pleasure. Then she…

"Look alive!"

"Huh? Whaaa?" Levi turned to see Matt had sneaked up behind him.

"That never would have worked pre-Grace. Still taking your power naps?"

"Yeah."

Stone wouldn't let him take any early-morning flights and forced him to take naps if he needed them. Even if he popped NoDoz and was hyped up on coffee, safety came first. For now, he was stuck with the later commuter-duty charter flights, and a flight lesson here or there.

"Can you take my flight to Tahoe tomorrow afternoon? I want to leave early to take Sarah out to dinner in Santa Cruz. It's a surprise."

"Sure." It was like the freaking *Love Boat* around here, except with planes.

"You could slow it down, old man." Levi slapped Matt's back. "I think you've landed her. She's yours and all that. Hooked and reeled in."

"I'm gonna let that go, seeing as your grandfather used to own a bait and tackle."

"Seriously, though, you're such an overachiever. You don't have to wine and dine her every night."

"Says who?"

"Great," Levi said. "Just one more reason I can't get married. Can't afford it, for one thing."

"She isn't my wife yet. Not going to lose her before she says 'I do.'"

"Not until you've got her tied up and shackled and thrown away the key, huh?" Levi winked.

"Gonna let that one go, too. Know why?"

"Why?"

Matt gave an ear-to-ear grin. "I'm one happy-ass man."

Levi gave him a hard shove. "Get out of here, you freak."

Stone stuck his head out of his office. "If you ladies are ready, we're having a meeting."

"Another meeting?" Levi moaned.

"This one is about the fund-raiser Emily has been working on for months—Pilots and Paws."

It was an organization Stone and Emily loved and supported, so they all did what they could to help. Levi brought up the rear as all three filed into the office. Emily, Sarah, Jedd and Cassie were already seated. "What are we doing for this thing?"

"We're…washing dogs for a donation," Stone said.

"That's easy enough," Levi said.

Stone winced. "We men have to do it with our shirts off."

Sarah clapped her hands. "Finally, a fundraiser I can fully support."

"You'll have to get in line," Cassie said.

"Don't worry about shrinkage, either," Emily said. "I checked the weather and we're good."

"Screw the weather. I'm not taking my shirt off unless Emily and Sarah wear bathing suits," Levi said.

"Fair's fair," Jedd said.

Levi sat through the meeting, led by Emily, who happened to be an event planner for her family's ranch when she wasn't flying for Magnum. Last-minute assignments were discussed and dispensed, since she'd already taken care of most everything. Levi wound up tasked with picking up pet product donations such as shampoo and the like, because he was single. Zoey, the owner of Pimp Your Pet in Fortune, was apparently also single and supercute according to Emily.

Not that she was trying to fix him up or anything. Still, that reminded him that he had promised to call Lily to follow up. He wasn't too excited about it, but he'd promised. One date. He could do one date. But this fake engagement Carly had roped him into might put a crimp in that. At some point, he figured, he'd have to settle down. Just like he had to go to the dentist every six months. Painful but necessary. Then when he got his itchy feet, as he expected he would any day now and want to move on, he'd have both Grace and a woman to remind him he was stuck. No reason to rush into anything. He and Grace had managed fine so far without a woman to direct their every move.

He was insulted that Irene thought he had to be married to raise his child properly. To be trusted to do a good job. Anyone who believed that was stuck in the dark ages.

Before his day was over, Levi donated some flying time to Pilots and Paws by transporting a rescue dog. The pup he flew home from the Fortune Valley Shelter to his forever family in Washington was a Chihuahua mix, so nervous he peed everywhere, even managing to squirt all over Levi's hand.

"Lucky for you, pup, I'm used to getting peed on."

He landed at the regional airport and unbuckled the nervous dog. "All right, c'mon…" He took a closer look at the collar around his neck. "*Bentley?* That's your name? Man, I'm sorry. Maybe you'll have better luck with these new people. People in California need to figure out how to name their dogs."

But when he got inside, an attendant told him that the people who were rescuing the dog hadn't shown up. "Don't know what to tell you."

Holding the shaking pup and praying he'd already unloaded all the water inside him, Levi dialed Magnum on his cell phone. Cassie picked up the phone, and after he explained what had happened, she handed the phone to Emily.

Who was crying.

"What the hell? What's wrong?" Levi asked.

"They changed their minds," she sniffled. "Oh, poor little Bentley."

He glanced at the tiny face and swore the dog's pupils were shaking. The whites of his eyes were showing. "You mean I flew all the fu—way here and now I have to bring him back?"

"It happens sometimes. Just bring him home. We'll figure something out."

He hung up. "Let's go, Bent— You know what? Screw that prissy name. I'm going to call you Digger."

His grandfather had owned a dog named Digger. It wasn't anything like this scrawny little thing Levi was afraid he might step on, but that dog had been a rescue, too. The only kind of dog his grandfather would ever own. Digger Sr. had been a retriever mix, a hunting dog that had never left his grandfather's side. That was the kind of dog Levi would get once Grace was old enough. A dog he couldn't risk stepping on in a million years.

"The name's a little badass for you, but I can't call you Bentley."

Digger Jr. shook all the way back to Fortune. Peed all over the seat, too. Levi wiped it up like he did Grace's spit-up. It was official now. He'd never cleaned up this many bodily fluids in his life, and he'd been through boot camp. The terrified pup was small enough to fit inside his jacket, so Levi stuck him in the front of his lightweight windbreaker and zipped it up. Maybe it was the additional warmth, but it cut back on the shaking a little.

"Where's the dog?" Emily met him at the entrance to the hangar. "Don't tell me you left him there."

Levi zipped his jacket down enough to reveal Digger's trembling head, eyes wide enough to pop out of his head.

"Aw." Emily smiled. "This is so great."

"What's so great? The forever family didn't show up to claim him. And you were crying."

"I know, but that was before."

Stone walked out of his inner office. "Would

never believe this if I didn't see it with my own eyes."

"What in the hell are you talking about? I thought you said this happens sometimes. The adoptions don't always go through."

"He doesn't get it." Stone came up to Emily and pulled her in with one arm. "Explain it to the newbie."

"Well, Levi." Emily stepped out of Stone's arms and reached to pet Digger's head. "You have just been adopted by Bentley."

"No way. And his name is Digger now. A Bentley is a car, not a dog. Am I the only one who understands this?"

Emily turned to Stone. "I rest my case."

"Yeah." Stone nodded. "You already named him, dude. Rookie mistake."

"No, no. Hold up." He threw up his palms. "I can't take him. I have a baby. Plus, this dog is nervous. And small. What if I accidentally step on him? Why do you think I put him in my jacket?"

"I think it's because you're a big guy with a protective streak and you sense that Digger needs you," Emily said.

"Liar." Levi ducked to find that Digger's head had disappeared inside his jacket. "No. Can't do it."

"Please, please." Emily put her hands together, prayer-like. "Please, Levi. Please!"

Shit. Levi glared at Stone, sending his brother

in arms a telepathic message: *save me before I kill you. Twice.*

"Don't look at me." Stone shrugged. "We have Winston. He's a hairy fart machine. The way I look at it, you got lucky, Airman."

"Yeah, right." Levi leveled Digger with an even, stern look. "This is just temporary."

CHAPTER TWELVE

WHEN LEVI ARRIVED to pick Grace up in the afternoon, Carly watched from the front window as he pulled something furry and small out of his truck. Something that looked a lot like a dog. She swung the door open to let him in. Upon closer inspection, definitely a dog. The teacup Chihuahua shook, and its eyeballs took up half the tiny face. She'd have to guess the pup was terrified by the looks of it, but to be honest, neither of them looked happy.

"I'll be right back. I need to get Digger situated before I come get Grace. Then we can talk."

Grace was still napping, as often seemed to be the case at pickup time, so Carly used the time to pace the kitchen and figure out what she would say to Levi. She needed the right words again, and as usual they were in short supply. He needed to understand that she'd done this for Grace. Not because she'd gotten carried away with all the kissing and the mind-blowing orgasm.

I went along with it because I thought an en-

*gagement sounded better than simply hooking up.
I couldn't let her know I'm the nanny.*

*I thought an engagement would signify com-
mitment and a stable family life for Grace.*

You were the one who was late!

*Levi, I've been under a lot of stress. I might be
having a nervous breakdown.*

No. She wasn't going for the pity factor. She'd
done this with the best of intentions. He would
just have to understand.

Levi returned within fifteen minutes and let
himself in. Though she appreciated the white
button-up Mcallister Charters shirt and black
Dockers, she also enjoyed the way he filled out
a plain cotton T-shirt. Hard not to notice the way
his wide shoulders strained at the fabric. The
well-worn jeans lying low on his hips were always a nice touch. And she didn't hate the way
he filled a room with his presence. With his alpha
attitude and energy. He oozed male sexuality,
and she wasn't immune to that.

Reality check. It was possible that she had a
little crush on her next-door neighbor.

"You owe me an explanation."

"Do you have a dog now?" He couldn't think
she'd ignore the creature she'd noticed in his
arms.

"It's only temporary. The owners backed out
of the adoption." He dragged a hand through
his hair.

Another pet adoption fail. Zoey had rescued three of those and found them new homes in record time. Except for Boo, whom she couldn't seem to find a home for yet, being that he was a one-hundred-plus-pound Great Dane.

"I hope it works out," Carly said.

"Nice try, by the way, but don't change the subject. You owe me. Explain."

She walked into the kitchen and he followed. "I'm sorry! I was only trying to help. Mrs. Lane recognized me. I thought it was kind of ironic that you had so many of the products we'd recommended on the website. Now it makes sense."

"But how did it get from that to us being engaged?"

Carly picked up one of Grace's empty bottles and turned to the sink to rinse it, her back to Levi. It might be easier to get the facts out while keeping her hands busy. And without facing him. "She talked about you. Not good things. You're a *playboy pilot*. You and Sandy were a *one-night stand*. And then…"

"Then what?"

"She saw my lucky ring and assumed we were engaged. I didn't correct her." The words came out in a rush. "Levi, she seemed very happy about you being engaged and settling down."

He made a very frustrated male sound, and she cringed.

"Why the hell is it that no one believes I'm capable of raising my own child?"

"I'm sorry! I can't change society for you."

"You could have told her you're the nanny."

The truth? Who told the truth anymore? Being a nanny wasn't sexy or exciting and, frankly, sounded like she needed the extra work to pay her bills. Not far from the raw and honest truth. And in her case, honesty wouldn't sell her company for top dollar. She had few true-blue fans, those who hadn't deserted after her mother's death. Mrs. Lane was one of them.

She didn't say anything for a beat.

"Carly," Levi pressed.

She whirled around, soap suds flying from both of her hands. "My company is in trouble!"

His eyes narrowed. "What kind of trouble?"

"The kind of trouble that happens when the founder of your company suddenly dies." She reached for a dish towel to dry her hands. "Think what would happen if Martha Stewart or Rachael Ray died. *That* kind of trouble."

"I'm sorry."

"I've been trying. Really trying to fix this mess and I'm extremely close. The last thing I want is for a fan like Mrs. Lane to get wind that I'm someone's *nanny*. How would that look? We've been trying to sell, so I can't afford for anything to go wrong right now."

"And I thought I hired a baby expert." He rocked back on his heels. "I didn't know you were selling the company. Might have said something."

"Why? There's nothing you can do to help. Look, I need to sell. For a lot of reasons. After my mother died, my father broke his hip when he was in Maine visiting my older brother. He had a total hip replacement, and the physical therapy bills have been through the roof."

"Jesus, Carly."

"It's all right. He'll get better. And I've learned so much from watching Grace. Actually raising a baby is a lot tougher than it looks. It's helped us both, in a way."

She threw the dish towel and it landed on the stove. Her hands shook with fear and nerves and a whole lot of other sensations that she couldn't quite name. This was only partly because Levi studied her, his blue eyes edgy and deep. Unreadable. She had no idea if he was about to kiss her or kill her. He calmly removed the towel from the stove, then stepped into her personal space.

"I wish I'd known about your dad. That's rough, I know."

"You should be mad at me. Furious. Please don't be nice to me right now." She bit back tears.

"One thing you should know about me. I'm not a *nice* man. I will disappoint you every time." He wiped away an errant tear with his thumb.

"I don't believe that."

"Believe it. What if Grace's grandparents are right about me? Did you think of that?" He cupped her chin with one hand.

"If that's true, then you need me to repair your image."

He chuckled. "I probably do."

She managed to crack a smile and bat her wet lashes at him.

"But I don't like lying. You should know that about me. From now on, we're going to have to be completely honest with each other. Get that?" Both hands slid down her arms and tightened. "Even if we're not honest with anyone else."

She nodded, somewhat shaky, but this time because he stood so close. His sensual lips were inches away from hers. They would be warm on her mouth. "I promise. No more lies."

"Now, what do you want to do about this fake engagement you got me into?"

"No one else has to know."

"A *secret* fake engagement?"

"The Lanes are only here for a month. How hard can it be to keep it under wraps for a few weeks?"

"So they're the only people we're lying to? The Lanes?"

She nodded slowly. "I think it could work."

"This is a small town."

"If we're careful, no one else has to know. Or find out."

"I don't know." Levi's heated gaze lowered to her lips. "I still don't like it. I'm not looking for a relationship right now, and suddenly I'm engaged."

"Well, what makes you think I want a relationship? Maybe you haven't thought about how hard this is going to be for *me*."

"Yeah?"

Her palms flattened against his hard chest. "You're not exactly the easiest person in the world to get along with."

He stepped back, lips twitching, and hooked a thumb to his chest. "Me? Why? What's wrong with *me*?"

"First, you're irritatingly punctual. Second, you throw Grace up in the air too high. I haven't wanted to say anything before today, and I'm sorry, but it's true. Third, you're way too bossy." She folded her arms across her breasts while she tried to think of more items to add to her list.

But the facts were she didn't know him well enough to list all of his faults, of which she felt certain there were many. And another thing: *I can never tell what you're thinking. Or feeling. Or whether you feel anything at all.*

"First, I was in the military, so sue me if it's still important to be on time. A hard habit to break. Second, Grace likes the throwing and I'm not going to drop her. Ever. Third, yes, I'm bossy, and I think you might like it sometimes."

She drew in a sharp breath and went all marshmallow melty inside. "I...I don't think so."

He tugged her in so that her whole body went flush against his. Breasts brushed up against rock-hard pecs. Liquid legs met his longer ones. His hand on her ass.

"I do. You might like it when I order you to come."

"Ha! Sorry, but I like to handle that sort of thing myself." Too late, she realized what that sounded like. As if she drove solo all the time.

He grinned. "Give me a minute while I picture that."

Her face flushed, and she cleared her throat. "I mean, I will decide how, where and when I... *you know*."

"Who's bossy now?"

Hot damn, she was kind of bossy around him. She didn't know why or how, but she kind of liked it. "When it comes to my body."

"Now, would you like to know what's wrong with you?" he asked, a too-wicked glint in his gaze.

"Not really," she managed to squeak out. She had a rather long list of her own and didn't particularly want to add to it.

"First, you're afraid of me." He tugged on a lock of her hair. "Second, you're too emotional.

Someone is going to take advantage of that. It won't be me. Third, you're a liar."

She froze. This wasn't who she wanted to be. His honest words cut so deeply that she wrenched away from him and stomped out of the kitchen.

CHAPTER THIRTEEN

LEVI HAD HIT a raw nerve, because Carly's eyes flashed with anger. She twisted out of his arms and walked away without another word. But someone so adept at lying shouldn't be shocked at being called out for it.

He understood little white lies. Not quite an angel, he'd told plenty of them in his not-so-distant past. *Baby, you're sexy. No, your tits are the perfect size. You're the only one for me. I think I love you.* All in his past. He no longer had room in his life for any kind of deceit. For years now, he'd been nothing but up-front and direct about what he wanted and needed from a woman. It was ugly but real. He found that women could stomach real better than he'd ever believed possible.

She'd stomped into her bedroom, and he followed, stopping to brace one arm in the doorway.

She turned and pointed to him. "I'm not afraid of you!"

It was difficult not to laugh. "*That's* what you're upset about? Not that I called you a liar?"

"First, I'm not afraid. Second, I'm *not* too emotional. I'm a girl. Anyway, it's better than keeping feelings locked up tight. That's going to give you an ulcer one day. And third, lying is new to me. A hazard of my trade."

He quirked an eyebrow. "I didn't know you were in politics."

"No, but close." She plopped onto her bed.

He waited patiently for more, assuming she would give it to him once the silence stretched between them. She probably didn't want to be alone with him in her bedroom and run out of things to talk about. Not here. Because that would be scary. For her. When that happened, they might both have to face the sizzling chemistry between them. Clearly, she didn't *want* any of this. And he got that. He wasn't sure he liked this deal, either, so she could join his club.

"You don't really want to hear this," she finally said.

He met her eyes. "Actually, I do."

"It's…a long story. You have to understand that I've spent most of my life hiding the truth. Every time a teacher asked me to stand up and read, I developed a bad case of laryngitis. Every single time. I listened to books on tape and I learned to memorize parts so I wouldn't have to read them. I had my coping skills. Either way, it was a long time before anyone realized I had dyslexia."

Levi's stomach dropped. He'd had a buddy in high school with dyslexia. Really bright kid who had a difficult time with reading comprehension. Not only had he had a tough time in school, but kids made fun of him. It was ugly, because kids could be so damn mean. Levi had gotten in trouble more than a few times for sticking up for his friend.

The discarded instructions to the crib took on a different light. "Did you get any help?"

"It took a long time, but yes. I was well behaved, so they said I was capable, just wouldn't apply myself. They didn't even want to test me for a long time. But finally my parents fought the school and got me help in my junior year."

He was no expert on the matter, but that seemed a little late. "So you graduated."

"Barely. And after a few years, I went to the Fashion Institute of Technology in New York City."

"Been there many times. Great city." The city buzzed with an excitement and energy that was contagious. Not the place he wanted to live, but he understood the draw.

"You know how the song says something like being able to make it anywhere if you can make it there? Well, I didn't make it there."

"I'm not much for Broadway show tunes." He moved to her bed, where he sat beside her, like he would stay awhile. "What happened?"

"Nothing. That's exactly what happened."

More waiting, then. He let the silence fill the room while he studied her. Contrary to popular belief, he wasn't so much an icicle as a patient man. Learned the hard way.

"I screwed everything up because I didn't believe in myself. Or maybe the lying caught up with me." She picked up a pillow and hit it once. "Look, there's a lot of selling that has to go on in any career. On a job interview, for instance. But when it comes to a competitive edge, I wasn't all that good at selling myself. Or my work."

"So with RockYourBaby you've chosen to lie your way to success."

"Not *lie*, exactly." She squirmed next to him. "Create an illusion that the real baby expert simply passed the torch on to her daughter. And because my illusion is all done behind a computer monitor, maybe it's a bit easier for someone like me. I didn't mean to drag *you* into this. But I also helped you. Irene likes me, and it can't hurt for her to think that we're together."

And he'd dragged her into his issues by asking her to bring Grace to the park. By letting her know about Sandy's parents when he might have kept it to himself. Because it wasn't like him to overshare. Maybe he'd done so because she'd helped him in a pinch, or maybe because he noticed how she truly cared about Grace, but either way, he'd shared more with Carly than was his custom. His fault.

"Is it that crazy an idea? For us to be a couple?"

"You were the one who called us stupid. We wouldn't make a good fit."

He and Grace needed calm and quiet in their lives. Not all this chaos and emotion that surrounded Carly. All the lies. She was going through a tough time. Frankly, she worried him as much as she frustrated him. He already had Grace to take care of, and it had been a cold night in Texas the last time he'd tried his hand at being a woman's white knight. Hadn't worked out so well then, either.

"I would have to agree." She took a breath. "Except for, you know, the kissing and…stuff."

"You mean the orgasm. We're engaged. I think you can just say it."

"Yes. The orgasm."

He tugged her in tight. "So we're in this together until the Lanes go back home. But between you and me? No more lies."

"No…more…lies."

Damn. Her eyes. They drew him in every time. Made him want things. Complicated things. But if he did this, if he went along with this little game, he'd put some parameters of his own into place. Not just for her. For himself. He didn't want to be sucked in by the likes of Carly Gilmore. Definitely, one hundred percent not ready for *this*.

"And we both need to remember this *thing* between us isn't real."

Yeah. Just keep telling yourself that, buddy.

She nodded. "I'm not likely to forget, since I'm the one who made it up. And after they're gone, we go back to how things were before."

"And no one gets hurt." He squeezed her hand.

He'd been in this place too many times to count. Temporary relationships. Hell, even his permanent ones had a temporary feel to them. And wasn't he sick of all that? Because he'd learned that even temporary had risks. Even temporary carried with it lifetime consequences.

Carly was staring at his lips. He should tell her that wasn't helpful. But because no one had ever called him wise when it came to women, he kissed her, taking the kiss deeper when she opened up to him.

"Wait." She suddenly pulled back. "What are we doing?"

"Practicing. Because it should look like we're comfortable around each other. If we're going to keep lying, anyway, and make it look good."

"Oh, right."

And also, because she tasted so sweet, too good. He knew she'd swallow him up whole if he let her. She was dangerous to his peace of mind, meaning he'd be playing with fire for the next month. This would be different, playing at a real relationship while knowing he'd easily walk away at the end. No harm, no foul. He'd make sure not to hurt her, or that she could ever get close enough to hurt him.

Game on.

CHAPTER FOURTEEN

ON SATURDAY, LEVI got ready for the pet wash. He gathered Grace's and Digger's assorted crap. For someone who could live for a week in the woods with the contents of one backpack to sustain him, carrying along this much stuff for the day felt unnatural. But he did it, because all the books said he should do it. All the so-called baby blogs, of which he was trying to read more since learning about Carly's.

He shook his head, reminded himself he was an idiot, then got busy packing a change of clothes for Grace. Several diapers, baby wipes, a pacifier—which she hated, but hey, maybe he'd get lucky one day—a bag of Cheerios, a teething ring, two bibs and some tissues. Of course, he also had to carry the fold-up stroller with him and the car seat. He briefly considered bringing the fold-up playpen his parents had shipped to him, but there would be so many women there today, Grace would probably get passed around for a while. For Digger, he simply brought his leash, some dog treats and plastic bags.

Man.

"It's a damned good thing you're so cute."

This he said to Grace, though technically it applied to both of them. Digger was cute, but not what he wanted in a dog. Levi preferred big, bad or at least somewhat threatening. But this was what he got, thanks to Emily. Once he'd snapped the leash on Digger's collar, all three of them were out the door.

A few minutes later, he pulled into the airport parking lot, where Cassie, Emily, Zoey and Sarah were already setting up. Signs were set at strategic locations, and three long hoses lay on the ground near big tubs with the Pimp Your Pet logo proudly displayed. Matt and Stone were nowhere in sight. Probably hiding inside, the cowards.

"Let me have Grace." Cassie reached Levi first, just as he opened the rear passenger door.

His experience the few times he'd had Grace around Cassie, Emily and Sarah was that they'd pass Grace around to get what they called their baby fix. Fortunately, Grace wasn't fussing at the moment, because when she did, they tended to hand her back. She was always his problem then.

He lifted her out of her car seat and handed her to Cassie.

Levi pulled out the stroller, then attached the car seat to it and rolled it toward Cassie. "Here, take this, too."

Cassie gave him a long look. "I see you brought the house again."

He would never again be caught without enough diapers. That one time had been a disaster. "And this." He set the diaper bag in the empty car seat.

"How are you, angel? What a good baby you are…" Cassie's words echoed in the October California sunshine as she pushed the stroller one-handed. She never sounded as sweet as when she had Grace in her arms.

He was going to take her up on that overnight soon. It was high time he had a real night off. He was still supposed to call Lily and arrange that date, but that wasn't going to happen now. Everything had changed.

"Come out of there."

At least his no-nonsense tone worked on Digger. He'd begun to respond to orders like a good enlisted man. Digger moved, his bulging eyes peeking from underneath the seat where he'd hidden. He crept out an inch at a time, like he feared he might soon face a firing squad.

"No one's gonna hurt you, Digger."

Great. Now he was talking to a dog as if he could understand English. Which meant he must be slowly turning into his grandfather.

"Aw." Zoey appeared at his elbow.

"Hey, Zoey."

She looked cute today, dressed in cutoff overalls and pink-and-white waders with strawber-ries all over them. Her dark hair was pulled in a ponytail high on her head.

"So… I heard about your engagement." She winked and gave him a thumbs-up. "Your secret is safe with me."

"Right." He picked Digger up, slapped the leash on him and handed him over to Zoey.

"You're going to get a free bath, little one." In two seconds, Zoey had led Digger away.

Levi made his way inside the hangar and to the Magnum offices to change. He found Stone and Matt hiding like a couple of scaredy-cats in Stone's inner office. They were both already changed into board shorts and wore short-sleeved T-shirts with the Pilots and Paws and Mcallister Charters logos.

"What the hell? Why aren't y'all out there helping?"

"It's early." Stone had his long legs stretched out on his desk as he fiddled with his phone. "We're doing all the work once we get going."

"Emily told him to get out of her way," Matt said with a smirk.

"What's your excuse?" Levi said to Matt.

"I was up late last night." He leaned back in the office chair and closed his eyes.

Stone glared at him. "Do I need to hear this?"

"Because of Shackles, smartass." Matt opened

one eye. "He snores louder than I do. How would *you* like a dog that snores?"

"How would you like a dog that farts?" Stone said.

"Would either of you like a dog that pisses on your hand and is so tiny it comes up to your ankles?" Levi changed quickly into his board shorts.

"Let me get out my violin," Stone said. "That dog is going to get you laid, not that you need any help."

Matt nodded, head back, eyes closed. "Yup."

"How's that?" Levi asked.

"Lots of women love those silly little lapdogs," Stone said.

"And then he's got Grace. Women love babies, too." Matt nodded in his sleep, apparently. "It's actually kind of unfair to all the other single guys out there, when you think about it."

If they only knew how Grace cramped his style. She was worth it, but he wouldn't call her a chick magnet. And now there was Digger. The first time a woman got her hand pissed on by his cute dog, she might not be all that thrilled with either one of them.

"I think y'all are giving me way too much credit."

"Yeah?" Stone arched an eyebrow.

"Neither one of you two were slackers when it came to picking up women. Just because you're settled down now, don't try to act all proper and shit with me," Levi said.

A few minutes later, there was a brief knock on the door and Sarah let herself inside. "We're ready for you." She smiled at Matt and yanked on his arm. "Take off your shirt, babe."

"If I had a nickel…" Matt stood and pulled it off, then threw it so that it hit Levi's head.

"Hey!" Levi threw it back at Matt's chest.

"We've already got a line forming. Women who want to see some skin," Sarah said. "The more skin, the bigger the donation."

They'd been experiencing an Indian summer that had stretched into October, and the temps were still in the low seventies with sun, just as the weather forecast had predicted. Sarah was right, and as he stepped out into a bright ray of sunshine, he noticed mostly women and one guy lined up with their pets. Big retrievers—his kind of dog—shepherds, beagles, poodles and…was that a pig?

The tubs were filled with sudsy water, and a short table near each one held all the pimping products. Levi scanned the area to find Grace and make sure she was still okay. She sat in her stroller, thumb in her mouth, staring with huge eyes at what appeared to be a bullmastiff. Digger was still off to the side with Zoey, who seemed to be giving him…a massage? Levi was officially in la-la land. Might as well get into this thing.

When in Rome… He pulled off his shirt.

"All right. Who's my first victim?"

CHAPTER FIFTEEN

OH, BOY, HE'S SO sexy.

He stood at the kitchen sink, holding a mug of coffee in one hand, facing the window. Shirtless. Even his back was drool-worthy, with a physique that was no gym rat's. No, these were working-man-who-lifts-engines muscles. Her favorite kind. Natural. She curled her arms around his waist and pressed her face into a warm, solid, masculine back. This one was all man. Oh, and he smelled so good.

"Good morning," she said to his back. Then she licked it, feeling his stomach tighten beneath her fingertips.

He groaned. "Didn't have enough of me last night?"

"Never."

He turned around in her arms to face her. "I can take care of that."

Levi.

In one hand, he had a diaper, and in the other, a baby bottle. "Did you feed Grace yet? Did you burp her?"

No! No! Not sexy! Not sexy!

"Jesus, Mary and Joseph." Carly rolled over and sat up in bed. "What's wrong with me?"

Wrong? Oh, nothing other than the fact that Levi had put a few suggestions in her head that were still bouncing around. He'd been sitting right on this bed when he'd kissed the living daylights out of her. When he'd set his boundaries. No one would get hurt. Even when this whole thing ended. She was totally on board with not getting hurt, by the way. The last thing she wanted was to get tied down to any man when she was about to finally be free. What she'd do with all that freedom was still up for grabs.

Besides, between Grace and her website, it felt like Carly had babies on her brain 24/7. If she wasn't working on the website, she was working with Grace. But even if what Carly really wanted was more dreams about Levi without his shirt on, she understood it wasn't a great idea. He'd been right to set limits. Even if what they had was only pretend, it would be fun faking for a little while. She didn't mind when he flirted with her and another orgasm would not be the worst thing to ever happen to her.

They had their stories straight. They had agreed they would pretend to have met first in New York and run into each other again when he moved to Fortune. From there, it had been one of those insta-love things no one believed in anymore. Neither did she, frankly, but it was going to have to work for their purposes. The only people who had to believe the story were Mr. and Mrs. Lane.

Carly had the meeting with Jenny scheduled via Skype in a couple days, and she'd see whether she could somehow work in a sales pitch of Rock-YourBaby. It was an opportunity, if nothing else, to tell her about the blog. To drop several hints that they might be interested in selling, in case Jenny knew of anyone. She worked to remind herself to contain the excitement. Jenny was a good contact to have in New York, and reconnecting with her could only mean good things ahead.

In the shower, Carly reviewed her options for today. She had some work to do because there was no such thing as weekends or taking time off when it came to running a small business. While drinking her first coffee of the day, she answered emails. A new photo of Grace wearing a pair of lace-trimmed jeans and a matching denim-and-lace headband had become nearly as popular and well received as the first viral blog post. She had definitely turned a corner with RockYourBaby.

She had a voice message from Mrs. Lane, who asked about getting together for dinner, the four of them. Carly would certainly have to swing that by Levi first.

She stared at the accounts-payable pile on her

desk and thought of all the bookkeeping that lay
ahead. Mom's favorite part. Facts were, Carly
had several hours' worth of work ahead of her
with her mortal enemy, Excel. But today was
beautifully sunny and warm, an unusual October day. She *should* skip the pet wash, but Zoey
would be disappointed. So she dressed in a soft
yellow summer shift dress and paired it with a
cropped long-sleeved denim jacket and her favorite strappy sandals.

Later, Carly sat in her car in the Magnum Aviation parking lot. *Why am I here?* Maybe it wasn't
a good idea to show up where she knew Levi
would be. It might be best to continue to keep
her low profile, at least until the Lanes were out
of town. Plus, she didn't even have a dog, so why
was she at a pet wash? Silly. She should be…
doing something else. Anything else. Using her
time wisely, for instance. Or she could go shopping for shoes with money she didn't have.

But even though she sat a little frozen by the
fact that she'd see Levi again—shirtless—the
facts were that she was here to support Zoey
and the pet adoption cause. Because as a general
rule, Carly had always supported every chari-
table cause in Fortune. It had always been the
Gilmore way. She was *not* here because Levi
would be here. Not wearing a shirt.

The first and last time she'd seen that, her jaw
had slackened and her tongue had disengaged

from her brain. She hadn't even known what it would be like to kiss him then, but now she did. Now she unfortunately realized that he kissed on par with what he looked like—not helpful knowledge for a woman looking *not* to get involved.

There was a knock on her window, and Carly turned to see Jill. "Are you getting out?" She cocked her head.

Carly stared from Jill to the leashed black Lab sitting next to her. Interesting, since Jill didn't own a dog.

She rolled down her window. "Who's this?"

"Henry." Jill nodded as if introducing them. "I'm dog sitting."

Carly grabbed her keys, hopped out of the car and bent to give Henry a pat on the head. He licked her from chin to forehead and nearly knocked Carly on her ass.

"Sorry. I should have warned you. Henry here is a licker."

Carly used the tissue Jill handed her to wipe her face. "Who are you dog sitting for, anyway?"

"Don't laugh, but it's for this guy I just met. He's low end of the Chris Scale but still a hunk and a half. I figured you met a Chris while baby-sitting. Who's to say I can't meet my own Chris while dog sitting? You never know—after the first kiss he might jump up several points on the Chris scale. It could happen."

They walked toward the hangars, where just

outside of one of them Carly noticed a line of mostly women with their pets. Most of them dogs, though there was at least one cat in the mix. Carly recognized many of the women, including Emily's grandmother and some of her Pink Ladies genealogical society friends, Marci from the Drip, and her third-grade teacher, Mrs. Olson. Sarah stood at the beginning of a long line, taking donations. At the end of the line, it split in three different directions.

"It's kind of luck of the draw which guy you get to wash your pet," Sarah said when Jill handed over a twenty-dollar donation.

All three of the men were wearing nothing but board shorts. For what it was worth, they all seemed to be doing a good job of washing the pets—and being good-natured about getting soaked when the dogs shook all over them. She noticed Levi bend to take a sponge to a wet golden retriever, the sun glinting off his tight shoulder muscles. Carly stared at his perfect body, knowing those abs were as hard as they looked.

Jill pointed in Levi's direction. "That must be him. Hot Dad."

"Yeah. That's Levi."

She elbowed Carly. "I don't blame you for watching the baby now. Good move."

"I didn't do it because of him." Carly put her hands on her hips. "I needed the baby. Remember?"

Jill rolled her eyes. "Yeah, yeah, I remember now. The baby. You needed the baby."

They moved up the line. Dogs were washed, toweled dried and primped. Off to the side, Zoey gave dogs massages. Emily and her sister, Molly, placed ribbons on the females and little plastic bow ties on the males. Hunter, Matt's teenage son, was taking photos with an old Polaroid camera and giving them to the owners. The whole thing was freaking adorable. A marketing genius must have come up with the idea.

Ahead of them, Carly noticed a beautiful blonde she recognized to be Joanne, owner of the only bridal shop in town, flirting openly with Levi. Naturally she'd be here, as she and Matt were parents to fifteen-year-old Hunter. She wore a short dress that showed a lot of leg and a pair of wedges with a ribbon that wound up around her thin ankles. Her long blond hair was loose, and every time she smiled at Levi, she tossed the mane of hair over her shoulder. She placed her hand on Levi's biceps, laughing when he squatted down to better pet the top of her toy poodle's head.

"Is Joanne...still single?" Carly said out loud.

"I think she's dating some semipro baseball player. Isn't she?"

"That's right." Carly nodded.

"Wait a second." Jill turned. "Hoo, boy. Look at you."

"What is it?"

"You're jealous."

"No. I'm not."

Totally not jealous when Levi laughed as Joanne said something near his ear and her stomach fisted double time. She was simply concerned that things could get complicated if Levi started dating someone else. Feelings could get hurt. Not hers. The other woman's.

"I think you're jealous. And why wouldn't you be? He's *your* fiancé."

"Shh!" Carly hissed and turned to see if anyone had heard.

Carly noticed Irene in the distance, walking with a man who looked about ten years older than her. He wore dark glasses and had a white beard.

Oh, God. Irene was here. With Frank, she had to assume.

"Carly!" Irene spotted her and waved in her direction.

They both walked toward Carly. She tried to catch Levi's attention, hoping she could send a silent DEFCON 4 warning, but he was too busy drying off Joanne's dog.

"Help." Carly pulled on Jill's arm and jutted her chin in Irene's direction. "Mrs. Lane is here. With her husband."

"Uh-oh," Jill said. "Just…act engaged."

"How do I do that?"

"I have no idea."

"You're a big help."

They were ready for this, sure, but a little warning would have been welcome.

"Excuse me, dear," a female bystander interrupted. "I see you don't have a pet with you. Would you mind watching Petunia for a minute? I have to get something out of my car, and I don't want to lose my place in line."

Carly looked down. The woman had a pig on a leash. "Um…"

"It's all right. She's a potbellied pig. Trained, just like a dog. Better than a dog. She loves her bath. Very smart." As if to prove it, she told Petunia to sit.

And Petunia did, just like a dog.

"Sure." Carly took the leash. It would give her something to do besides have a silent, nervous breakdown. "I'd be happy to."

Carly waited with Petunia. Maybe Irene and her husband were afraid of pigs and would wait until she could join them. It would be for the best if they could have any conversation away from any of Fortune citizens' big ears.

"There you are, Carly, dear." Irene walked straight up to her in line. "I want you to meet my husband. Frank, this is Carly, Levi's fiancée."

Frank grunted. "Pleasure."

She didn't know what she'd pictured for Frank Lane, but it certainly wasn't this. He was dressed in Bermuda shorts and a loud, clashing polo shirt and appeared to have just walked off a golf course.

"What are you...you two doing here?"

"I read about the pet wash in the local newspaper and I love small-town stuff like this. It's so Mayberry-like." She glanced at Petunia. "Is this *your* pig?"

"No, I'm only helping the owner because she had to get out of line."

"We'll wait with you." Irene planted herself next to Carly and away from the pig. "Did you get my message about dinner?"

"Yes." Carly swallowed. "I...I need to ask Levi about when would be a good time."

"While you women jibber-jabber, I'll wait right over there." Frank pointed toward a row of folding chairs that someone had set up under some shade.

"Fine, dear." Irene patted Carly's shoulder after Frank walked off. "He wasn't as excited as I thought he'd be."

How could Irene tell? The man looked like he had a permanent scowl etched on his face. "Why not?"

"Who knows?" Irene sighed. "He said something ridiculous like Levi would probably lie about this. Who on earth would lie about being engaged?"

Carly went still. "Jeez. Someone crazy, probably."

"Or desperate." Irene nodded. "Is Grace here?"

Carly pointed toward Cassie and Grace while simultaneously searching for Petunia's owner as the line moved forward. Ahead, Henry had already been dried and received a bow tie. Jill chatted it up with Hunter, who had taken photos of the dogs and flapped them in the air to dry them. Carly moved up the line and wound up pushed toward Levi. Irene lagged somewhere behind her, talking with Mrs. Olson about the wonderful weather in California.

Yes, yes. Stick to the weather. The weather and the appalling price of real estate.

Petunia squealed, and Levi turned to smile at the pig.

His warm gaze slid up to meet Carly's eyes. "Hey."

"Hi, babe!" Carly launched her body toward Levi and planted a big kiss on his lips.

She meant the kiss to be a quick buss for Irene's benefit, but Levi tightened his arms around her hips. He tugged her in tight and put some tongue in the kiss. Her fake fiancé was not shy about PDA.

Unbelievably. Hot.

"Oh, my." Irene laughed.

Levi pulled back, and his eyebrows went up at seeing Irene. "Hi."

"Irene came by to support the event. Pilots and Paws is such a worthy organization. They do such great work uniting pets with their forever families." Carly might be laying it on a little thick, but sue her for being a bit wowed by that kiss.

Levi squatted in front of Petunia and removed her leash. "Who's this?"

"Petunia. She belongs to someone who had to get out of line. I'm sure she'll be right back."

Like he'd been bathing pigs his entire life, Levi went to work on Petunia.

"Frank is here, too." Irene pointed in his direction. "Sitting right over there."

"Great," Levi said, and Carly couldn't tell whether this was a welcome development in his opinion. Only his shoulders showed some strain. He pointed. "Grace is here, too. You might as well say hello."

"Yes, we'll go ahead and do that." Irene walked toward Grace.

Levi lifted Petunia and placed her in the sudsy water. She seemed to like it, too, just like the lady said she would. She made a strange half-honk and half-squealing sound. Carly kept quiet and let Levi work. Quiet worked for her, too, especially when it involved watching Levi bend and, as his board shorts ran down low on his hips, reveal a patch of golden skin. He had a perfect ass. And it was official—Carly was boy crazy. Er, man crazy. She and Petunia, that was. The smart pig had rolled on her side, perhaps to make it easier for Levi to cop a feel. Carly would swear Petunia had batted her eyelashes at the man.

"You okay?" Levi squatted next to Petunia, rubbing her belly with a wet brush as he washed her. He cocked his head to Carly, waiting for her answer.

If he was talking about the other night, no, she was not. She'd been thinking about him way too much. "I didn't know they'd be here. She just… showed up."

"It'll be okay." He spoke smoothly and without an ounce of emotion.

That was Levi. Cool. Calm. No fear. She wondered if he'd give her lessons.

He rinsed Petunia off one last time with a large sponge, then lifted her out of the tub and straightened to his full height.

"She wants to know a good time to go out to dinner. What should I say?"

"Stall."

"Good idea. I'll tell her I'm too busy with work. You're too busy with work. We're both just way too busy."

"So long as you don't make it sound like we're so busy we can't take care of Grace."

"Right."

"I'm not worried." He grinned. "You've got this."

"Yes. Yes, I do. Okay. I should get Petunia back to her owner. Wait. Where's Petunia?" Carly turned in a circle. No Petunia.

"Shit." Levi stared in the direction of the airstrip, which of course was fenced off to the general public.

Petunia was headed for the fence where there was a strip of grass and dirt. Mostly dirt. Carly ran for the pig, but Levi, with his long legs, quickly outpaced her. Petunia squealed as if she'd finally tasted the sweet freedom of her ancestors. Dirt, straight ahead. Could paradise be far behind?

Carly heard a woman screech, "My pig! Petunia, come back to me. Come back!"

"I've got this!" Levi yelled.

"I've got this!" Carly waved to the woman.

Levi reached the pig first, of course, but Carly was right behind him. He put his hands on Petunia, but she snorted and, being wet, slipped out of his grip.

Carly tried to block her between them and got a hand on her once, but Petunia got away. Now she was slippery, wet and muddy thanks to the dirt. When she tried to make a run for it again, Carly threw herself on top of her. But it seemed that the harder Carly clung, the more Petunia wriggled. She squealed and snorted in a most unladylike way. And dear God in heaven, was Carly actually wrestling with a *pig*? Wearing her favorite Forever 21 summer dress?

"Aren't you going to help me? Put the leash on her! Levi. Hurry! I've got her."

But he simply stood over her, hands on hips,

grinning ear to ear. He'd been joined by the pig owner on one side, and Mr. and Mrs. Lane on the other. Mrs. Lane had a worried look on her face, but the amusement in Levi's eyes was impossible to miss. The owner bent to leash Petunia.

Levi grinned and held out his hand. "Didn't anyone ever teach you never to wrestle with a pig?"

CHAPTER SIXTEEN

A FEW MINUTES LATER, Levi tried his damnedest to school his expression into something resembling concern. *Do. Not. Laugh.* His grandfather had not laughed at him the time he'd tried to milk a cow and been rewarded with a spray of milk that had covered his eyes. His mouth. His ears. Pop hadn't laughed. He'd coughed, turned and excused himself to get a towel. Probably had a good long chuckle on the way to the kitchen.

Carly sat on a chair in Stone's office, streaks of mud on her chin, cheeks and nose. Blond hair wild and unruly. Short dress muddy. Even her sandals had been through the wringer. She looked like she'd been in a fight with a...well, a pig. Which told him two new things about this woman: she did not give up easily, or mind getting a little dirty in the process.

Good to know.

He wiped mud off her chin with the wet towel Emily had given her and bit his lower lip. "There's an old saying. If you wrestle with a pig, you'll get dirty. And the pig will only—"

She held up her index finger. "Don't finish that sentence."

He grinned.

"You're enjoying this, aren't you?" She grabbed his hand from where it was busy cleaning off her nose and brought it down.

He took control back and went back to wiping at her cheeks. "*Enjoy* is probably not a strong enough word."

"This is so embarrassing. Petunia was supposed to be trained, like a dog. That's what her owner said."

"You can take the pig off the ranch, but you can't... I forgot how that one goes."

"Thank God."

"You're pretty sexy when you're mud wrestling, you know?"

"How can you laugh about this? I looked like a fool in front of the Lanes. That can't be good."

"Nah, you just looked like someone who takes her responsibilities seriously."

"That's what I was going for."

"I'd say you got it done."

She brought his hand down again, and this time he allowed it. "Thanks for taking care of me like a good fiancé might do."

"No worries, though I don't think they noticed me bring you inside. They're with Cassie and Grace now."

"So no one saw us come in here?"

"Don't think so. Matt's washing twice the number of pets right now, which is fine with me."

"If I haven't said it enough, I'm sorry. I didn't mean to make life harder for you, pretending to be my fiancé. I should have considered you might be interested in or dating someone else. It was shortsighted of me, I know. I just…reacted. I'm really sorry."

"Being your fake fiancé is not the worst thing to ever happen to me." Not even the second or third, but he wasn't going there.

"Were you dating anyone here?"

Seemed like a crisis of conscience had overcome Cute Stuck-Up Girl. Cute Sexy now. "A coffee date with Lily Hamilton. I was supposed to call and follow up for dinner."

She closed her eyes, then opened them again. "Lily. She's so nice. I'm so sorry, Levi."

"It wasn't a thing. And you should know, anyway, after you and I kissed, I had no intention of calling her. I haven't had time to…date. Or anything." And it had been far too long without the *or anything.* Also not going there.

"Me, too. I think I forgot how to act around someone of the opposite sex."

His gaze heated. "You did fine the other night on the couch."

She coughed. "Yeah. Thanks."

"What's wrong? You don't normally wrestle a pig in front of a guy? Because that can be a mat-

ing call in some countries." He managed to keep a straight face.

She rolled her eyes at him. "No. I don't have the most stellar history with men."

"Get out. My fiancée? How did you catch me, then?"

She didn't laugh. "I wouldn't normally go out with a guy like you, anyway. Guys like you don't go for girls like me."

"Guys like me?"

"I know I'm not sexy, or anything."

"Yeah, you are," he said. "Otherwise, I don't think we'd be engaged."

"That isn't funny."

"It's a *little* funny."

She didn't say anything for a beat, but then stood. "I have freckles and wild wavy hair that won't do what I tell it. I'm a little chunky. Oh, sorry. Curvy. I guess maybe your type is someone like Joanne."

"Joanne?"

"Never mind. Forget I said anything. It's just that I…don't want you to think this pretending has to go on behind closed doors. You don't have to act like you find me attractive. Or…tongue kiss me in front of Irene."

"Oh, yeah. She saw that, didn't she? Seriously, Carly. You've got to be kidding me if you have any doubts about how sexy you are. When I said

you drive me crazy, I meant every word. You're a knockout."

"I'm not fishing for compliments, and you don't have to say that."

"I know I don't have to. Not like you're going to break up with me if I don't. This is just me... being honest. Like we said we were going to be."

"Okay." She let out a long breath. "Thanks."

"But I'd seriously like to kick the ass of whatever guy made you feel like you weren't."

There was definitely something there, given the suddenly guarded expression in her gaze and her lack of response. Bingo. A dude. An idiot. Possibly someone a hell of a lot like...him. He didn't want to believe it, but it made sense. It was there in the way she carried herself, with a heartbreaking bravado he saw right through.

"Here's what you need to know. Most of us are jerks. And we wouldn't know a good thing if it hit us in the nut sack."

"Not all of you." She rubbed her knee, which hiked up her dress higher, not that he should be noticing.

But okay, he did. He *noticed* everything about her. The way she subconsciously rubbed her ring when she was nervous. Scared. For whatever reason, she was still wary of him. Afraid to be alone with him, maybe. Not that he blamed her. He was a little out of his element here, too, if he was honest. He'd dated plenty of beautiful women in the past. Then there was Carly. She was nothing if not beautiful, but here was the thing. She was also…so damn real.

He stepped into her space again, drew her in by the nape of her neck and, for a moment, just stared into those liquid amber eyes. She had him feeling protective about a woman for the first time in a long while. Caring about her feelings. He'd dragged her into an office and cleaned her up so that she wouldn't be humiliated.

He didn't know what had gotten into him lately. "Don't do that. Don't ever think that you're not perfect the way you are."

"That's easy for someone like you to say."

"Like me?"

"You have a mirror, don't you?"

"So you think I'm a hunk?" He grinned.

She wouldn't look at him directly, as if he was the sun and she'd forgotten her shades. "You're okay."

He liked the way she gave him shit. Definitely not making it easy for him. Even so, he leaned in closer. Zeroed in on her lips.

Lifting her up, he backed up and set her on the desk, hiked her dress up to her hips and stepped between her legs. The smile slipped off her face, replaced by a heated gaze in her beautiful amber eyes. He kissed her, hard, trying to communicate in one kiss all he wanted to do to her. Ravage her for hours. Listen to her scream his name. All he needed were a few uninterrupted hours and a little privacy.

She moaned when his hands lifted her up enough to cup and squeeze her ass. "We…can't do this here."

"Not here, no," he said against her collarbone, nipping her. "I have big plans for you."

Her hands came around his neck, tugging him closer. "And I have some for you."

He pulled back and took a minute to just study her. How had he never noticed how beautiful she was? Nothing *cute* about her. She was devastating. He'd had knockouts before, but Carly was hotter than all of them put together. Sweet. Loving. So soft.

A knock on the door he'd neglected to lock had him separating from her quickly. Carly straightened the skirt of her dress.

"Levi?" Sarah's voice.

"Come in," he said, then cleared his throat.

Sarah opened the door, and her intelligent eyes seemed to make a quick assessment that she'd interrupted something. "I wanted to check on Carly. Everything okay?"

"I'm fine." Carly hopped off the desk and headed to the door. "Just a little muddy, but I'm all cleaned up now."

"The lines have died down, so we're good with just Stone and Matt."

"I should go find my friends." Carly walked past Sarah, then turned to Levi. "See you later."

He cracked a smile and watched her go.

Sarah caught Levi's gaze, hands on hips. Not saying a word. Women. She wanted to say something to him, so what the hell was she waiting for?

"What?" Levi finally asked.

"You know what," she said.

Matt appeared behind her. "You're *engaged*?"

Crap. Levi slid a hand down his face. "Where did you hear that?"

"Mrs. Lane told anyone who would listen. Everyone in my line wanted their dog washed and the scoop on whether you'll be registered at Target or someplace else."

"What the hell?"

"That's right," Matt said. "What the hell, Levi? I've saved your ass so many times I've lost count. You're going to get married and not tell *me*? Your compadre? Your bud?"

"Please, Matt," Sarah said. "If anyone should be upset, it should be me. I could tell them all the best places in the area to register. We just did."

Levi closed his eyes and pinched the bridge of his nose. "I don't need any help registering. There's no wedding."

"Well, that was quick," Matt said. "You're a little too fickle, dude."

"Oh, you're enjoying this, aren't you? Watching me squirm."

"Definitely not true," Matt said with one of the widest grins Levi had ever seen on him. "I'm here for you. Nasty breakups are no fun."

Levi groaned. "Everyone's a comedian. Not. Getting. Married."

"Then why does Mrs. Lane think you're engaged?" Sarah asked.

"That's because...*she* thinks we are."

Matt nodded. "Sure, sure. That makes about as much sense as anything else."

"Look, Carly's just going through some...hard stuff right now, and it made sense," Levi said. "What Mrs. Lane doesn't know won't hurt her. She seems to like Carly, and that sort of helps me, too. By association."

"About that," Matt said. "Sarah told me something about an emergency screening you almost lost your cookies over?"

Levi glared at Sarah.

"Hey, I sleep with him. What do you want from me?" Sarah excused herself and left the office, leaving Levi alone with Matt.

"I didn't want you and Stone to worry about me. I've got it covered."

Matt shut the door. "Yeah, I know. You don't need anyone's help. You're fine on your own. You can do it all. Super Dad. I know."

"Never said that. Anyway, the whole thing's been scrapped. Thanks to Carly."

"Yeah, so here's the thing. You might have wanted to swing this one by me. A noncustodial grandparent has few rights in California. It's not like I was married to her, and Joanne never had to take me to court over anything, but you know my dad. He wanted to make sure. So he researched the crap out of custody law. And unless it's changed a lot in the last fifteen years, I don't see how the Lanes could have requested an emergency screening. There has to be a mistake."

That didn't exactly compute. Mrs. Lane had seemed sincere enough at the park. Unless the person behind the scenes and causing all the angst was the one person he hadn't spoken to yet.

Mr. Lane.

No doubt about it. He and Mr. Lane were going to have to sit down and have a talk. Man to man.

"Somehow I doubt it's a mistake." Levi shoved past Matt, nearly shoulder checking him when he did.

"Right behind you," Matt said.

Levi had had enough of all the shit. He'd been deceived first by Sandy, when she'd never bothered to tell him he would be a father. Now Sandy's father had it in for him, obviously trying his damnedest to destroy whatever slice of peace Levi could grasp. Hold on to for a minute. No. This had to stop, and he'd be the one to stop it.

Like a bull about to charge, Levi made his way outside. But though he scanned the crowd three times, Mr. and Mrs. Lane were already gone.

"Too bad," Matt said. "And I was ready to see some blood."

"Shut up." Levi found Grace with Emily and allowed himself to breathe again. At this point he shouldn't put anything past Mr. Lane. "Everything okay here?"

"Perfect." Emily sighed, eyes half-mast. She was in what Levi called her baby high. Seemed that babies were the drug of choice for some women. "I want one."

"You can't have this one."

Emily blinked. "I'll get my own, thanks. I've got Mr. Studly right over there and he loves to practice."

Stone grinned at Emily from a distance, unaware that his bride-to-be was already plotting against his freedom. Poor sucker. Levi sure hoped he had a head start on a healthy savings account. At least he wouldn't be blindsided.

"Where's Carly?" He scanned the crowd again. Not a beautiful and self-conscious blonde in sight.

"She went home," Emily said. "And by the way, when did you get engaged and why am I the last to know?"

CHAPTER SEVENTEEN

AFTER GETTING HOME, taking a shower and getting all the mud out of her hair, Carly forced herself to take care of some bookkeeping. But her mind kept going back to Levi in the office at Magnum Aviation.

I have plans for you. Not here.

Oh, she wanted to hear more about those plans. Considering she had arranged for his engagement without his knowledge, anything else that happened between them after that would have to be his idea. She'd already done enough. And worse, when her tongue had become disengaged from her brain and she'd told Irene they were engaged, she'd failed to consider any women Levi might be dating. What did that lapse in judgment say about her?

Maybe it said that the desperation she'd felt for so long about selling and getting her father some help had spilled over into all areas of her life. Little did Levi know when he'd brought Grace over here to ask for a favor that he'd be swept up into her plans and not the other way around.

But at last this baby business was thriving again after months of being dead in the water. So she didn't need Levi and his hot kisses and orgasms right now, not even as a nice distraction. Even if, at the moment, a nice distraction and a little bit of fun wouldn't kill her. But she didn't need the kissing that made her feel awake for the first time since Mom's death and Dad's accident. The touches that made her legs weak enough to match her resolve. She didn't know if she could stay away, but she had no business getting involved with a single dad.

For the first time in a while, New York was a little seed of an idea taking root. Maybe Dad was right and she hadn't given it enough of a chance. Jenny was obviously still in the city, so Carly would know at least one person there. She'd checked, and Alec was no longer teaching at the FIT—not that she should let him stop her from enrolling again, anyway.

But she did love Fortune. Loved the small-town mix of rural and suburban. The old working farms and vineyards that butted up against newer housing developments. The residents, nosy, but supportive of every worthy cause that came along. They were good people. She had history here. Good friends like Zoey and Jill. Life was simple here. Easy.

But maybe easy wasn't what she needed.

Later that evening, she was in the middle of

an episode in season two of *The Fall*, wondering if she should break out her sewing machine and work on a few more dresses for Grace instead of watching a show about a serial killer while alone, when she heard a rustling sound outside. She went to the door, going first by the kitchen to grab her sharpest butcher knife in one hand, cell phone in the other, thumb poised to dial nine-one-one. She peeked through the peephole.

Nothing. *Paranoid much?*

She went back to the kitchen to put the knife away, then grabbed a soda and stepped out into the fall night. Even if the days had been unusually warm for October, nights were a wake-up call that they were smack-dab in the middle of autumn. Soon, the weather pattern would shift and change. The clocks would be set back, and the days would shorten.

Taking a seat on the tiled porch step, she set her unopened soda can to the side. The night was dark and filled with stars, and the air carried with it a chill that gave her second thoughts about the long-sleeved cotton shirt she wore. Carly closed her eyes and pictured New York City. It would be much colder there now. No one walked outside without a sweater, least of all a native Californian. The sounds of sirens and traffic would fill the air, and neon lights would stay on all night long.

She jumped at the sound of a door closing and turned to see Levi. Hands shoved in the pockets of his jeans, he stared into the velvety black night. She turned in his direction, drawn to him with a pull she couldn't ignore anymore.

"Hey." Levi crossed their shared lawn.

He sat next to her on the step, bumping into her thigh. Grinning, too, as if to make it clear it had been no accident. Not saying another word, he reached for her soda, opened the top and handed it to her.

"Where's Grace?"

"She's with Cassie tonight."

Oh, boy. That meant he had a free night. Wide-open. She wondered what he had planned for it and if there was any room for a fake fiancée in his short-term plans. They sat in silence for a few minutes, during which time Carly passed him the soda.

He took a swallow and handed it back to her. "Found out something. Mr. Lane lied to me. There's no court date. I'm an idiot for letting them spook me the way they did. I know better."

"Don't blame yourself. You're new to this, and they're not making it easy on you."

"No, they're not." He spread his legs and his long arms hung between them.

"I can imagine it's harder for Mr. Lane. Fathers and daughters sometimes have…complicated relationships."

Carly's father had always worried about her, but especially after Mom's death. They were separated now by several thousand miles, but the distance worked. Because she had to do this on her own. He would have only tried to rescue her from the tough work she'd had to do by herself, just like Mom had done.

"It's the only slack I cut him. Can't imagine what he went through."

"When my dad fell and broke his hip…at his age, it's dangerous. We worried we might lose him, too." She fought for control of her shaky voice. Not going to let her emotions take over, and risk him feeling sorry for her.

"I get it. My parents travel all over the world to places where American civilians often have no business being. I used to worry about them all the time." He took a big breath. "But it's one thing to lose a parent. Another to lose a child. Even if they're grown."

She nodded. "I can't possibly understand."

He studied her. "Tell me about your dad."

"My dad? Oh, he always had my back. It's hard to see him like this. Hurting. Not willing to work to get better."

"Physical therapy is rougher than you might realize. I've had a couple friends go through it. It can be not just physically debilitating, but mentally. Only the mentally strong get through it."

"And he won't get better if he doesn't try to adapt to the new hip. My brother says he fights them at every turn. He hates the pain."

"They all do. But no pain, no gain."

"I've heard that before. Every time I went to the gym."

"Physical therapy is like the gym on steroids. You know that trainer you love to hate? It's like that."

"So no use fighting it, right? Get through the pain and to the other side."

"Sounds like you've been there."

"No, just nearby."

He laughed, and she loved the sound of it. His laughter rang into the night and touched her special places with a sharp, hot slice of desire.

"Tell me."

"In a way, New York was sort of like physical therapy for me. Painful, but I needed to get through it."

He squinted. "How's that?"

"Never mind." He didn't need to hear about her problems. "Nothing to tell. It just didn't work out for me."

His easy acceptance of that, without forcing her to say more, surprised her. All of her friends had pressed, Mom and Dad included. Only Zoey and Jill knew the honest truth. Alec had built her up, just to tear her down.

She'd simply been...devastated.

"Plan B can be interesting. Grace is my plan B."

Carly was still working her way to plan B. "What was plan A?"

"Plan A, since I was eighteen, was always the air force. My first love. My dad was army, so he gave me a hard time. But I wanted to make my own way. I was going to die there, or stay until they forced me out."

"I'm sorry, Levi." She leaned against his shoulder and listened to the pattern of his breathing.

Steady. Measured. So much like the man.

Levi had lost so much. His dreams. They were both, in different ways, readjusting to a new reality. But while she'd struggled to regain her footing, he'd seemed to hit the ground running. Carly admired that about him. He didn't waste time feeling sorry for himself or blaming Sandy for not contacting him about Grace sooner.

"It's all good. Still get to fly. I wouldn't have planned it this way, but I'm still okay."

She wondered if anything truly upset Levi Lambert. His emotions were cool and guarded, rolled up tight.

"Even with Sandy's parents in the picture? It's still okay?"

His jaw seemed tight, the only clue she had that he felt something. "I know how to fight, and she's worth fighting for."

She wanted to tell him that she realized it couldn't be as easy as he made it look. Wanted to let him know that he could confide in her. Tell her everything. Unwind. But she could see in those fathomless blue eyes that Levi Lambert was not an open book.

He reached across her lap, his warm hand brushing against her thigh, and reached for the soda. "What were you doing out here?"

"I thought I heard a noise." She had heard a noise, but in reality she'd come out here because the four walls were closing in on her. And maybe because, on some level, she'd hoped that Levi would join her.

He quirked a single eyebrow. Opened his mouth, then closed it again.

"What? I would have dealt with whatever I found out here. I'm not as weak as I look."

"Didn't say you were weak."

"I can take care of myself, I mean. I have a good butcher knife. I don't need a man."

He groaned. "Pay no attention to me. That's the sound I make when I'm replaced by a kitchen utensil."

"A *butcher* knife. Big and strong and…sharp."

His blue gaze slid from her eyes to her lips. "You're not making me feel any better."

He'd flustered her, and she fought for the right words. "You know what I mean. I…I don't need a man to fix my problems. I don't need to be rescued."

"Tell me. Is there *any* reason you need a man?" He grinned, a wicked glint in his gaze.

"I think we already established that."

"Uh-huh."

"Oh, c'mon. Something tells me you don't need me to soothe your fragile male ego."

He snorted. "Ouch."

She was going from treading water to drowning. "What can I do to make this better?"

He sat beside her, all broody and alpha male testosterone filling the night. His eyes had switched from light and humorous to a dark and heated gaze that had her resolve melting like a chocolate bar left in a hot car. God, she did need him. Now. Not to slay her dragons but to remind her she was alive. A woman.

He stood and crooked his finger.

Oh, boy. He looked so incredibly sexy. A sliver of moonlight glinted in his blond hair. He had that tousled natural look. So…inviting.

She didn't know what she was—what they were—doing. Still, her feet took her in his direction as if they were the ones making all the decisions now.

She'd been in Levi's house only once and even then briefly, so now she took it in. A similar floor plan to her own. A brown leather couch dominated the great room, and even though touches of a little girl were everywhere Carly cast her gaze, the overall impression was of one hundred percent American male. The plasma TV was large and in the center of the living room. She noticed a Dallas Cowboys throw on a rocking chair and decided she'd have to forgive him for that.

He was smiling when she turned to him. "Meet with your approval?"

"That's a big TV."

He lifted a solid shoulder. "I'm from Texas. We do big…everything."

While she let that simple statement register, one of his arms reached for her and tugged her in close. And that was the thing about Levi. She imagined that all children and dogs and women everywhere would melt in his arms. He was utterly male. Such a protector. Warm, hard and… safe, somehow.

Then he pulled her farther into the room and toward the laundry, where he opened the door. "Except for Digger. He's not Texas size."

She followed him into the laundry room, where there was a small dog bed now occupied by Levi's even smaller dog. Digger wore a teensy-weensy blue-and-green dog sweater from Zoey's store that read I've Been Pimped, which made Carly smile. He lifted his trembling head, showing her the whites of his eyes, then curled into himself as if he could roll tight enough to disappear.

"Aw. Poor baby."

"I think he likes the warmth from the dryer." Levi nodded toward the dog.

"He's shaking."

"That's why I got him the sweater. Believe

me, I've never put a sweater on a dog in my life.
Seems wrong. But I think it's nerves more than
anything else. He still isn't sure about me."

"Maybe he was abused by his previous owners."

"If by abused you mean dropped off at the shelter because he has an uncontrollable bladder, then
yes." Levi squatted in front of him and held out
his palm. Digger licked it. "Hey, Digger. This is
my friend Carly. Carly, meet Digger."

Carly one-finger waved. "Why Digger? He's
been digging in the yard?"

"No, but thanks for that image. Maybe something to look forward to. I nicknamed him after
my grandfather's favorite dog. That was before
I realized Emily would take that as some kind
of a sign."

"Why?"

"When I flew him out to Washington for
his adoption, the family didn't show up. Emily
thought that meant Digger and I must have been
meant for each other. She had zero mercy on me
when I reminded her that I have Grace."

Carly bent low beside him to pat Digger's bony
head. "That's okay. Kids need pets."

"Maybe so, just don't know about babies. When
I introduced them, her eyeballs got as wide as if
she'd seen a monster. Digger stared back. Then
he peed all over my hand, and I'm pretty sure
Grace did the same in her diaper."

Digger turned in a circle over his doggie bed

three times, then plopped down with a satisfied doggie sigh.

"It's nice of you to take him in."

"Well, it's only temporary."

"Sure."

He sighed. "Yeah. I guess I'm going to get too attached to the little thing. I haven't stepped on him yet, so that's promising."

She tried not to stare at this man who was such a mix of things she'd never expected to find. He had the outward appearance of someone who'd been plucked out of one life and thrown in an alternative universe. One in which he was suddenly a family man, with a baby and a dog to boot.

Levi closed the door to the laundry room and shoved his hands in his pants pockets. "Carly, I don't want you doing anything you don't feel comfortable doing. Like being here. Alone with me."

"I said I'm not afraid of you. Why won't you believe me?"

"So…you're okay with all this?"

"Like the orgasms, you mean?"

He gave her a slow smile. "For starters."

"I'm not exactly a virgin. I know what I'm doing with a man."

One arm came up on either side of her and caged her near the wall. "I know, but are you ready to take orders?"

"Um." She squirmed.

"No. Not ready yet."

"Neither one of us is looking for something permanent." She wanted…needed another kiss from Levi. "But what if I want some small part of…this?"

In case there was still any question, she licked her lips.

He cupped her chin. "What part?"

"You."

With a slow grin, his hands settled on her hips and in one swift move he pulled her flush against him. Every inch of her in close contact with his body. Close. So close. He thrust one powerful leg between her thighs and kissed her. Not shy, and not at all tenderly or with any hint of hesitation. Instead, his plundering and madly wicked tongue promised her a wild ride. His hand slid down her back to cup her ass and lift her to him. She kept kissing him, over and over again, unable to break away.

He tasted so good she almost forgot that she wasn't quite dressed for seduction. She'd walked over here wearing a Green Day T-shirt that had seen better days and her old and faded jeans. Not exactly the outfit she'd love to wear to seduce a man. But right now, right here, Levi was all she needed. Wanted. She wasn't going to think about anything else. Not RockYourBaby, not Grace, not their fake engagement and not New York. Nothing but this moment.

No one gets hurt.

She broke the kiss. Hands wrapped around his powerful neck, she gazed into warm blue eyes. "Levi."

"Yeah."

"Let's not stop this time."

She wrapped her legs around his hips, wanting to climb him like a monkey. She buried her face in his neck, licking him while he carried her into the bedroom. When he tossed her on the bed, she bounced and rolled on her back. A quick glance around the room, and she noted the baby monitor on the nightstand. But no worries that Grace would interrupt them tonight. No, Carly had him all to herself.

When Levi pulled off the gray sweatshirt he'd been wearing, she stared at his incredible, hard body, a little awestruck by him.

"I've wanted to do this for a while." He chucked the shirt to the side.

A little humiliated about her lack of sexy lingerie, she quickly tugged off her jeans and T-shirt, hoping the lack of push-up bra didn't matter. Nope, she didn't have the sexiest choices tonight. No bra, push-up or otherwise, and she wore light blue panties with pink hearts.

His gaze swept over her, and he groaned.

She went for her panties to remove them before he noticed they were whimsical and not at all sexy, but then noticed that he wasn't moving. Just staring. "What are you looking at?"

"You. Just you."

She sucked in a breath. Levi wanted her, just the way she was right now, lack of sexy lingerie included. And a moment later, when he pulled off his boxer briefs, she saw firsthand how much he wanted her. He was gorgeous, hard man.

"This isn't going to be fast," he said with a lazy smile. "Or easy."

CHAPTER EIGHTEEN

THE ROOM BUZZED with an almost unnatural quiet. So quiet Carly could just about hear the hum of the refrigerator in the kitchen. And her body as it vibrated. Purred. Fully awake. She'd never been so turned on by a man in her entire life and she didn't want to stop. Not now. Ever. She wanted him inside of her, making her feel something again. She'd missed this. Being so close to a man. Connected. He was Mr. Right Now, and she didn't want to think about anything else. She felt protected. So wanted for the first time in forever.

Levi crawled up her body, covering her with openmouthed kisses. Knees, inner thighs, stomach, breasts. And everywhere he touched shook with warmth. With need.

He cupped her jaw and met her gaze. "You okay?"

"Yes. I'm good."

"I want you, Carly." Without waiting for her answer, he tugged on her earlobe hard enough to make her moan.

He reached between her thighs to touch her

right in the middle of all her hot, damp need, then gave her an easy smile. "And you want me, too."

No use arguing there, since her body had spoken for her, but oh, boy, he was so confident. And correct. She didn't answer but bucked against him, making him groan.

"Tell me," he demanded.

"I want you." Reaching for him, she wrapped her hand around his shaft, showing him how much. "You know I do."

He groaned and kissed her deeply, using one strong arm to brace himself above her while his talented fingers teased her as they dipped in and out of her wet core. She writhed and moaned, losing herself. His kisses were an experience unto themselves, and not just a means to an end. He kissed her like his life depended on it. Like she was his oxygen.

Meanwhile, his fingers continued their sweet torture and she came seconds later, her body shaking and trembling. And if she'd come like that with his fingers, she had a feeling she might spontaneously combust when he got inside her. Willing herself to get a grip, she stopped gasping and whimpering and rolled on top of him.

He let her, gripping her hips tightly when she straddled him. "I think you liked that."

"Okay. Maybe I did." Couldn't let him get too cocky.

She slid down the hard length of his body, feeling his taut muscles tense under her touch as her tongue circled one pec and then followed down to his abs and the light smattering of hairs leading to the V of his pelvis.

"Oh, yeah," he moaned and fisted a hand in her hair.

She smiled and gave him one long lick before she took him into her mouth. His body went rigid and he groaned, his hips bucking as he lost some of his control. His breathing became ragged; he cursed and then moaned in pleasure.

"Stop. You've got to stop."

"Why?"

"Because I'm not ready for this to end. Remember I said it had been a long time? And I want inside you. Condom. Now."

She sat up and looked wildly around the room. "Right. Where is it?"

"I don't know."

"You don't *know*?"

He sat up and rummaged through nightstand drawers. "You're supposed to be flattered. It means I wasn't sure about you. Also, did I mention it's been a long time?"

She joined him, jumping out of bed to search the dresser drawers. "Well, I sure don't have anything, because if you think it's been a long time for you..."

"My wallet!" He reached into his pants and

pulled out his wallet, and a moment later there appeared a cellophane-wrapped dream.

"Check the expiration date."

"Way ahead of you."

She closed her eyes, hoping, really worked up for this. For him. Ready as she'd ever been. A moment later the sound of plastic ripping open. She almost forgot to breathe.

He took control then, rolling the condom on and moving them both to tuck her under him. "I want to see your face."

Yes. Oh, yes. She wanted to see his face, too. And his beautiful eyes. His gorgeous, expressive mouth with a smile that made her feel like he could see into her fantasies to know what she was thinking.

With one swift move he slid deep into her, making her cry out. "Levi."

"Right here." He bent down to meet her lips in a fierce kiss.

He moved above her in even and slow devastating strokes, so gracious and strong. His powerful thrusts rocked her world. She felt hot. Wild. She met his heated gaze, seeing his eyes now dark with desire, and she shifted her hips to take him deeper still.

He threw back his head, pleasure etched in every angle of his face, the cords in his neck drawn tight. "Carly."

Amazingly, she felt the pressure inside her

grow quicker than it ever had before, and for a moment she felt a trickle of fear. She couldn't lose complete control, not with him. Not yet. But she tossed that thought to the side, a little bit crazed by the way her body responded to him. She lifted her hips to him again, crying out when he went so deep. He pumped into her harder, driving her to the edge. When she couldn't stand it a moment longer, she told herself it was okay to let go. Just this once. He had her. She came again, fiercely this time, her body pulsating in little quakes as she cried out his name. It was a moment later when she realized they'd come together.

A first for her.

She lay beneath him, spent and sweaty, wondering if she looked as ruined for any other man as she felt inside.

Levi pressed his forehead to hers. "You still with me?"

Not sure about that, she simply nodded and fought to catch her breath. Feeling her heart rate come down from cardiac-event levels, she forced in an even breath. Levi took his weight off her but didn't move from his position braced above her. Still inside her. He grazed her jaw before he kissed her lips again and again.

"I like kissing you."

He moved off her, rolled and tucked her beside him. She lay in his arms, eyes wide-open, wondering if this was normal for him. Did he always wreck women like this, or was she just particularly weak?

When she shifted in his arms to get up, his grip tightened, and he grazed her neck with his lips.

"Not yet."

Carly relaxed into his arms, a smile tugging at her lips. "You're a cuddler, Levi. Color me shocked."

"What? I don't look like a cuddler?" He smiled against her forehead.

No. He didn't. More like the guy who would take what he wanted and let himself out the back door. She knew she wasn't being fair to label Levi. Just because what little she knew of his history with women was less than monk-like didn't mean he'd never been tender. Loving. He'd proved that tonight.

"Hmm." She let her fingers graze down his pecs to his abs and back again, gratified when his muscles tightened in response. "I appreciate you not ordering me around."

"You weren't ready." He chuckled softly. "But the night is still young."

He was right about that. She didn't need to limit fun to the hours before midnight. No, she was in charge of her own life and had all night with Levi if she wanted it. She'd sleep tomorrow.

CHAPTER NINETEEN

CARLY WOKE TO morning light filtering through the bedroom window and blinked. It was morning, but she still didn't want to get up. She'd been having such a great dream…

Who knew orders could be such a turn-on? But when they involved her pleasure, she wasn't going to argue with the man. She snuggled closer to the star and reason behind her erotic dream, only to find a pillow in his place. No Levi. Wiping the sleep from her eyes, one thing became clear. She'd overslept. In Levi's bed! Her plans, hatched sometime during the wee hours of the night, had been to wake just before dawn broke. She'd write him a sweet note, something to the effect of "thanks for the memories" but much better than that. Oh, she'd come up with the right words. Just give her a few hours and a deadline. After composing the perfect note, she'd planned to quietly slip next door so when he woke up he could miss her.

Not…not *this*.

Levi was missing from his own bed. What did

that mean? He wanted her to go? A note—which she certainly hoped was his grocery list—sat on the nightstand, tucked partially under the baby monitor. She sat up, tucking the sheets around her naked body, and read the note.

Went for a run with Digger. Be back soon.
—Levi

So...damn. He'd outwitted her in the note department. Kept it short and sweet. That was certainly one way to go. Wouldn't have been her choice, because he'd left out details. Should she wait for him here? Go next door and try again for her miss-me approach?

Was there coffee?

All the important stuff. Missing. She climbed out of bed and picked up her jeans and shirt off the floor. Her panties had to be stuck somewhere in the covers, but after struggling with sheets and blankets for several minutes, she found nothing. Fine. More underwear was waiting for her next door. It wouldn't kill her to go commando.

But then she heard the front door open. Levi was back. And she was naked and still here, since he'd ruined her grand exit. He owed her a grand exit. And something told her that morning sex would be off-the-charts hot with Levi. Might as well not waste her presence here. One more time with him ought to do it, and then she'd get this ridiculous crush out of her system for good.

She wrapped the top sheet around her, smoothed her hair into place and stepped outside the bedroom door. There, she turned her backside in his direction and dropped the sheet, bracing one arm in the door frame. À la Marilyn Monroe, she tossed her hair back and gave him a full moon.

"I'm ready for more orders, Airman!"

"Carly?"

Carly froze because that was *not* Levi's voice. She quickly picked up the sheet and turned to see Cassie, a huge smile plastered on her face as she held Grace and covered the baby's eyes.

"Sorry!"

She'd traumatized the poor, motherless child. One night with her father and she'd been ruined. Great job, nanny of the year.

Carly backtracked, tripped over the sheet and hit her head on the bedroom door frame. "I'll be right with you."

Her panties had materialized out of the sheets in all the chaos. She pulled them on and dressed in yesterday's clothes.

She gazed in the bathroom mirror only to be rewarded with her bed-hair look. Might look sexy in bed but not so much in the kitchen. And she would have to join the real world a little sooner than planned. She finger-combed her hair and brushed her teeth with her finger and a little of Levi's toothpaste.

Carly met Cassie in the kitchen, where she sat at the table, Grace in the high chair. She was gumming some Cheerios and didn't look too traumatized.

"Good morning."

"And a *very* good morning to you." Cassie rose and poured some still-brewing coffee into a mug. "Apparently."

"I'm so sorry that you had to see my ass like that. Poor Grace. What can I do?"

"Please. She won't ever remember this. Have a seat." Cassie poured some creamer in her mug and stirred. "Let's have some coffee."

"I'm just going to go because I'm right next door." Carly hooked a thumb in the direction of her house and turned to leave. But she didn't even make it out of the kitchen.

"So you and Levi, huh?"

She whirled back. "I know what this looks like, but we're not really…together."

"Oh, I know you're not engaged. That part is fake. But this? I might be an old woman, but I know exactly what *this* is."

Carly did, too. It was fun with a capital *F*, and she didn't know if she was quite done with it. But she'd have to be, because there was too much to lose. They were neighbors and friends. No one got hurt—that was the deal. Besides, she was beginning to care way too much about Levi...and Grace. More than a nanny probably should, and more than she ever wanted to admit. Publicly, she adored babies. Privately, she didn't like or understand babies. This was just a job. An obligation and nothing more. The babysitting had helped the business. She'd helped Levi. Sort of.

And the facts were, she was very likely headed back to New York City. Her confidence was growing more every day. She didn't need to get attached to these two, only to have to leave them. Levi didn't need that, either, even if she had a difficult time picturing him getting too attached.

Carly glanced over at Grace, and the baby's drooly smile kicked her right in the gut.

"And how's your daddy doing?" Cassie changed the subject.

Kind people in town asked on a regular basis and she usually made up a few sentences to make it sound, if not good, at least passable. *Making progress. One day at a time. He'll get there.* No one really wanted to hear bad news. And Dad's PT was just another thing in her life she couldn't control and had given up trying. The important thing was to keep after him to do his exercises and keep the bills paid so that it could take as long as it had to take to get him better. The way Daddy kept stalling, it could take years of PT, and every delay made it less likely he'd achieve a complete recovery with the new hip.

Carly didn't answer for a beat, and Cassie took that as an answer in itself. "Man's as stubborn as a mule, isn't he?"

"He is." Carly stared into her coffee mug.

He wasn't all that different from Carly sometimes. But while he pushed her to step outside her comfort zone, he wasn't willing to do the same. Frustrating.

"Back to you and Levi."

"No, let's not."

Cassie reached to pat Carly's hand. "I want you to give him a chance."

"Give *him* a chance?"

"Don't just find something wrong with him, like you do with all the guys you've dated."

Carly snorted. "That sounds like something my mother told you about me."

"Yes. What was wrong with that sweet man you dated for a while? Antonio, was it?"

"You mean the guy who was cheating on me with three other women? That *sweet* guy?"

Cassie made a face. "Then what about Rick? I thought you two were really getting along last year."

"We were, until he borrowed five thousand dollars to start his stupid beer delivery business, took off to Idaho and never paid me back."

"Such a shame. He had lovely dimples. And he seemed like a nice man."

"He wasn't."

Then there was Alec, not a nice man at all, but she didn't talk about him. He was just a blip on the radar of her love life, anyway.

"Well, you finally hit the jackpot. Levi is different. Special."

"I didn't hit the jackpot. We're neighbors and I'm his temporary nanny and fake fiancée."

"And…this morning?"

"Onetime thing. He can go ahead and be special because I'm not looking for special."

Cassie squinted and leaned in like she hadn't heard right. "What, now?"

"Maybe I want a little fun for once." She took a gulp of coffee. "Besides, the thing is, I'm probably going back to New York City."

"Yeah?"

"Sure, as soon as I wrap everything up here. I want to finish what I started there."

"Makes sense. And I know you'll tell Levi your plans so he's not left hanging when you go."

"He's supposed to be looking for a new sitter anyway."

Cassie's eyebrows went up. "That's *not* what I meant."

Levi came through the front door. He wore sweats, a windbreaker and a backward baseball cap. But more than what he wore, Carly zeroed in on his eyes. They were filled with a kind of strength that she'd never found so attractive. He was big and bad. Strong and solid.

"Hey," he said, taking in the kitchen scene with sharp eyes that never seemed to miss a single detail.

"Hiya, cowboy," Cassie said.

Carly zeroed in on the fact that Digger was not with him. "Digger?"

He pulled a worn-out-looking Digger from under his jacket. His eyes were no longer wide with fear but more like half-mast. On the good news front, he looked too tired to shake.

"He's not much of a runner." Levi set him down, and he scurried off in the direction of the laundry room and the safety of his pillow. "I would have been here sooner, but he slowed me up."

"It's the short legs." Cassie dropped a kiss on Grace's forehead and patted Carly on the back. "I'll leave you to it, then."

"Hope she wasn't too much trouble," Levi said. "Thanks again."

"No trouble at all."

They exchanged goodbyes, and Levi walked Cassie outside.

"No trouble at all." Carly turned to Grace. "Seriously?"

"Goo." Grace held a Cheerio in between her two fingers with the intensity of a doctor performing brain surgery. When she got it into her mouth, she gummed it with nothing less than abject joy on her face.

"If only my life could be that simple."

"Pfft," Grace said.

"Yeah, okay. I get it. There's no comparison."

"What's no comparison?" Levi smiled from the entrance to the kitchen, where his lean and built body was braced in the entrance, one arm on either side of the frame.

"Uh, nothing." Carly stood. "Time for me to go now."

But he stopped her when she tried to move past him, his hands sliding down from her waist to her hips. "Sorry about this morning. You were sleeping so soundly. I figured I wore you out."

"I'm the one who's sorry. I thought I'd surprise you, so I walked out of your bedroom in nothing but your sheet. Dropped it right in front of Cassie and Grace."

He groaned and gripped her tighter. "And I missed that. My day sucks so far. Digger did his business on a neighbor's lawn when he should have been running. And me, without a doodie bag."

"I can't say much for my morning, either."

"But last night." He pressed his forehead to hers.

Last night. And in the early morning hours before dawn's light. She'd thought Levi would be exhausted from sleep deprivation. But no. He'd more than surprised her with his boundless... energy.

"Last night." She pulled back to stare at his lips.

Crazy. She was greedy with desire for him. As if he knew it all too well, damn him, he grinned with a cocky self-assurance and tugged on her lower lip with his teeth. She rose to her tiptoes and kissed him back. Lingering. Her fingers twisted in the short hairs at the nape of his neck and she pulled him closer. The kiss went longer and deeper and had her forgetting she was in a kitchen with Grace sitting only a few feet away in her high chair.

Grace babbled happily, reminding her that they were not alone.

"Levi." Carly broke off the kiss, breathless, fisting Levi's shirt for balance. "Are you still looking for a nanny?"

"Yeah." He kissed her neck, then stepped toward the edge of the counter and a stack of papers sitting there. "I have résumés from a reputable agency. Want to help me go through them?"

"Of course." She accepted half the stack from him.

"Where were we?" He stepped into her again, his skilled hands skimming up her spine.

A male voice called out, "Where the hell are you?"

"Damn it," Levi said. "I can't catch a break today."

Matt Conner appeared in the kitchen holding a pink box. "Doughnuts."

"What's up?" Levi's voice had an edge to it that stated he wasn't too ecstatic to see his friend.

That made two of them, doughnuts notwithstanding.

Matt possessed rugged good looks that reminded women everywhere that smart could also be devastatingly sexy. He grinned as if he realized he'd interrupted something. "Take it easy, Ice Man. Have a doughnut. It's either this or a Midol."

Levi simply grunted something that sounded like, "Shove it, genius," and moved toward Grace, whose little legs had been kicking hard since the moment Matt had walked into the kitchen.

He opened the box with a flourish and presented it to Carly. "Ladies first."

She brought up the résumés to her chest. "I was just leaving."

"Take one to go," Matt said.

Because they looked to be from the new bakery in town, and she wanted to support local business, it was only the right thing to do. Carly grabbed a chocolate-sprinkled doughnut. "Thanks."

"You don't have to rush off." Levi now held Grace. With his blue eyes and unshaven just-rolled-out-of-bed look, he looked so much better than a doughnut. That said a lot.

"I've got to prepare for my meeting tomorrow." She met Levi's eyes, but his expression was, as usual, unreadable, at least to her.

She'd just spent the past few hours on top of him, under him and in every other position listed in the Kama Sutra. And she still couldn't tell if he wanted her to stay. Not that she would give him a choice. They'd both agreed that nothing would change between them, and even in the short time she'd known Levi, she'd come to value his friendship. With that knowledge, doughnut in one hand and résumés in the other, she said her goodbyes and rushed next door.

CHAPTER TWENTY

"You have lousy timing."

Levi didn't know if he was pissier with Cassie, who clearly hadn't knocked before dropping Grace off, or Matt. Matt, who had a sex life any man would envy. His son, Hunter, was already practically grown, and even if Matt kept insisting that a teenager was on the level of a toddler, Levi wasn't buying it. Lack of privacy was a nonissue. It was the reason locks had been invented. Speaking of which, he was going to start locking his front door during the day.

"Tell me about it." He had the decency to look guilty. "Still not going to feel sorry for you."

It wasn't like Levi thought he'd be able to drag Carly back to bed with Grace wide-awake. He just hadn't wanted Carly to go. That single thought stopped him short, because it wasn't at all what he was accustomed to feeling when it came to women. Usually he'd be happy to take a break after great sex. Let a woman miss him. But it was different with Carly. He wanted to cook her breakfast and talk to her. Shit. Maybe it was because he felt some sort of bond to Carly now, given their connection with Grace. Yeah. That had to be it. Made sense, too.

Either way, he was in a bad mood. Digger had started it all with his short legs and lack of cooperation skills. Levi woke with the bright idea to go for a run, something he rarely had the chance to do anymore. He was full of the kind of energy and passion that he hadn't felt in months. Carly had looked down for the count. He'd tried to wake her, but she'd mumbled something like, "Five more minutes," then snuggled under the covers. Being that he'd kept her up half the night, he gave her a break. Big mistake he wouldn't soon forget.

He'd thought the run would maybe teach Digger how to be a *real* dog. The result was an epic fail, lack of doodie bags included. But if Levi didn't adjust his attitude, he'd be guilty of needing that Midol soon. Since Grace's chubby legs were kicking and she was leaning out of his arms like she'd seen her best friend, Levi handed her to Matt. For unexplainable reasons Grace adored "Uncle" Matt.

Levi helped himself to a doughnut. "Why are you here?"

"Happy to see you, too."

Grace patted Matt's cheeks and squealed in delight. Matt made a loud smacking kiss sound on her plump cheek, and she squealed some more.

"What is it about you?" Levi squinted.

"I'm like a big teddy bear. That's what Sarah says."

"Nah, that's not it."

"Face it. Guess I'm just adorable." He smiled with such conceit that Levi wanted to hit him except for the fact that he was currently holding his baby girl.

"Whatever." Levi inhaled the doughnut in two bites. Then helped himself to coffee, his fuel these days.

Matt sat at the table, bouncing Grace on his knee. "Truth? Sarah made me come by. She and Emily went cake tasting for the wedding. I was all set for a day of couch surfing and watching the game when Sarah gave me the look."

"What *look*?"

"The look that says I could do better with my time than watching sports all day."

"For sure now, I'm never getting married."

"Figured we could watch the game over here."

"Deal." Levi held up his coffee mug in weekend warrior solidarity.

Matt, more than any of his friends, relieved him with Grace on the occasional weekend. Stone and Emily did, too, joined at the hip that they were. They'd usually come over and shove him out of the house for an hour or two, but he felt guilty staying out for longer, even if Emily swore they needed the practice. Sarah was hit or miss because of the Pandemonium art gallery shows in town that happened on weekends. Now Cassie had been thrown into the mix. If it wasn't for the occasional relief on weekends, he'd have long ago gone ballistic.

"But you didn't have to drop in. I'm good. You know that."

"What I know is that you wouldn't ask for help if you were lying on the ground bleeding. You'd probably just stitch yourself up with a needle and thread and keep going."

"This is my deal. You guys help enough, believe me."

"We're happy to do it. Anyway, none of us are of much help, since I'm the only one who's had a kid and I didn't see much of him in those earlier years."

"And you're sure you want another one?" Levi asked.

He lifted a shoulder. "Whatever my bride wants. You know how it is."

"Right."

It was only one of the many and varied reasons he would need to stay single. He liked making his own decisions. No one would tell him how to raise Grace or how to spend his weekend—if he ever got a free one again. And if he wanted to spend the entire weekend from his couch, damned if he wouldn't do just that.

"So," Matt said, letting Grace chew on his knuckle. "You and Carly."

He took a gulp of coffee and grimaced at the bitterness. "I wondered how it took you so long to get there."

"Giving you space. Didn't I tell you it wouldn't take long? You got Digger. And Grace is a big attraction."

Levi didn't think so, at least not with Carly. Grace had helped with her business, and that was about the extent of her attraction to him because of Grace. Which, to be honest, was something else he liked about her. She wasn't one of those women who glommed on to babies like they were trying to suck out all their oxygen.

"It's nothing. Just...we're having some fun."

Matt slid him a significant look. "Yeah? And does she know this?"

"Hell, it was her idea." He bit into his second doughnut and inhaled it in three bites. "Neither one of us is looking for anything permanent."

"I don't know her deal, but I know yours. And you need to remember that you're in new territory. Just because women couldn't hang with the life of an AF pilot doesn't mean that's going to be the case anymore."

It wasn't as if Levi hadn't tried long-term relationships in the past. Twice, in fact, with women he believed he loved at the time. But when neither one could tolerate the long absences without cheating on him, he'd given up. Either long distance didn't work for anyone, or he was simply easy to leave.

"Thanks for the 411. I'm good."

"You don't want an angry nanny on your hands."

No, he didn't. Levi glanced at his phone. Speaking of angry…

He had to call Frank and give him hell. The man wasn't returning calls and messages. How did the Lanes expect to build trust when they kept lying to him? The lies had started with Sandy. And the first conversation he'd ever had with her father had begun with a lie. He'd told Levi in no uncertain terms that Grace was the child of Sandy and her boyfriend at the time. They had the birth certificate to prove it.

But in fact, Levi had been contacted again by social services after the birth certificate had been found. He'd wasted four weeks he could have had with his daughter. Now he was caught in Carly's lie, which she thought would help him, too, but, in his opinion, was far more about her company.

"WASN'T THE PET wash wonderful?"

Irene didn't think she'd seen a cuter event in her lifetime. A pet wash event to raise money for a good cause. The buffed and hunky shirtless young men washing the pets was a nice touch, and eye candy even for a senior citizen. But she wasn't going to mention that to Frank. He'd stopped going to the gym or caring about anything months ago. He sure didn't want to hear that Levi had a physique that any man would envy. Not to mention that he was engaged to Carly Gilmore, Pearl Gilmore's daughter!

Since the moment Irene had digested that information, she hadn't stopped floating on imaginary pink clouds. Grace, despite her rough beginning, would be all right. And wasn't that really all they should care about now? They couldn't do much about how they'd wound up here, but they could do their best with what remained. Surely Frank would understand now that Levi would do right by their granddaughter. He'd listen to her now and abandon this joke of an emergency screening.

"Frank? Are you *listening* to me?"

Given that he was staring straight ahead as he drove them to their budget hotel from Sunday brunch at a local diner, she couldn't be certain.

"I heard you." He grunted.

That grunt meant *you have got to be kidding me*.

"You're so naive," Frank said. "Tell me you don't honestly believe Levi the playboy pilot is already engaged? And how can you be impressed with a woman who would wrestle with a pig?"

"It was a potbellied pig. People keep them as pets."

"She should know she was simply giving the pig a good time. Ridiculous."

"I don't know, Frank, maybe she didn't grow up on a farm."

"Why are you defending that woman? Everything just got a lot more complicated for us."

"I'd say it got a whole lot better. We can relax now, knowing that Grace is with a woman who's a first-rate baby expert. You know how I love RockYourBaby. And so did Sandy, by the way. She bought everything that Pearl Gilmore recommended as rated best for baby."

"And because of her, we're going to lose our best chance at getting Grace back."

"Face it, honey, we never had much of a chance anyway. Who would award grandparents custody of a baby when the father is perfectly capable? It's not as if he's a meth addict or an…an unemployed actor."

Frank snorted. "Think about it. It's a little too perfect. He's engaged to a baby expert. How did that work out? It's more than a little convenient, if you ask me."

"We've been over this. You don't actually think anyone would lie about being engaged? Really!"

"I wouldn't put anything past him."

Dear God, it was hopeless. Why did she bother anymore? "I want you to cancel the emergency screening. I insist. No judge in their right mind will think anyone should fear for Grace's safety."

Frank didn't speak for a moment. "Okay."

Irene was so pleased that for a moment she didn't know what to say. Maybe she would get her husband back after all.

"Thank you." She squeezed Frank's hand.

Later that day, after Irene had checked in with the kids and gone to the hot tub alone once again, she came back to find Frank asleep. He did far too much of that, a clear sign of depression. And yet he refused to see a grief counselor. She'd been seeing a lovely woman for months now, and it was really helping. But much as she'd beg Frank to go, he insisted he could handle this on his own.

Handling it meant he'd taken a leave of absence from work, usually woke at 11:00 a.m., spent time on the computer doing God knew what, then took a long nap in the afternoon. She knew this wasn't healthy but couldn't get through to her once strong husband. He'd turned into a man she hardly recognized.

She shook him to wake him up. "Did you cancel the emergency screening?"

He opened one eye. "Don't worry about it."

"I am worried. Shouldn't you at least email the lawyer? We don't want to waste the court's time."

He didn't answer.

"Don't you think it's a waste of everyone's time and energy to show up? Won't the judge be upset with you?"

"For the love of God, Irene, stop nagging."

He rolled out of bed. "There's nothing to cancel. They don't allow grandparents to file for emergency screenings in California."

For a moment, she couldn't speak. "So...you lied to me? To all of us."

"I had to make him believe it. This only works if he thinks we have him cornered. I expected him to back down. The fiancée thing threw me for a loop. How could I foresee that would happen?"

Frank's voice was like a faint humming in the background as Irene tried to breathe. In and out. In and out. *I'm still here. Still alive and breathing. Thinking and feeling.*

"This...this goes beyond anything I could have imagined you doing. How...how could you?"

"I just need a better strategy. I'm meeting with a real shark on Monday. Calm down."

She sat on the edge of the bed before she fell down. "No, you need a doctor, not a better strategy."

"I'm fine."

"You're not fine! Let's leave Levi and Grace alone for a while and go back home. We'll work this out."

"I'm not going to that new age doctor you have. Bull hockey."

"She's helped me. I lost Sandy, too. You don't see me giving up."

"Maybe because she wasn't *your* daughter."

Irene felt sucker-punched. She stood on two

shaky legs because Frank had just hit below the belt. Sandy was not her flesh and blood, but she might as well have been. There were still days when the grief hit her like a fist to the heart. The smallest things set her off, like the TV shows Sandy used to love as a child. A macramé plant hanger and other Mother's Day gifts she'd made for Irene. On those days, she'd cry quietly so as not to further upset Frank. She'd call her daughters, her son, and speak to the grandchildren. Anything to remind herself there were still reasons to be alive and happy.

"I loved her like my own."

As she'd long suspected, Frank had punished her for moving on. For wanting to live and not dry up and die in her grief. From somewhere deep inside, Irene found the strength of the younger woman who had married a single father with a twelve-year-old daughter. A daughter she'd tried her best to raise like she was her own.

Irene moved to the closet and began to pack her suitcase. Unworn dresses she'd brought to go out for a nice dinner or two—dinners she now knew would never materialize. Her pumps. Lingerie Frank didn't notice. The swimsuit.

"Where are you going?" Frank demanded.

"I'm getting another hotel room. And you're paying for it."

"Are you out of your mind? We should be saving money now."

Anger, unbridled and free, took the place of her pain. Why not? Frank had taught her how. She snapped the lid of her suitcase shut. "I guess that's your problem now, isn't it?"

And this time she meant it.

BY MONDAY, LEVI was back to work. He put in some more work on the mechanics of the sidelined plane with Jedd, took a few flight lessons and a flight to San Diego. He was alert and well rested.

That was a lie. He was alert but not well rested, and he'd blame that on his neighbor. He'd almost forgotten how much he loved sex. At least this time he was exhausted for all his favorite reasons.

Cute and Stuck-Up was not cute at all. She was freaking gorgeous. He knew this now because he'd explored and been up close and personal with every soft and sweet part of her—and there were a lot of sweet parts. She made tiny moans when he had her close, and when she finally let go for him, her whimpering sounds drew him right to the edge before he was ready. He'd had to fight hard to keep control.

"Oh my God, what's wrong? Are we going down? Are we crashing?"

He was going to get Stone to stop handing him the difficult runs just because he was the new guy. Mary Helen Zelinski had a fear of flying she'd been working on for years. Her therapist had finally gotten her to the point where she could get inside a plane that wasn't moving. That was last week. Today, Levi had calmly gone over the flight process and procedures. All of their many safety measures. Given her his credentials and flight record. They'd been in the air for ten minutes, Mary Helen white-knuckling it all the way.

"We're fine, ma'am," he said in his most assured, calm pilot voice—the same voice he'd use to announce, "We're going down." He left that part out. It was never going to happen, but still. No room for emotion in the cockpit. Fear or otherwise. It was the way he'd been trained and the way he lived his life.

"No! You can't fool me. I've been watching you and you look distracted. Nervous. You keep checking that controller thingy. I saw *Sully*, too! It was part of my therapy. I read that all you pilots are like blocks of ice, so we're probably all about to die!"

Levi had handled plenty in his decade-plus of flying, but he'd have to say that a panicked passenger seated directly behind him with her therapist was not one of them. Still, he wouldn't let it rattle him. Or inform her that if there was any distraction at all here, it had to do with multiple orgasms and nothing else.

"Calm, Mary Helen, calm," her therapist instructed. "Remember what we talked about. Our pilot has an impeccable safety record—"

"Which could end at any time!"

"Breathe."

"We'll head back now," Levi said.

"Why does he suddenly sound like a robot? Dr. Campbell, if you make it, please tell my husband I love him. Also, I left him his favorite casserole. I knew this would happen."

"We're flying safely home," Dr. Campbell said.

"Should I request an ambulance to meet us?" Levi said and immediately regretted it.

Damn. He was really off his game today.

"An *ambulance*? I knew it!" Mary Helen shrieked.

"For *you*, ma'am," Levi said. "The rest of us won't need one."

"That won't be necessary." Campbell now had a definite edge to his voice.

Mary Helen went into overtime with the breathing. "I'm on a beach in Maui. I'm on a beach in Maui."

Shit. So was he. On a sandy white beach with a gorgeous blonde… Carly. He executed his smoothest landing and taxied slowly enough to have been given a tranquilizer, all for Mary Helen, who now laughed and babbled about how she'd reached yet another milestone. He congratulated her, accepted her hug and silently hoped she'd never fly with him again.

He followed his passengers through the hangar. Mary Helen had a small group waiting for her with signs that read You Did It! and Partay Tonight!

"We need to talk," Levi said through a tight jaw when he caught sight of Stone.

Stone simply nodded in the direction of his office. This would be good. Levi would tell Stone in no uncertain terms that he was sick of being used. Just because he was the NFG didn't mean he got to have all of the shit assignments. He'd paid his dues. No more hysterical women. Or nervous dogs. He was drawing a line and that was final.

He stepped into the office, ready to tear Stone a new one, when he saw Mrs. Lane. She sat in a chair, hands folded on her lap. Eyes red rimmed. She'd been crying.

Super.

This one he couldn't blame on Stone. "Something wrong?"

"I'll give you two a few minutes alone." Stone shut the door to his office.

"Yes, something's wrong. My husband! He's taken official leave of his senses. I'm sorry to have to tell you this, but there was no emergency screening. He lied to all of us."

Levi swallowed, relieved there was no more bad news. "I know."

"When did you find out?"

"Saturday."

"I pressed him to call the court and cancel it.

He kept saying there's no need. And then he finally confessed. I suppose he expected you to think we're such great people for letting it go, but all he'd intended to do was make you miserable. Force you to hire an attorney and spend money. God only knows what he possibly thought he could achieve with this. He's done nothing but use fear tactics on you since the moment we found out you were the father."

Levi couldn't argue that point. He'd tried to understand it was the grief talking, but Mr. Lane had only made everything between them far worse. "There's no reason you two can't have a relationship with Grace. I never wanted to keep her away from her grandparents."

"But that's not enough for my husband. He's depressed, and lately the only thing he does in his spare time is feed on his anger. What happened was horrible and we won't ever quite get over it. We can't do much about it now, but Frank won't get help. He wants to beat himself up about what he could have done to have a better relationship with Sandy. But we tried. We always tried. She didn't want to have much to do with us after she left home."

"You've both been through something no parent should ever have to go through."

She sniffed. "I sometimes wonder if Frank wants Grace or if he just wants to keep her away from you. All he thinks about is punishing you for taking Grace from us. But he forgets that Sandy made a choice to be with you at some point. And it wasn't fair that she never let you know about Grace. I'm sorry for that, too."

"Thank you."

Damn, that was a first. He'd never expected sympathy from Sandy's parents for his situation, but it was true that what she'd done was wrong. Every time he thought about the fact that, had circumstances been different, he would never even have known about Grace… She would have been raised as another man's daughter.

Still, Levi felt guiltier than ever before. The problem with temporary, with no strings, was that it wasn't really true. Was it? He'd been kidding himself for years. Or maybe he'd just been lucky in the past and his luck had run out. Sandy was someone he'd been with for one night. Someone he'd never know now, but he had a child with her. Grace had half her DNA from a woman he'd never get a chance to know. He was tied to her, through their child, through her parents.

Mrs. Lane took a breath and dabbed at her eyes. "Sorry to bother you with all this. I know you're busy planning a wedding and everything."

Levi coughed and hit his chest. "Um, yeah. That's mostly Carly's deal."

"Of course. You men just get to show up and look suave and dapper." Mrs. Lane stood. "Anyway, I wanted to tell you the truth as soon as

I could. I want to see Grace, of course, every chance you'll give me."

"And Frank?"

"I don't know or care what that old man is doing anymore. We're getting a divorce."

CHAPTER TWENTY-ONE

CARLY TOOK ONE last look in the mirror and tossed her hair back. "Wish me luck. I think I've got this."

"Pfft," Grace said from the bouncer, where she was busy sucking on her big toe.

The interview today would occur via Skype, and Carly had dressed for success. Even if Jenny wouldn't see them, she had on her good-luck shoes, the kick-ass green suede booties with cutouts. Carly's wavy hair was tamed to within an inch of its life and fell perfectly around her shoulders. Check. Makeup, including a soft and nonthreatening shade of pink lipstick. Check. Matching pastel-pink rayon shell with a little pearl necklace handed down from Mom. Check. Argyle pencil miniskirt and black tights.

"Check, check and check. All set."

Carly had taken to talking to Grace all day long. It was better to fill the silence between her and Grace with real words instead of silly baby talk. She'd sometimes go through an entire day explaining to Grace everything she was doing or about to do.

It's time for your bottle. Snack time. Would you like the applesauce today or the apricot? Okay, apricot it is. Is it time for your nap yet? No? Think again.

For her part, it was kind of cute the way Grace seemed to understand the words and actually tried to respond at times. And even if her only response was in the form of *da-da*, *ba-ba*, *ta-ta* and *pfft*, Carly couldn't help thinking she was really trying to communicate, going by the earnest look in her bright and intelligent blue eyes.

The interview with Jenny had been set for three o'clock. By the time Jill arrived to watch Grace while Carly conducted the interview, she'd worked herself up into a small panic.

Jill bounced Grace on her knee. "This is the most anxious I've seen you since you got back from New York. You were a mess then."

"What? I look like a mess? Why? Where?" She ran to the bathroom mirror to check.

Still professional. Not a hair out of place. *My past failures do not mean I'll have failures now. This is different. Mom's company.*

"Chill. I didn't say you *looked* like a mess." Jill rolled her eyes. "You're going to do fine. That's a cute outfit. Love the boots. You're rocking it. Yada yada yada."

"I know, I know."

"Da-da, ta-da," Grace said loudly, as if she, too, wanted to add her support.

"So what do you think she wants to talk to you about?"

"I have no idea, but it's my job to take the initiative and find a way to bring up and pitch Rock-YourBaby. Maybe she'll know some people who might be interested in buying." Carly twirled and stuck her arms out. "Sure I look okay?"

"The pearls might be overkill," Jill said. "You're not Donna Reed. That was your mother's look. You're the young, hip version of RockYourBaby. Lose the pearls."

"Really?" Carly fingered the soft, smooth pearls.

Jill lifted a shoulder. "Without them, you've got the whole California hipster look going on. But your choice."

It was just one opportunity, one networking contact, maybe even the first of many. Why was she so nervous? Answer: she couldn't blow this. She'd brought the company back from the brink of bankruptcy and into something profitable and desirable again. Worthy. And Jenny had noticed. Why else would she have called Carly?

Once Jill and Grace were out the door for a walk around the neighborhood, Carly sat in front of her laptop and signed in to her Skype account. Then she simply waited. She removed the pearls, then put them on again. She drummed her fingers and practiced her smile. It looked frozen on her face, so she tried for a more even look that didn't make her look so eager, or quite so desperate. She rubbed her ring for good luck. Then stilled her fingers and concentrated on her breathing. Even. Slow.

I've got this.

When the Skype call rang, Carly was ready for it. This was the time. Her moment to shine and sell, sell, sell RockYourBaby. She'd never been more prepared or in a better place. She pressed to accept the incoming call, prepped to smile. And her laptop died. Apparently her battery had run out of juice, and she'd literally hung up on Jenny.

"No! No! I didn't mean to hang up." She nearly tripped over her own feet doing it, but she managed to plug her cord in and power up.

She quickly pressed Call Back, and Jenny's face appeared. Speaking of smooth and professional, Jenny had always had the countenance of a clear, placid lake. Clear green eyes filled with warmth. Short, raven-black hair in a perfectly straight pageboy. Carly, on the other hand, felt like the ocean during a hurricane and thought she might have just suffered a small stroke.

"Hello? I'm so sorry about that," Carly said, trying to smile. "I lost you."

"No worries. We can't always rely on the best communication because of spotty Wi-Fi."

Yes. Let that be it and not that she'd neglected to check that her battery was fully charged.

"I'm so glad to see you again! You look great," Jenny said. "And I was so sorry to hear about your mom."

"Thank you."

The best parts of New York were coming back to Carly, including talented and sweet people like Jenny. Carly had envied Jenny's talent and confidence, and her fashion poise. But one thing about Jenny was that she'd never let any of her success at school go to her head.

"Fashionista Baby was pure marketing genius. I'm in awe."

Carly cleared her throat. *Accidental marketing genius.* "Oh, yes. Thank you. So much time and effort went into that one."

Lie number four hundred and twenty.

"I'll bet. And the model you've been using? That baby is simply precious. You couldn't do any better. Those bright blue eyes. Like the Gerber baby all over again."

"Uh-huh." Carly swallowed hard. She didn't like lying to her friend. "Actually, speaking of RockYourBaby." She patted the folder she'd received from her accountant. "We're poised to do a record last quarter. I don't know if you heard, but we're selling the blog and our brand. And after that viral blog post, we're likely to get a lot of offers soon."

Jenny held up her palm. "We're not interested in RockYourBaby."

Carly forced a frozen smile on her face. If they weren't here to talk about RockYourBaby, then what were they here to talk about?

"What I'm interested in is you."

"Me?" Carly wasn't a believer in false modesty, but honestly she had nothing to offer a company like the Cutting Edge. Not yet, anyway.

"I absolutely love the designs on your baby model. That's all you, isn't it? I recognized your work."

"Yes, but I was just fooling around a little."

"Ironic. Because it's just what I've been looking for to suggest for the new label."

Jenny went on about the new children's fashion line they wanted to create, the demographics they wanted to reach. Millennial mothers Carly's age who were interested in dressing their babies and young children just as fashionably as they dressed themselves.

There was a light buzzing sound in the room as Jenny kept talking. The thrumming, light sound of Carly's fingers as they drummed uncontrollably on the table. Her leg jiggled, too, practically keeping time.

Carly interrupted Jenny. "You do know I never completed the program?"

"I know." Jenny scanned the room and leaned

in closer to the screen. "Do *you* know that you're not the only girl he messed with?"

She so did not want to go there. Alec did not have privileges into this conversation. "You, too?"

"Oh, hell no. But a few of my friends. He preyed on the students with the least amount of confidence. Built you up just to tear you down. Didn't he?"

Carly nodded. Why did people do that? For kicks? A power trip? She didn't know which, but right now she hated more than anything else that she'd let him win.

"I always thought you were talented. And I swear to you, Carly, had I known what was going on, I would have said something to you. I only found out after the fact."

Carly believed that to be true. Jenny would have intervened. She had that kind of chutzpah and determination that Carly had always wanted. Instead, she'd run home and wasted valuable time. Worked at the Drip. Questioned everything she'd ever wanted to do with her life. All because one teacher/boyfriend had humiliated her. And wasn't she so sick of herself?

"Is he still teaching?"

Jenny tipped her chin up. "Not at FIT."

"Good." Even though Carly knew that from the school's website, it was reassuring to hear.

"Come back, Carly. Don't let the bastard win. If you're game, I'll take this to my director. Put a portfolio together of more of what I've seen on the blog and send it to me."

"I don't have much. I've just been having fun with it right now," Carly said. "There's so much I have to do with RockYourBaby."

"Forgive me for saying so, but maybe it's time to walk away from RockYourBaby. Your blog really seems to have taken off since you started posting photos of your baby clothes. That's where your heart is. You're still a designer."

"I do want to come back to New York." She'd just thought it would be to finish her degree.

"Put a portfolio together that I can present to my director, and we can go from there."

"That's…generous."

"I love your work, Carly. I always did. Maybe you need some time to digest."

Digest. Digest and possibly regurgitate. Because Carly's leg had not stopped jiggling the entire time she'd been speaking to Jenny. She felt as though she'd run a mile but not moved a single inch. Jenny had *noticed* Carly's work. Maybe it hadn't been the floor-length gowns she once dreamed she'd design for a movie star to wear to the Academy Awards. But it meant something that she'd caught Jenny's eye. Jenny was kind, but Carly also knew that she wouldn't compliment her unless she meant it.

She'd been worried about what she'd do after selling RockYourBaby. Worried about what direction her life would take. Now she could go back to school and finish, knowing that Alec couldn't hurt her anymore.

Knowing she wouldn't let anyone else hurt her ever again.

CHAPTER TWENTY-TWO

"WHERE HAVE YOU BEEN?" Carly snapped. By the time Jill showed up with Grace an hour later, Carly had been about to call nine-one-one and put out an all-points bulletin on a tall redhead and an adorable baby.

"Take it easy. I figured I'd get my steps in, so we took an extra long walk." Jill unbuckled a sleeping Grace.

"Let me." Carly bent to pick Grace up and carry her into the house.

She walked carefully into the spare bedroom, where she'd set up the crib, and set Grace on her back as recommended by the American Academy of Pediatricians. Yep. Carly knew her stuff. More and more each day. Grace had the face of a cherub in her sleep, sweet and soft pink cheeks. Enviable long lashes. Carly spread a blanket over her in case she got cold, and gently stroked her plump cheek with the back of her hand.

She turned and left the room, nearly bumping into Jill just outside in the hallway.

"What are you doing?" Jill narrowed her eyes.

"Putting her down. What does it look like?" Carly whispered.

She shut the bedroom door and tiptoed into the kitchen, Jill following.

"How did it go today?"

"She didn't even want to hear about Rock-YourBaby. I couldn't pitch it."

"I'm sorry. Don't worry, there'll be other—"

"She wants *me*."

"You?" Jill clapped her hands. "That's great! Wait. It's good. Yeah?"

"No, dummy! Not good." Carly reached into the cabinet and took down her blender. "I need to sell Mom's company. And time is not my best friend right now."

"But...what about their offer?"

Carly lined up the fresh fruit. Bananas, apples, blueberries. "It's not an offer. She'd like me to send a portfolio of all the clothes I threw together for Grace so she'd look cute in the photos. Maybe something would come out of it, or maybe not."

Jill laughed. "But that's great. You finally found your niche in the fashion industry."

Carly threw in a banana and pureed it. She dumped it out into a bowl, where she mixed it. Later, she'd put it in the small containers she'd bought so that Grace could have fresh baby food.

"I never thought I'd design baby clothes."

"Sometimes life surprises you." Jill leaned against the counter. "You don't hate it, do you?"

"No. Actually, I kind of like it. Weird, I know."

Jill slid a significant look in the direction of her baby-food making. "And by the way, what the hell are you doing?"

"Making Grace her baby food."

"I know *what* you're doing. I just wonder why."

"Why?" Now Carly turned and went hands on hips. "And you used to be an au pair! It's the healthiest way to feed a baby. Natural. Home-made."

"And that's usually the way parents do it. Not *nannies*, or at least not unless we're asked. You don't mean to tell me that Levi asked you to do this."

She shook her head.

"So, basically, you're doing this out of the kindness of your own heart. Because you are so invested in her health and well-being."

"Uh, well. Actually...I—"

"Stop." Jill held up her palm. "This is exactly what I was afraid of. You stroked her cheek when you laid her down. You're making her fresh baby food. Fake fiancée or not, you're getting way too attached."

"No." Carly shook her head. "I'm not getting too attached to Levi."

"I don't mean *Levi*."

LATER, CARLY CHANGED Grace's diaper for the nth time that day. "Jill is ridiculous."

"Ba-goo," Grace said.

Pretty sure that meant she agreed. She'd been up for a couple hours now. After Jill had left and Grace had woken from her nap, she'd engaged in her usual babbling alternated with crying jags. Eventually, she'd calmed down some after Carly had walked her in the backyard to look at the flowers and trees.

Of course Carly wasn't getting too attached to Grace. It was a ridiculous suggestion. Babies were sticky and needy and always hungry and wet. It wasn't her fault that she was a good person and wanted to feed an innocent baby fresh food. She supposed if it were up to Jill, Grace would eat baby food filled with additives. She carried Grace into the living room and set her on the play mat she adored. Second favorite after being outside.

Carly picked up one of the nanny résumés from the stack on her coffee table and took a look. This was a chore she'd been avoiding, but getting someone else was the responsible thing to do. Her work here was done. Obviously, the website and blog were much more successful when she stuck to her wheelhouse—clothes. Even if they were simply baby clothes. The blog had never been so popular since she'd started posting photos of her new outfits almost daily.

The first few résumés were adequate but pretentious. Why should someone who had her degree in child psychology think she was the perfect nanny? What? No one else understood what made a child tick? Please. When Carly picked up the résumé of a woman who had studied child development in both high school and college, was working toward obtaining her teaching credentials, spoke Spanish as a second language and had a minor in art, Carly assumed she'd found the perfect nanny. Given the dates of her graduation, she was around twenty-five. She would probably be perfect.

For reasons she couldn't explain in a bazillion years, Carly tore up the résumé.

Carly's phone buzzed, and she reached for it as a text message from Levi scrolled across the screen.

Buckle up, buttercup. On my way home and Mrs. Lane is following me.

Carly furiously texted back, Why? What does she want?

His reply came quickly.

It's not good, but I'll explain later. For now try to act like a good fiancée who's completely in love with me.

You're hilarious.

Spare key under the mat. Meet me at home.

Carly threw her phone down. She should text-argue with the man, but her house was not fit for company. She had unopened boxes from UPS crowding the great room and she hadn't cleaned up her kitchen yet. She'd told Mrs. Lane they'd go out sometime for dinner, but tonight wasn't going to work. She just wasn't prepared to act like Levi's dutiful fiancée. Not tonight.

Tonight she'd planned to phone her brother Kirk and ask him for an update on how their father was really doing. Maybe have a genuine conversation about options.

"Okay, girl. This is for both of us. Showtime." Carrying Grace next door, she bent to find the key under the mat and slid it in the keyhole.

When she let herself in the door, it became clear why Levi wanted to meet her here. While her home was in its usual state of chaos, his place was immaculate. How did he do it? She'd assumed the other night when she'd been over that it had been a fluke, that Grace had been with Cassie and he'd had time to straighten up. But he'd left the house this morning, and the only thing out of place was a single coffee mug in the sink.

They were so different. He was neat, she was a mess. Ditto emotions. His were tightly controlled and she was wound up like a top half the time. She often had no clue what he could be thinking, beyond getting her naked. That was where he became obvious.

With her, there was never any doubt what she felt about any situation.

He tossed Grace up in the air, so certain that he'd catch her. Carly was only the nanny, but she pureed fresh fruit so Grace could eat healthier.

And were they supposed to be living together now, in his home? Because she didn't see how Irene would believe that a woman lived here in this…testosterone-filled house. There were no touches of femininity. No flowers or pastel colors. Either way, she'd take Levi's lead and go along with it. It was her fault they were engaged in the first place.

When she heard Levi's truck pull into the driveway, she took a seat on the leather couch, Grace on her lap, poised for their entrance. Lights! Camera! Action!

Levi opened the door and held it for Irene, who walked through.

"Hello," Carly said to both of them.

Grace squealed and held out her arms for Levi. Irene seemed to believe the excitement was for her, and not because Levi stood directly behind her.

"Grace!" Irene picked her up and kissed her plump cheek, then turned to Carly. "I hope I'm not intruding, but I've had a terrible day and Levi offered."

He did, did he? "No worries. It's good to see you."

"Hey, babe." Levi pulled her in for a squeeze. "How was your day?"

Carly stared up at him. He seemed natural in this domestic bliss scenario. She, however, was clueless. "Uh, good."

"Dinner ready?"

Okay, that was a damn glint of mischief in his eyes. He was having some fun with her.

"There was a bit of a failure on that end."

"Uh-oh. Burn it again?"

Carly glared at him.

His lips twitched.

"Please don't go to any trouble for me," Irene said. "Maybe we can just order takeout. You're both busy professionals, after all. I don't know how you do it."

"Carly prides herself on a home-cooked meal every night," Levi said. "She works all day, then spends her nights cooking and cleaning. I try to get her to stop and take a break, but she won't listen to me."

She was going to kill him.

"Super Mom." Irene smiled. "Grace, you're so lucky."

"I'm the lucky one." Levi grinned.

Well, he wouldn't feel so lucky when she relieved him of his manhood. "What can I say? I try."

"Oh, she does more than try. I'm one happy man." He kissed her, a long, deep kiss that had her losing both her footing and a tiny piece of her mind. It was an 8.0 on the Richter scale of PDA.

"Oh, my," Irene said.

When Levi finally broke off the kiss, for the second time that week, Carly turned to see a grandma shielding Grace's eyes.

"Babe, we've talked about this." Carly smiled through gritted teeth.

He threw up his hands. "I'm sorry, I can't help myself."

"Oh, yes, yes, you can." Carly said. "By the way, babe. Your gym bag? I threw it and all the stinky clothes in it away. I was worried about toxic smells near the baby."

His eyes narrowed. "I needed a new gym bag anyway."

"Men," Carly said, plugging her nose. "I invest heavily in air fresheners and scented candles."

"I'll order us a pizza," Levi said, taking a step away and pulling his phone out. "Okay if I put anchovies on it? Carly wants me to eat fish once a week. You know, for heart health."

"If you don't mind, dear, I'm allergic, so I'd rather not," Irene, God bless her, said. Then she elbowed Carly and whispered near her ear, "I'd enjoy this affection while you're young. Believe me."

She glanced at Levi, who now stood facing the sliding glass door to the backyard, phone to his ear.

Her entire childhood had involved being teased and humiliated by her two older brothers, who never missed a chance. And since she'd learned at the feet of the masters, she'd never been a slouch in the department.

She would need some time, but oh, how she'd plot her revenge.

CHAPTER TWENTY-THREE

BEFORE THE PIZZA ARRIVED, Carly busied herself setting the table. It took her three tries to find the cabinets where Levi kept his dishes. She guessed at the utensil drawer twice. Eventually all of them gathered at the table to eat. Grace babbled as she sat in her high chair next to Irene, who talked on and on about Grace.

"I'd like to help contribute toward her care," she said.

"We're doing fine," Levi said.

"Anything you two need, just name it. I'll be taking Frank to the cleaners, so I should have some money."

"Excuse me?" Carly asked.

"Yes, I'm divorcing the ass." She covered her mouth. "Excuse me. Little ears. The man. I'm divorcing the man."

Levi stuffed his mouth with another giant bite of pizza, but his eyebrows were drawn in concern as he listened.

"That seems…sudden," Carly said.

Irene sadly shook her head and patted Carly's

hand. "I know how much you and your mother believe in family and lasting bonds. But this is something I have to do. God knows we can't all be Pearl Gilmore."

Now she was speaking Carly's language.

"I hope you're not doing it on my account," Levi said. "Because I'm willing to put the misunderstandings in the past."

"That's big of you. But no. It's not just the lies. It's everything. I'm only sixty-two, and I've got a lot of living left to do. I want to live for the rest of my life, and I think he's ready to shrivel up and die. He's grieving, like I am, but he hasn't reached out for help. And he needs help because he's only dealing with his pain by hurting people around him. The people who care, like me. I honestly don't know what else I can do."

Poor Frank. And poor Irene. She was being so brave about it all. Carly couldn't imagine what it would be like to start over at her age, and after what she assumed was so many years of marriage. To give up would have been unthinkable to her parents.

Carly wanted, more than anything, what her parents had for so many years, but it seemed elusive. That kind of bond didn't just happen. One didn't go out and place an ad for it. It was kismet, serendipity. All that gobbledygook no one believed in anymore. Someday, she wanted a marriage based on love, and honesty, and passion.

Until the day her mother died, her father had called her his bride. It seemed so unfair that two people who still loved each other so much would be taken from each other, while the Lanes were just throwing it all away.

Levi continued the conversation, asking about the important things, like Sandy's medical history and whether he might get her records at some point. Things he should know, for Grace's sake. All things he should be concerned with, and Carly was proud of him for thinking of them. He might have teased her earlier, but it was clear that Levi had a plan that involved more than the two of them playing house.

God, he was amazing. Raising his daughter on his own. His blue eyes were intent and bright as he listened to Irene. Brimming with intelligence and curiosity, just like his daughter's. This wasn't fair. They'd both wormed their way into her life and her heart. And maybe Jill had been right. Carly was going to get hurt, and hurt badly, when Levi found himself in a real relationship and not this cat-and-mouse game they'd both been playing. When she sold Mom's company and moved on to New York, he'd replace her in no time. Her feelings might be real and growing fast, but she didn't think the same could be said of Levi. He was clearly intent on doing it all on his own.

He needed Carly to be his eyes and ears during the day, but almost anyone trustworthy enough could do this job. Anyone at all. Cassie had, the other night. Pull Carly out of this situation and insert anyone else and there would be no real difference. Grace would have her diapers changed by another nanny, and Levi would…find the occasional comfort with that nanny, too? Hot kisses and the occasional friends with benefits?

I hate when I feel sorry for myself.

Eventually, dinner and talk were over and Irene asked if she might be allowed to bathe Grace and put her to bed. After getting them settled, Levi stood at the end of the hallway leading to the bedrooms, hands shoved in the pockets of his black cargo pants.

"You said I stink."

"You made me sound like a servant!"

"Okay, fine. We both had our fun. Truce."

"Do you think she bought it?" Carly whispered. "Us?"

He stepped into the kitchen. "Might have been more convincing if my future bride hadn't acted like I was mauling her when I kissed her."

She'd done no such thing and was shocked to think he even cared. But more important, her heart had stopped on the word *bride*. "*What* did you say?"

He didn't answer for a beat. "You're not comfortable with PDA, I take it."

"*Bride*. You said *bride*. Don't throw that word around like it doesn't mean anything."

His eyebrows knit together, and he looked genuinely confused. "It was your idea, babe."

Yes, yes, it had been her idea. It hadn't bothered her at the time, just a means to an end. But now things were different. She just didn't know why.

"You don't have to remind me," she said, going toward the front door. "I know how much you hated the idea. It won't be long now that we can at least stop pretending."

He stopped her by grabbing her wrist. "Hang on. Where do you think you're going?"

"Home."

"Not yet, you're not."

"I think you can handle the rest of this without me."

"Who says I want to? I'm not a great liar."

"You seemed to be doing fine earlier."

His eyes twinkled, but his lips were only twitching as if they wouldn't fully commit to a smile. "That's different. I was teasing you."

"I'm so glad you had fun." If her voice bristled a little, she couldn't help that. She'd had a terrible, no good, very bad day.

"What's wrong?" He still hadn't let go of her wrist, and now his hand slid up the inside of her elbow and stroked her.

Her body betrayed her with a tingle she definitely did *not* want to be feeling right now. His gaze pierced hers with interest that seemed genuine. He wasn't pushy, no, but clearly he was not going to let this go. She'd forgotten for a moment that her own thoughts and feelings were always so clearly displayed for the entire world to see.

"There's still no real interest for RockYour-Baby. People are not exactly lining up to buy it."

"Yet," he said.

"Yet." She stepped away from him to where she felt a bit safer from the electricity pulsing between them. "Levi, we have to do something about the Lanes."

"Like what?"

"We can't let them give up on each other. They came to Fortune married, and it seems like they're leaving separated. It doesn't seem right."

"And...it's also none of our business. There is that."

"But they're Grace's grandparents. We should care."

"We?" He grinned.

She felt warm and flushed. "Can I help it if I care about people?"

"No, you can't. And I kind of like that about you. A whole hell of a lot."

"Well...thank you."

Suddenly Levi's eyes, so guarded and hooded to her before, were having an entire conversation with her. Interesting the way those blue eyes could speak when they wanted to. But maybe now she needed an interpreter, because they were telling her things she was afraid to believe. Taking this relationship to another level would complicate her life too much. She didn't need him. Or want him.

That was a lie. She wanted him, oh, how she wanted him. But that by itself wasn't enough.

"She's asleep," Irene said from behind them, startling Carly. "Such a sweetheart. I just wish her grandfather wasn't such an ass. He could be here with me now. Instead, he's probably still sulking. Watching TV and sulking."

A few minutes later, Irene had gathered her purse and jacket and Levi had walked her to her car. Carly could go home. She'd been free to go as soon as the rented sedan drove off. So why were her feet rooted to this spot by Levi's window?

She moved to the door and watched Levi's hot body, broad shoulders looking tight, as he stood like a statue observing the car drive away. He turned to her, catching her gaze. The porch light illuminated him, causing his blond hair to appear even lighter. His eyes bluer. He stepped inside, his gaze never leaving hers. Once inside, his eyes grew dark and filled with a longing and desire that matched her own.

Carly might be leaving Fortune, but she wasn't leaving tonight. Tonight stretched out before her with plenty of possibilities. And she didn't want to be alone.

He grinned as if she'd said her thought out loud. Then her phone buzzed.

Her brother was calling.

CHAPTER TWENTY-FOUR

"I NEED TO take this."

If she thought she'd have some privacy, Carly was absolutely wrong about that. Because Levi stood no more than a foot away from her and didn't move. Strangely, her body didn't want him to, even if her brain said he should let her take this call. Alone.

Because Kirk didn't call unless there was a problem.

"Hi," Carly said into the phone, staring at Levi's lips. "Is everything okay?"

"Not so much," Kirk said. "Dad might need another surgery."

Carly sucked in a breath and turned her back to Levi. "What's wrong? What do the doctors say?"

"Same as usual. It's not healing and his lack of participation in physical therapy hasn't helped. Taking him to the specialist again next week, and we'll take it from there."

"Keep me in the loop. I want to hear everything the doctor has to say. And if he needs another surgery, he'll get it."

Kirk sighed, and she could hear the tension in his voice stretching across the miles. "Carly, this time I'm going to need more help. I can't swing the deductibles alone this time. Sharon and I—"

"Of course," Carly said. "I'll help, you know I will. Anything you need."

"I need you to sell the company." He cleared his throat. "How's that going, by the way?"

Carly closed her eyes and made a meal out of her fingernail. "It's…going. We're getting there. I have a couple of possibilities lined up."

"I'm sorry. I don't mean to… It's just, well, you know Dad."

"He's having another bad day?"

"He has too many of those. I'd have you talk to him, because that always seems to cheer him up, but he went to bed early complaining that the whole world was going to hell."

"I need to get him out here. Maybe I can be the one to—"

"He's better off here for now. We said we'd revisit when we saw some improvement."

Kirk was right, but that didn't mean she thought their dad could make it through another Maine winter. And they were already in October. This year had gotten away from her.

"But the cold weather." Just the thought of her dad out in Maine, missing his wife and hurting both physically and emotionally—it was enough to choke her words off.

"We'll manage. You just worry about selling the company. And of course, you realize we're at the point where we need to take an offer. *Any* offer."

She sighed. "I know."

I won't cry. I won't cry.

Carly made promises to call next week with an update and wrapped up the call. She turned to find Levi studying her.

His arms came around her immediately, circling her. "What's wrong?"

She was that obvious. But she blew out a breath because she didn't want to talk about this anymore. He already knew her company was in trouble. Already knew her father needed help. If she told him any more, he'd only feel sorry for her, and she couldn't take that right now. "You have your own problems."

"Which are under control." Grabbing hold of her hand, he spun her into his arms. "Tell me."

Her palms went up against his warm, hard chest, but no matter how sexy he was, no matter what he ordered her to do, she'd already said enough. "No. And stop giving me orders."

"Don't think of it as an order." He lifted her chin until her eyes were forced to meet his. "Tell me?"

"You can't help. What's the point?"

"You know you want to tell me." He grinned,

a slow and easy smile filled with cocky self-assurance. "And you will."

"Why should I?"

"Because I can help. It's your dad again, isn't it? He's worse."

"Yes."

"Hip replacement, right? Titanium?"

"How'd you know?"

"Maybe I know some innovative treatments after hip surgery."

"He's got good doctors. I'm sure they've tried them all."

"You don't know that."

It was true. She didn't know much of what treatments they'd tried, and if Levi could help... if there was the slightest chance he could make a difference, she'd be an idiot not to let him try.

"How do you know so much about broken hips?"

"A buddy of mine. He has a titanium hip."

And she had to guess that she didn't want to know why, so she didn't ask.

Levi kept talking. "The recovery was rough."

"I bet." But she'd guess he was younger, too. Age made a difference in recovery rates. Even she realized that much.

"Listen, Carly, you don't have to be this strong person who keeps everything inside. You have friends and people who care about you. Everyone loves you. Why won't you let them help?"

He had to be talking about himself. Not her. He was the one who kept his emotions in check, who had control of everything in his life. A tight schedule. Always on time.

On the other hand, he'd accepted her help. Or more like he'd been forced into it out of desperation. But she could see he had an army of friends in the community. So strange. It appeared he'd managed to have a greater support in place than she did.

Strong as he appeared to be—and he was strong, by all accounts—Levi did allow some people in.

How far in still managed to be a question mark.

"I don't keep everything inside."

"Just with me, then."

That hit her front and center and might as well have been a punch to her gut. He was right. She'd held back from him from the moment she'd decided she would sleep with him. Because she didn't want to get attached. She didn't want Levi and Grace to be more commitments and obligations in her life.

Because I always manage to screw those up.

"No." She shook her head, not wanting to admit it. "That doesn't sound like me."

His thumb traced her bottom lip. "Then stay with me tonight."

"We don't have to pretend anymore."

"This isn't about the Lanes. It's about you and

me." His hand palmed the nape of her neck and he drew her closer, until she was just a breath away.

"Don't you have to work—"

"No early flights tomorrow."

But we said no one would get hurt. And I'm very likely leaving for New York.

She didn't want to make it any harder than it would be to leave, and Levi and Grace were already complicating her life. Far more than she'd ever intended.

"But I—"

"Do you need your toothbrush? Because I'll go get it."

"Levi," she said on a laugh.

"I mean it." He tugged on a lock of her hair. "Unless you're still too scared of me. Which I understand."

"I never said I was afraid of you."

"You didn't have to." He brought their joined hands up together and brushed a kiss across her knuckles.

He was right, in a way. She was afraid of the control he kept around her at all times, because she understood all too well how some of that could just…snap. When someone who'd held all their emotions in for so long just cut loose, there was usually a lot of damage after the fact. It had happened in New York. Her teacher, her friend. Alec had been so encouraging and patient with her questions. Then he'd just snapped. The tirade he'd thrown in front of the class was so embarrassing Carly hadn't been able to show her face again for days.

Levi studied her now, his brow furrowed in concern. She did trust and feel safer with him than she had with any man in a long time. He seemed sincere about wanting to help, and he was sweet to be concerned about her father. And with that single effort, he'd managed to reach inside and squeeze her heart. But she was so not ready to do this little dance again. Especially not with him. She was leaving and didn't want to hurt him or Grace.

His lips grazed her jawline, and he brushed a kiss on the corner of her mouth. Talented hands were busy sliding down from her hips to palm and squeeze her ass. In another minute, she wouldn't be responsible for what she'd do. And she needed him out of her system, but not like this. Not by staying the night and imitating what a committed couple might do. Wake up together. Have breakfast. Grace would be here, too. They'd be like family, but not a family.

"I need to go."

"Are you sure?"

She met his eyes and found a strength there that stunned her. "Yes."

He stepped back, no hurt, disappointment or recrimination in his gaze. Just a quiet and calm acceptance as he held her hand and led her out his front door.

"You're not mad?" she said to him outside her home.

He cocked his head and smiled a little. "No."

"Why? Don't you *ever* get mad?"

"You really don't want to talk to me after the Cowboys miss the playoffs. Again."

"I'm serious."

"So am I."

"You have so many reasons to be angry about what happened with Grace."

"I am angry," he said calmly.

How could he tell?

He wasn't asking for an explanation or an excuse, but she still wanted to give him one. Give him something. Because she wanted him too much. "It's not you, Levi. I—"

He put out a hand to stop her. "Let me stop you there. No one likes a sentence that starts that way."

She got flustered. How many times had she heard that coming out of a guy's mouth? And now here she was saying those ridiculous words. The problem was, she meant them. She was the problem. Not him. She'd thought he was the playboy pilot, the single father on the prowl. The commitment-phobe.

But maybe that was her.

"That's not where I was going with this. I'm not…not turning you down."

"No?"

"I just need a little time. To think. I've screwed so many things up in my life because I didn't take the time to think before I leaped."

"Sometimes thinking is overrated."

"You don't believe that."

"Guess not." He gave her a long look. "The important thing is whether you regret the other night."

"No! I have no regrets. But we said no one would get hurt in this."

"I remember. And no one is getting hurt."

Easy for him to say. He could keep those pesky emotions controlled and locked up tight. Separated and compartmentalized. She could not.

"Yes, that's exactly what I plan."

It was her decision to say no tonight, and she needed to slow this train down. Because Levi was sort of perfect in so many ways. Strong but kind. Funny. She wasn't the type who could separate love and sex like some of her girlfriends could.

But she couldn't say that she'd completely given up on trying. "Can we revisit this sometime?"

He smiled. Easy. Relaxed. So self-assured and calm she wanted to fall into him. Because it would be so easy.

And easy is not what I need right now. It was

hard not to reach for him, but she didn't. *Not a good idea.*

"Anytime. Anywhere. You know where I live."

CHAPTER TWENTY-FIVE

LEVI HAD SO far enjoyed an email moratorium from Mr. Lane. While the nasty emails might have ended, Levi didn't want to leave the situation this way. Unsettled. One would think that the fathers of two daughters, each forever connected to the other, would have something meaningful to discuss. He'd spend more time on that, but now it was up to Mr. Lane.

Irene had done her part to make Levi feel comfortable around her. He'd trust her with Grace in a heartbeat. She was a good woman, interested in Grace's welfare and well-being above all else. His perfect idea of a grandmother. Irene would be a great addition in Grace's life. But there was someone else missing from this equation, someone who could tell Grace all about her mother. What she was like when she was a little girl. Everything she'd someday want to know. Until Mr. Lane fought his own demons, Levi didn't know if he could help.

Meanwhile, he could help a certain woman who had burrowed under his skin. Carly had se-

crets she still wouldn't share with him, but he
was a patient man. One who understood holding people at a distance. He more or less had a
graduate degree in the sport. That she'd chosen
to put up a wall with him didn't feel right, but
he'd deal with it. When her eyes were filled with
heat mixed with what resembled fear and uncer-
tainty, she killed him twice. He didn't know if her
distrust was directed to all men, or simply him.
But it was there, and she couldn't fool him. She
held back from him, not because she didn't want
him. But one thing was clear—she didn't want
to feel the way she did.

It was Wednesday before Levi had a chance to
connect with Eric Taylor.

Levi had first met Eric at a wounded warrior
event. Eric had been in special forces at one time,
but when Levi met him, he was using a wheelchair. Two years later, Levi caught up with him
after the total hip replacement. He still walked
with a slight limp, but he'd married. Found work.
Let the bitterness go, and Levi knew that hadn't
been easy. He hadn't been there in the trenches
with Eric, watching him bust his balls every day
to learn how to walk with his new hip. But he'd
certainly heard about it.

When Levi finally tracked Eric down, he'd
interrupted something loud. In the background
he heard the distinctive sound of squeaky shoes

against a polished wood floor. Very familiar to a former high school guard.

"What's up?" Eric said. "I'm at the kid's basketball game."

They exchanged quick updates on life. Eric had the expected response Levi got from most of his friends when they first heard about Grace. Temporary shock, followed by sympathy.

"You're gonna love being a dad."

"Already do. But I'm calling for a different reason. How's the hip?"

"Ah, you know. I still call myself the bionic man, but I'm good. Sometimes on cold and wet days I feel rusty. No better word."

"I've got a friend who's struggling with PT. Wonder if you'd give him a call."

"PT, my old nemesis. No problem, dude. I owe you. You took me out of some dark times by just treating me like a human being and not a freaking celebrity."

One of the worst things about the injury for Eric had been the medal he'd received. Like too many soldiers, he had survivor's guilt and the medal hadn't helped.

Eric had once told Levi in a quiet moment that he'd always have Levi's back. And ironically, he'd called in his marker for Carly's dad. He'd ask Cassie for contact information, and given that she was the oracle of Fortune's senior citizens, she would have Mr. Gilmore's current phone number at his son's home in Maine.

Because, of course, he'd gone behind Carly's back on this one. He didn't want her feeling like she owed him anything. No, when and if his fake fiancée ever wound up in his bed again, it would be because she wanted to, not because she felt grateful.

"Thanks, man. We'll talk again soon." Levi hung up, satisfied, and glanced at his watch.

He'd missed the lunch wagon because he'd been returning from a flight, so he popped his head in the office. "Hey, I'm going out to the deli to get a sandwich."

"I'll take a turkey and avocado," Cassie said from behind her desk.

"Bring me one, too," Matt said as he walked into the room. "Ham on rye. Sarah wants a turkey on wheat."

"I like the meatball sandwich," Stone said, coming out of his office. "Might as well get Emily something, too. She'll be back soon. How about a salad?"

"Wait. Am I picking up lunch for all of you?"

Matt handed him a twenty. "This ought to cover us."

Stone handed him another twenty. "See if Jedd wants anything."

"What the hell? Didn't the roach coach come by today?" Levi said.

Stone and Matt exchanged glances.

"I'm hungry again," Matt said with a shrug.

Stone smirked. "Yeah. Same here."

Levi got it. It was typical NFG treatment, and he was NFG. It had been a long time since he'd been one, but like any good airman, he wouldn't complain. After taking Jedd's order, he hopped in the truck and made his way to the deli. As it happened, he didn't mind picking up a second lunch for his buddies, although they'd be damned lucky if he didn't spit in it.

No worries. He had a good job. Had a little girl and no more pressure from the grandparents. Had a fake fiancée, which, at some point, could work out to be a little bit of a problem, but so far so good. He still, however, had a stack of résumés sitting on his kitchen table to go through. Last night, he'd flipped through a few of them and lost interest after a couple minutes. On paper, everyone looked great. But no one jumped off the page. No one had interesting hobbies or had studied at a fashion institute. How was he supposed to find an adequate nanny now when Carly had spoiled them both the way she had? No one was ever going to be good enough from now on. He doubted anyone else would puree fresh baby food, put up with Grace's crying and take her for long walks simply because she loved trees.

In the grocery part of the market, he ran into Emily's grandmother Jean, and she held him up several minutes talking about Texas. Her son, Emily's father, owned a large cattle ranch in Texas and spent half his time there. Strangely, because Levi was from Texas, she seemed to think he might know some of their ranch hands in Lubbock. He did not.

After what felt like twenty minutes, he'd finally received the last of his large take-out order from the deli. He turned and nearly ran right into Lily.

"Hi, Levi." Her words were friendly, but her tone said: hello, *jackass*.

He'd forgotten he was supposed to follow up after their one and only date. "Hey."

"Don't worry about not calling," she said, tone heavy on the sarcasm. "You must be busy, what with your engagement and all."

He coughed. "That's— Well, yeah. Sorry."

"Yes, you *are*." With that she pushed her shopping cart past him, nearly shoulder checking him when she did.

He had no idea why she would be this upset, since it had been one date. There had been zero chemistry between them, and he was pretty sure she'd sensed that, too. But he'd meant to call. He'd just been a little busy with life and his... engagement.

The thought pissed him off more than the huge sandwich order. He'd been bamboozled into an engagement with a woman who drove him crazy in all the good ways but happened to have a little problem with lying. Secret engagement, his ass. There were no secrets in a town like Fortune, and he knew that better than most.

Levi threw the bag of sandwiches and one chicken salad onto the passenger-side seat.

"Well. That was awkward."

Jill stood just behind him, holding a bag from the market.

"Heard that, huh?"

"I did. I will say that I'm impressed you've been loyal to your fake fiancée, by the looks of that encounter."

"Secret fake fiancée."

"Yeah. Sure." She shifted the bag's weight in her arms.

"Can I help you with that?" Sue him, it was the way he'd been raised.

"No."

"Then I'll be on my way. I'm the lunch delivery guy."

"Wait."

Seconds away from a clean getaway. No such luck. "Yeah?"

"You and Carly."

"Me and Carly." There was more, much more, so why wouldn't she just come out and say it?

She eyed him, suspicion and distrust heavy in her eyes. "I'm not sure I should say anything."

"That makes two of us."

"Okay, look." She sighed and shifted the bag again.

He desperately wanted her to put it down, because it made him look like a chump to let her stand there and struggle with it. "You sure I can't help you with that bag?"

By the grace of God, she set it down and put both hands on her hips. "I realize you don't know me. And I don't know you. But I know my friend. And I trust Carly."

And not him. He understood. "I'm not going to hurt her, if that's what you're worried about."

Her squinty-eyed look gave him pause. She didn't appear at all convinced. "Carly is sweet. And kind. And she's...had a rough time."

"I know." It wasn't as though he'd exactly had the smoothest few weeks of his life, but he recognized something fragile and a little lost in Carly. He also saw a steely strength in her that maybe her friends were discounting. She was stronger than even she realized. "I see that."

"She's weak now and maybe a little vulnerable. So go easy on her."

"You realize we're not actually engaged."

"Don't even try that with me, mister. I saw the way you kissed her. The way you look at her. I saw you drag her into that office on pet wash day."

"Guilty." He liked Carly. Liked her a lot. There was nothing wrong or illegal about it.

"I'm just saying, be careful."

"You wouldn't be a best friend if you didn't say something."

"Exactly." She picked up her bag. "Remember that."

"Yes, ma'am."

He drove off, sulking all the way. While he'd been surrounded by friends since he'd arrived in Fortune, all of that came with its detriments, as well. He never seemed to get any real privacy. Everyone was in his business. Damned if sometimes he wanted everyone to get out of his life and let him live it in peace. Let him fly planes. Raise Grace. Let him and Carly…what?

Hell, he didn't know what, but something told him he better figure it out.

CHAPTER TWENTY-SIX

"WHAT DO WE do with this?" Carly lifted the item out of the box and set it on the floor.

The UPS guy had just delivered a package from a local company holding a prototype of a baby chair. Basically, it was a pink, molded plastic chair with a tray attached. The opposite of a high chair, it essentially looked like a *low* chair.

"What the heck is this used for?" Carly said, puzzled.

"Baba!" Grace said. She was rocking on all fours on the play mat nearby.

Carly didn't think Levi had one of these. Was there any use for it? There was a sheet with instructions and a short request.

Please consider using our new and improved baby chair and reviewing it on your site. We're a new company in Southern California. All of our products are made in the USA. We'd love your feedback.

It was good to know someone still cared about her opinion.

"Let's try this out, Grace."

Companies were still sending their products, even if the direction of RockYourBaby had shifted from product recommendations to fashionable baby clothes. She'd been contacted by the local newspaper for an interview and expected to answer questions about the changing direction of RockYourBaby. But maybe it couldn't hurt to have a new product recommendation squeezed in among all the #fashionistababy photos. For some of Mom's loyal fans who'd stuck around through the transition.

Carly had never seen a molded baby chair before. She wasn't even sure why a baby would need one, but there had to be a use for it or they wouldn't have made it. She picked Grace up and put her in the chair, then cinched the belt. Once she attached the tray, Grace seemed to think she should have something on the tray. It seemed too much like a high chair not to have food there. She banged her little fists on the tray.

"Baba ta dada!"

She needed some grain cereal like what Cassie had been feeding Grace on Sunday. She'd loved it, and Carly had picked up a box at the store specifically for Grace. Hurrying into the kitchen, she grabbed the box from her cupboard. She froze with her hand on the box when she heard a piercing scream, dropped everything and ran.

Grace had climbed out of the chair and lay

facedown on the ground, one of her little legs still caught in the belt.

Oh, God. Carly raced to unbuckle her and release her little leg, then pulled her off the floor. Grace screamed as if her leg had been cut off, which made Carly check both of them. Three times. They seemed to be intact with no bruising, thanks to the coveralls she'd been wearing. But her little face was another story. Her lip and nose were red and bruised.

Should she call nine-one-one? Drive her to the hospital herself? Call Levi? With no time to waste, she grabbed her purse and keys and was out the door without another thought.

THE TRIAGE NURSE at St. Louise Hospital did not seem to understand the seriousness of the situation. Granted, in her car seat on the way here, Grace had calmed down. That did not help Carly get across the importance of her being seen immediately.

"But she fell! See her lip?"

The nurse stared over her glasses. "Did she fall from a height?"

"Of course not! Well, a small height. It was a kind of Bubba chair."

The nurse squinted her eyes. "What's a Bubba chair?"

"Can I talk to the doctor?" Carly demanded. "This is an emergency!"

The nurse scowled, left and came back in a few minutes with a pouch of ice. "Here, ice it while you wait."

Carly found an available chair near a man who seemed to be bleeding. Grace gummed the bag of ice happily. She'd apparently forgotten she'd just had a near-death experience.

"She's a cutie," the man said.

"Thank you." Carly shifted in her seat. "They're not seeing you? You're…bleeding."

"Ah, it's nothin'." He held up the hand he had wrapped in a cloth and called over to the nurse. "Let the baby go ahead of me."

The nurse ignored him.

"They're not very friendly around here," Carly muttered.

"What happened to the baby?"

How humiliating to confess to this stranger that she'd turned her back on Grace for one second. One second too long, and now she had a bruised lip and nose. God knew what kind of permanent damage she'd done.

Carly bit her lower lip and studied the pattern of the floor. "She fell."

"Oh. Well, she looks okay."

"Looks can be deceiving. What if she has a concussion? Do you think they'll do a CAT scan?"

How would they do it on a baby? She'd scream bloody murder. The man gave her a weird look,

like he couldn't believe she'd been so careless.
Had he never made a mistake in his entire life?
And where was Levi? She'd called—hands-free,
of course—from her car, but Levi had been up in
a plane. Cassie had said she'd give him the message. She'd also told Carly to calm down and
breathe. Not that she'd done any of those things,
nor would she, until someone in authority told her
there was nothing wrong with this baby.

The man smiled. "Tell the truth. This is your
first baby, isn't it?"

"Yes, but she isn't—"

"My wife was the same way. First kid she
boiled everything. Bottles, pacifiers. Believe
me, by the third kid you pick up the pacifier and
just blow on it to make sure there's no hair on it.
Germs are good for kids."

Finally, after what felt like hours, she and
Grace were seen by a doctor.

"Well, hewo wittle baby. How are woo?" The
doctor, a grown man with white hair for the love
of Pete, said this with a straight face.

Carly already wanted someone who would take
all this a little more seriously. "We don't talk to
her like that."

"Woo don't?" He was dressed in a typical
white lab coat, with a stethoscope around his
neck, which was supposed to inspire trust and
confidence, she assumed. Still, he would talk to
Grace like a human being if Carly had anything

to say about this. He bent to inspect Grace's lip and nose and squinted.

"Woo have a wittle boo-boo?"

Carly sighed. Where was a grown-up when she needed one? "She fell. From a kind of Bubba chair."

At this, the doctor straightened and met Carly's eyes. "Those things are hazards. They should be outlawed. We'll need a full battery of tests immediately."

Now, this was more like it. "Could she have a concussion?"

"Possibly." He rummaged in a drawer and came out with a plastic toy elephant that fit on his index finger. "Would you please undress her down to her diaper and put her on the exam table?"

Carly did all that quickly and stood by, holding Grace in place, as the doctor had her follow the elephant. "Checking for signs of concussion."

"Good."

"She looks fine. You were lucky. Did you know that last year two children had cracked skulls from those things?"

"Oh my God!"

"Didn't you read the instructions? You're never supposed to put it on a high surface. Where was it? A table? A counter? The couch? How high up?"

The doctor had gone from Mr. Rogers to a police detective shining a bright line on her in a closed interrogation room.

Carly's voice shook. "It wasn't high. It was on the floor, of course."

The doctor froze. "It was on the floor. I don't get it. How did she fall?"

"It was just one second. I went into the kitchen and…"

He nodded. "That's how it happens."

"She must have tried to climb out of it. I don't know. She hurt her lip and nose, see?" She pointed.

"And…that's *it*?"

"What do you mean, that's it?"

"Woo just have a wittle boo-boo." The doctor bent low and tweaked Grace's nose. "No pwoblem."

"Are you sure she's all right? What about a possible concussion?"

"Where? On her lip? Nose? No, I don't think so. She just needs a little ice, which I see you already have. This will resolve itself all on its own. Make sure you get rid of that chair when you get home, just to be safe. What is wong with Mommy, wittle one? Tell her woo okay. Woo okay, wight?"

Grace squealed with laughter.

"Something tells me this is your first," the doctor said. "Poow Mommy. She wuv her baby giwl."

"Pfft!" Grace said.

The nurse slid the curtain open. "Your husband is here."

"He's not my—"

But it was too late for explanations. Levi had obviously come straight from the airport, and wore his white Mcallister Charters button-up and black cargo pants, his aviator shades propped on his head.

The doctor shook Levi's hand. "Don't worry, Daddy. First-time parents are always rushing to the ER for every little thing. Seems she bumped her nose. She'll be just fine. Won't we, sweetheawt? Woo a cutie!"

Carly almost screamed at the man to stop making a fool out of himself, but Levi smiled, actually *smiled* at the strange doctor. Grace reached for Levi, of course, so he strode over to her.

Soon after, they were alone.

"I'm so sorry."

She expected a lot of things. Possibly to be yelled at because she'd screwed up this gig, too. Certainly a few stern words from Mr. Pilot, the guy who managed to throw Grace up in the air and catch her without missing once. But instead of harsh words, Levi's eyes were soft as he pulled Carly into his arms.

CHAPTER TWENTY-SEVEN

LEVI HAD LEFT for the hospital the minute Cassie had given him the message. But as he'd driven to St. Louise Hospital in the next town over from Fortune, he hadn't allowed his imagination or emotions to take over. Kept his cool. Not too hard to do, since it was his MO. He'd learned it from his parents at an early age and lived his life by it. He'd learned not to cry as a young child when his parents left him with his grandfather all summer so they could work for the World Health Organization. It wouldn't change the outcome.

He didn't know what had happened to Grace, and until he knew what he was dealing with, he refused to panic. He'd simply gone through the motions, even if a little faster than normal. When he'd arrived, he'd explained his situation to the ER clerk, then followed a nurse to the emergency bay. One quick look at Grace and he could see she was fine.

But Carly was another story. Her eyes were red rimmed. Cheeks tearstained. Hair tousled like she'd run her fingers through it a dozen times.

She had clearly overreacted, which told him one thing: she'd behaved like a typical first-time parent. He saw all the signs, having been in her position a few short weeks ago. Something in his chest shifted uncomfortably, and for the first time since he'd become a parent, he didn't feel like he was in this deal all alone. His friends loved and cared for Grace, and they'd do anything for her. No doubt about it. But not one of them was as invested in her well-being as Carly had become. Which made her the perfect woman—uh, he meant *babysitter*—for him.

He'd also come to depend on her, far more than he had on anyone else in a very long time. Which was why somehow, against all reason, he'd wound up comforting Carly. Hell, he hadn't lied. Raising Grace was by far the toughest gig he'd ever had, and he'd made plenty of mistakes his first weeks.

Once he'd received the discharge paperwork and been assured by the doctor once more that Grace would be fine, he carried Grace in his arms and followed Carly to her car. It was near the ER entrance, where she'd parked rather haphazardly.

He put a hand on her shoulder. "You sure you're going to be all right?"

"Would you stop asking me that?"

"Look, I'm not going back to the airport. Emily took my last flight of the day."

"You had to get someone else to take your flight? I'm so sorry I bothered you over this."

"Don't be. Anyway, she didn't mind at all."

When she unclicked her car lock with the key fob, Levi opened the door for her. She came around and stood between the door frame and the car. "When I think of what could have happened…"

"But it didn't."

"How can you be so calm about this? I screwed up."

"You overreacted. Not quite the same thing."

She sighed and got behind the wheel. "Raising a baby is so hard. I don't know how you do it."

He grinned. "With a lot of help."

He could admit that now. Even if a sense of pride kept him thinking he could do this on his own, he wouldn't have survived the first two weeks without his friends. Matt and Sarah. Stone and Emily. Cassie. Who in the world ever raised a child in a vacuum?

Her smudged green eyes met his. "Thanks for being so cool about this."

She tried to shut her door, but he put one arm out to stop her.

"Carly."

"What?"

"You have to drive Grace home. I don't have the car seat with me."

She clunked her head on the steering wheel. "Of course."

He leaned into the back seat, strapped Grace in, then shut the door. "See you back there."

LATER THAT EVENING, for the first time in weeks, Levi felt four walls closing in on him. After feeding Grace, bathing her and rocking her to sleep, he fed Digger. Levi had finally taught him to roll over on command, and he'd discovered that the dog was incredibly smart when there were dog treats involved. Eventually, Digger grew tired and retired to his pillow, taking his latest treat with him.

Levi plopped on the couch feeling out of sorts. He wanted…something. Company, maybe. Carly. What he wanted were those green eyes searching his again with a hunger and vulnerability that made him ache. He wanted to hear the soft moans she made when he was buried deep inside her.

But, as Matt had warned him, Levi needed to proceed with caution. Much as he liked Carly and the way she took care of Grace like her own, she'd already demonstrated she could lie with the best of them. His least favorite character trait. He told himself that she wouldn't lie to him again. She'd learned her lesson, but on some level that didn't ring true.

She was a little hysterical, too. A bit lost. Troubled about something she wouldn't share with him.

And had no idea how beautiful she was.

He could get a woman. He could get a lot of women most of the time. The problem had always been keeping them, though not much of an issue since he'd stopped trying. His long absences had made a permanent relationship impractical and impossible. Granted, everything had changed since his AF days. He was grounded and would be for the foreseeable future. But what was he supposed to do with a girl-next-door type like Carly? He had no idea what she really wanted other than selling her mother's company, or if what she wanted could ever possibly be him and Grace. Carly might not be able to hang with him through the difficult times ahead of raising Grace.

A few minutes later, his doorbell rang and he opened the door to find Carly, a tinfoil-covered pan in her hands.

"I made you brownies. A peace offering."

He waved her in. "Hey, I told you. We're cool."

Still holding the tray, she walked to the kitchen and set it on the table. "It's okay. I love baking once in a blue moon. There's a routine to it that's reassuring. And if you follow the directions precisely, it always comes out."

Between the doughnuts and brownie deliveries, he definitely needed to figure out a way to play basketball again. Or teach Digger how to run.

Her back to him, she hung her head. "I screwed up. I should have just phoned the doctor's office before running to the emergency room. You must think I'm such an idiot."

"Not even close." He pulled on her arm so she'd turn and face him. "People make mistakes, babe.

You're talking to someone who has made some big ones in his life, so I'm not judging you. Grace is all right."

"But—"

"You didn't judge me, did you?"

"That's different."

"You want to tell me why you think you're such a screw-up? Because something tells me it goes beyond what happened today."

Her eyes narrowed. "Okay, look. I brought you the brownies, and I'm seriously sorry about today. But that doesn't mean you get to psychoanalyze me."

"Got it."

"Just eat the brownies, Levi. That's what they're here for." She pulled off the tin foil and underneath lay a small work of art.

Brownie art. They had green icing on them and what appeared to be chocolate shavings on top. Beautiful, and he didn't want them. Not now. He simply studied her, feeling a smile tug at his lips. She did that to him, even after he'd had a crap day. He could admit now, so many times he'd come home after work to pick up Grace, he'd been looking forward to a lot more than seeing his little girl. Just a few minutes with Carly picked up his day. She was sweet. Witty. Not to mention, after one night with her, impossible to forget.

"You...don't want the brownies?" she asked.

He folded his arms and leaned back against the counter. "They look great."

"They are, in fact. All my life, any time I was scared or nervous about anything, like a test, I'd bake. In New York, I had enough inventory to open my own bakery. Too bad I never wanted to do that for a living, since I'm pretty good. My roommates were certainly happy. Aren't you even going to taste one?"

"Later."

"Well, fine, suit yourself. I think I'll have one if you don't mind. You're actually in great shape, and I don't think one brownie is going to kill you." She scooped a brownie out and took a bite. "How's Grace?"

"Still good."

She nodded, and he didn't miss the way she let out a long breath. Maybe that was why she'd come over. The brownies were an excuse, because she was still worried about Grace. It killed him a little bit that she had taken it so hard, and he wanted more than anything to make it better for her. To fix this. Permanently. He wanted her to see herself the way he did for once. Capable. So beautiful. Intriguing. He wanted to take whoever had shattered her self-esteem and rearrange his face permanently.

She finished the brownie and licked her finger. He groaned inwardly.

"Levi…maybe…maybe it's time you find another babysitter."

"So you're bailing on me."

"You should have fired me." She poked a finger in his chest.

"For overreacting? Listen, I know I'm new at parenting, but I'd be more inclined to fire someone who underreacted. You did everything a newbie parent would have done, and that's what I want. That's what Grace needs. Someone who cares about her as much as I do. And I don't want anyone else."

"You haven't even tried to find anyone, have you?"

Now she had him. Why would he when he had her? *Correction. You don't have her, Grace has her. There's a difference.*

"I've been busy."

"It was supposed to be temporary."

"But now we're engaged." He walked past her and picked up a brownie.

"Secret fake engaged."

"Whatever."

He took a bite out of the brownie, which, as it turned out, was a moist, chocolate-and-mint-flavored piece of utopia. This brownie tasted like sex. The best kind of sex, the kind you didn't want to end. An all-nighter. He nearly grabbed the edge of the counter to ease the intense pleasure of this brownie. His mouth had just had an orgasm.

Carly smiled. "Good, huh?"

He swallowed. "Not bad."

"I have my talents." She slid him the look of a confident woman, chin up, and damn, he loved that look on her. "Look, I wasn't honest with you. Not completely. When I took this job, I said I was a baby expert. Which wasn't entirely true. Although I know an awful lot. It's just not the same in theory. Which is funny because I've always been better at hands-on. I was never all that good with books and tests."

The dyslexia.

She waved a hand. "You got me sidetracked. I'm trying to say that this baby business is so much harder than I thought it would be. And I think you and Grace deserve better."

"I've got better." He took a step closer, but not before picking up another piece of sex…er, brownie.

"What you've got is the owner of a popular baby website who can write about baby products and recommend them. But that's a far cry from someone who really understands babies."

"I don't need someone who understands babies. What I've got is someone who understands Grace."

"What you've got is—"

"Someone who doesn't do baby talk because she obviously thinks my daughter is smart enough to understand real words. Or maybe just wants to teach her real words. Like I do."

She gazed at him, eyes soft. "Why do people do that, anyway? I think she should learn the word right the first time. If she can't say it, she'll just keep trying."

"Exactly," he said, taking hold of one wrist with his free hand. "Now you see why I can't let you go."

Of course, she thought he was talking about the babysitting gig. And he was, partly. Mostly.

"I see your point. But surely there are other babysitters out there like me. Not everyone says *woo* for *you*. Jill doesn't. Mrs. Lane didn't. And anyway—"

And that was it. She needed to stop talking, because he'd much rather be kissing her. He stuck the rest of the brownie in her mouth while it was open. It was not the first thing he wanted to do with that mouth of hers. Not even the second thing. But he still enjoyed the wide eyes, the pink cheeks as she chewed and studied him. He enjoyed *her*. When both of his hands drifted down to her hips and tugged her close, her expressive eyes went from surprised to the soft yearning look he'd seen in his fantasies.

She swallowed, and her tongue flicked out to lick her lips.

"Got that? Because you have something…right

here." His tongue licked one side of her mouth, then the other.

"Levi," she breathed. "What are we doing?"

"Anything you want."

CHAPTER TWENTY-EIGHT

THERE WAS ONLY one thing Carly had found she loved more passionately than her better-than-sex brownies with mint-chocolate frosting and chocolate slivers on top. Sex. With Levi.

Anything you want.

His voice was smoother than butter and richer than chocolate. The combination of her brownies and Levi's kisses had her in sensory overload. Her heart kicked up and she fisted her hands in his cotton shirt, then her fingers skimmed down his abs until she rested them on the waistband of his jeans.

Levi shouldn't promise things he couldn't deliver. He couldn't give her anything she wanted, because what she wanted was for the world to go away. She wanted responsibilities and obligations and even long-held dreams to disappear for now. Even for a moment. Maybe then she could be alone with Levi. She could be decadent and careless and luxuriate in soft cotton sheets and the feel of his bristled jaw against her neck. In between her legs. Everywhere.

"Tell me what you want," Levi said, dropping openmouthed kisses down the column of her neck, on the soft spot behind her ear.

"Um…this is a good start."

"More detail." His fingers reached into her hair and tilted her face up to his.

She met his eyes and saw the raw heat in them. "I want you to kiss me. I like the way you kiss me."

Her lips parted under his, and he stroked her tongue. "What else?"

Her breath caught, her legs went liquid and she couldn't speak for a moment. "More."

"Good answer," he said with a wicked grin and tilted her chin up with one finger. "But whatever we do tonight is going to change everything. I won't share you with anyone."

His hands slid down to rest at the small of her back and he pressed against her.

He was hard, and she shivered with anticipation. "That goes for me, too. I won't share you."

"Understood." He smiled against her mouth.

"Wow," she whispered. "That was easy."

"I'm easy. When it comes to you." His hands glided down her arms and cuffed her wrists.

Not to be outdone, she got busy touching him everywhere, something she loved. Her wandering fingers flattened against his abs, which tightened in response. Seconds later, she wound up hoisted in his powerful arms. He threw her over his shoulder in a firefighter's hold.

"Levi," she said on a laugh. "What are you doing?"

"I'm saving you," he said, moving toward his bedroom. "Always wanted to do this."

Her upside-down view of the world was amusing. For one thing, Levi had a great ass, in his jeans and out of them, in case she'd forgotten. She hadn't. They wound up in a tangle of limbs on his bed, both fully clothed, Levi on top. Going by the feel of him pressing against her stomach, he had to be busting out of his jeans. She wanted to remedy that and remedy it fast. When her hands drifted down lightly and tugged on his pants, he reached for her hands and stilled them.

He brought their joined hands up to his lips and brushed a kiss across her knuckles. "Slow down."

When he reached for his T-shirt and pulled it over his head with one arm, her pulse kicked up into triple digits. He had the most magnificent body, all hard, inherently male angles. Hard… everything. She pulled off her shirt, too, revealing the cami underneath. Still no sexy, push-up, demi bra. She cursed her lack of lingerie and swore she'd go to Lu Lah Lah tomorrow and stock up for the winter.

Levi didn't seem to mind the cami. He locked eyes with her, his blue ones searing her with desire and need. His fingers circled her breast through her sheer cami and his thumb tweaked her nipple. He pulled her cami over her head, then grazed his teeth over her lower lip.

He took in her body, as if he was trying to memorize her, and this time she wasn't as self-conscious.

"Enjoying the view?"

"Always." He bent to draw a nipple in his mouth. Licking and nipping, he had her writhing under him in minutes.

"Stop teasing me." Her fingers dug into his forearms.

"Never." He went back to her nipples, sucking and licking like he had all the time in the world.

"Levi." She sank her fingers into his hair and held on for the ride. And he would take her on a hell of a ride. "Tell me you have a condom."

He met her eyes. "I have a big box."

"Oh, good." Wait. A box? "Why a *box*?"

"I was hopeful." He stopped to meet her eyes, and his were on fire with heat. "About us. You and me."

It got her all hot and bothered picturing Levi buying those condoms. Thinking about her when he did. Because he'd wanted her again. That first time hadn't just been memorable for her. The thought fired her up with renewed desire and an aching longing that spread to every nerve ending. And that was the thing. He wanted her just as much as she wanted him. It had been so long since she'd felt this desired. This wanted. And he'd managed to make her feel this way with just one look from his blue eyes. A gentle touch from his calloused hands. And some not-so-gentle touches that were as amazing and breathtaking.

He kissed her again, his mouth demanding and possessive. His tongue hot and wild. He stopped only to bring his hands to the waistband of her jeans, where he unbuttoned and unzipped. She helped by lifting her hips to shimmy and wriggle out of them, and he pulled them the rest of the way off.

He gave her a slow smile. "Wriggle your hips like that again."

"Like this?" Now wearing only a sheer white thong, she was nearly naked as she undulated her hips for him.

The smile slipped off his face. "Do you know how sexy you are? Look at you, babe. You're so damn hot."

"Yeah?"

He swiftly removed that one last piece of gauzy material between them, then he kissed her in the middle of all that heat. He worked his tongue and lips on her, doing incredible things and driving her right out of herself. She clutched at the sheets, rocking her hips.

"Levi—" she gasped. "I'm going to…"

"No. Not yet. Don't come yet."

"But—"

She couldn't speak. Could barely formulate a thought in her head. Holding back was costing her so much. She was on the edge of a precipice, hanging on and wanting to fall. Let go. Levi continued with his slow torture, his tongue and mouth on her, doing wicked but wonderful things that made her feel…everything.

Finally, finally, when she thought she would scream, Levi said, "Come."

Then he did something incredibly wicked with his tongue and she was gone. Just gone. Her body shook and trembled and she cried out his name.

When she'd come back down to earth and remembered how to breathe again, she found that he'd crawled up her body and had a condom packet in his teeth.

He ripped it open with an easy, slow smile, then a moment later, he slid into her, long and deep. "Stay with me."

She did, meeting him thrust for thrust in incredible pleasure. The delicious pressure built up quickly inside her, Levi sliding slowly into her in a rhythm that worked for both of them. Oh, how it worked. He gripped her hips and drove into her, his own breathing becoming ragged and uneven.

"I can't stop it. I'm coming," Carly said.

"Do it," Levi said, and just like that they both went tumbling over the edge, falling hard.

CHAPTER TWENTY-NINE

LATER, CARLY LAY spooning with Levi, trying her damnedest to push away all the anxiety that crowded her mind. Thoughts of her father's injury, New York and all her unfinished business were taunting her because, for the first time in a long time, she was happy. Too happy, for a change. She deserved this, damn it. It didn't matter for how long. She had this now, and it was so easy with Levi.

But maybe easy isn't what I need.

She should tell him right now. Explain that, while she'd be going back to New York City, it didn't have to be the end of this. He could visit her. Often. Eventually she'd return, and they'd pick up where they left off.

"I can hear you thinking," Levi said, his deep voice utterly sexy and muffled against the nape of her neck.

"Huh?" She turned on her back to face him.

"Something's on your mind."

Maybe the guilt she felt, realizing that everything had changed between them. She was no longer fooling around, and she sensed he wasn't, either. This little fling between them had taken on a life of its own, and she still wasn't being completely honest with him.

"Just so much on my mind." *Is it technically a lie if I don't tell him I'm thinking of leaving?* "I…wish I hadn't given up on my degree at the Fashion Institute."

"What do you think? Why did you give up?" He tucked a strand of hair behind her ear and gave her a slow smile.

"What I think," she said on a long exhale, "is that I'm not good at school, and that's why I didn't finish."

"No other reason?"

"I thought I was doing pretty good." She thought back to that exciting time in the city she'd come to love. All that energy and excitement crackling through the very oxygen she breathed. She'd been young and alive. So many possibilities. "Actually, I was sort of the teacher's pet. One of my instructors took me under his wing. We dated, too, a couple times."

"Yeah? So how old was this guy?"

She lowered her head to say the rest of the hard truth into his chest, because, even after all this time, it was still a little embarrassing. "He wasn't old. Seven years older than me. I slept with him."

"I don't need to hear that."

"Only once. It was a stupid mistake and things

were weird after that. But I thought we were doing okay at school. Then one day I made a mistake, just a small one, easily corrected. It wasn't anything no one else had done before. Alec went ballistic. He screamed at me in front of the entire class. I couldn't show my face for days, but I did go back. It wasn't the same, though."

Levi's arms tightened around her. "I don't like where this is going."

"I didn't finish. My confidence was wrecked, and my mom sent me a one-way ticket home. She said I just needed some time to regroup and think about my next move. Of course, I never told her about Alec. She would have wanted to sue the school."

"She would have sued, but all I want to do is beat his ass."

"It's not all his fault. I shouldn't have slept with my teacher."

"Bullshit. I don't want to hear that."

"I take responsibility for my actions. I was young, and maybe I liked the attention he gave me."

"Yeah, and he was seven years older than you *and* a teacher."

Everything Levi said was true, and she'd heard it all before. Jill and Zoey had wanted her to write to the school to complain. And now Carly realized that she should have. She could have stopped him from making any other girl feel so small.

Levi kissed her shoulder, then lingered there while his hand skimmed down her spine. "Is that loser still there?"

"He's not. So either he was fired, or he left on his own."

"I could find him."

"No." She sat up straight and met his gaze. "You're not going to do anything."

"I've got skills you don't know about." He simply lay back, a wicked grin on his face, hands splayed behind his head. Nothing but the thinnest white sheet covered him, just below his abs.

"I'm sure you do." But if he hadn't shown her all his skills, she hated to think he'd been holding back. Any more of those skills and he'd give her a stroke. "Special *service* skills?"

"Yep."

"Seriously?" She straddled him, hands splayed across his abs. "You're going to hold out on me?"

"Only until you beg. Then I won't be able to resist."

"You think I'm going to beg?"

"I know you're going to beg."

"Try again. I don't beg."

He locked eyes with hers, his own gaze blazing hot. "I'm going to do that thing I do. Then we'll see how you beg."

"What thing?"

"That thing where I ruin you for any other man."

"Oh. *That* thing."

Then he flipped her, rather skillfully in fact, displaying some of those skills. "I'm going to make you feel so good that you're going to forget anyone who ever made you feel less than the gorgeous, sexy, *smart* woman you are."

Her heart ached just hearing those words. Another thing he couldn't do, but how she loved that he wanted to try.

"Promises, promises."

And then he proceeded to show her, inch by inch, and kiss after mind-blowing kiss, just how well he kept his promises.

CHAPTER THIRTY

"Girl, you need to stop smiling like that," Jill said from behind the counter at the Drip. "You're making me wish I had a boyfriend."

"Sorry."

"Just hope I meet someone that makes me smile like that someday."

Carly yawned in response, and Jill glared at her. "Oh, stop it. You couldn't be more obvious."

"What happened to your good-looking neighbor?" Carly said, paying for her mocha latte.

"Men are dumb."

Fortunately, Jill said this over the loud cacophony of the espresso machine, so Carly thought most of the customers sitting nearby probably hadn't heard her. Hopefully. She walked over to the other end of the counter to wait for her drink, pushing Grace's stroller forward. The Drip was fairly empty after the lunch rush. It was a good place to do homework or write and there was a long bench table in the back usually filled with students and writers.

Jill slid the mocha in Carly's direction. "He's

married. I took his stupid dog to the pet wash and walked him three times. The last time I brought him back he thanked me for walking his wife's dog while she was on a business trip. You'd think he could have told me that the first time, don't you?"

"That's terrible, but it *was* very nice of you to do that."

Jill rolled her eyes. "And a little mocha for the baby girl!" She handed over a small paper cup filled with whipped cream for Grace.

"That's the organic whipped cream, right?"

"Of course."

Grace squealed in delight when Carly put it in her hands. Carly had started the training early, but for now it was a mocha-free zone for Grace.

"What time is Grandma coming?" Jill asked.

"She should be here any minute."

"You're going tell her today?"

"That's the plan." Carly pushed the stroller to an empty two-chair table and set her drink down.

She hoped that Irene was as open-minded as she seemed to be, because Carly wanted her to walk out of the coffee shop rethinking all of her plans. Despite the fact that Levi thought it was none of their business, Carly couldn't, in good conscience, allow Mrs. Lane to walk out of her marriage of more than twenty years without a fight. Real love was always worth fighting for.

It was worth overcoming every obstacle. She'd make Mrs. Lane see that, one way or another.

Irene wanted to take Grace to the local petting zoo, and Levi had agreed. This would give Carly some free time today, as well. Since Grace had started to sleep less during the day and more at night, Carly's days had become difficult to juggle.

It wouldn't be much longer before RockYourBaby was sold. They'd recently received an adequate offer, and though it was for far less than she'd hoped, they now had a solid and viable option. Kirk had agreed they should sell at the lower figure. It was time. Now they simply had to take care of the paperwork and contracts. RockYourBaby would become part of a larger and more profitable baby website. Apparently, Your Beautiful Baby even hired professional journalists to write their articles. They'd decided not to buy the RockYourBaby trademark name, and instead, planned to capitalize on Fashionista Baby because of the popularity of the viral post.

The door chime dinged, and Carly looked up to see Mrs. Lane walking toward them. She had a backpack slung over one shoulder and wore a windbreaker, long pants and hiking shoes.

"Hey, you two." She bent to pat Grace's head and took the empty chair. "I bought diapers and I've got water bottles and snacks. I didn't want you to go to any trouble."

So much for the diaper bag Carly had packed

with fresh fruit and healthy organic snacks. "That's okay. Take this anyway."

"Thanks," Mrs. Lane said, accepting the bag. "And thank Levi for me again, too. I'll take lots of photos of her today because I'm going back home next week."

No. That wasn't enough time to get these two to come to their senses. "Do you have to?"

She smiled then, kind and reassuring, and patted Carly's hand. "Oh, I see what you mean. That's kind of you, honey. But I've got a house to get ready to sell and so much to do. More than twenty years of marriage. I'll probably need one of those big green metal trash bins."

"But…but what about Mr. Lane?"

"What about him? If he wants to give up, that's his business."

"Maybe you should talk to him."

She leaned back in her chair. "Talk? I've *talked* until I ran out of words. He doesn't want to hear me *jibber-jabber* anymore, as he calls it so eloquently."

"But twenty years. Don't you…love him anymore?"

"Oh, honey. You're so young. Well, of *course* I love him. But sometimes that's not enough."

Since when?

"What if I talk to him?"

"You?" Mrs. Lane seemed to consider it, then

shook her head. "I can't stop you from wasting your breath, but if you want to, go ahead."

"How do you know when it's over? Really?"

Most of Carly's relationships had ended before they'd even started. But she'd never seen her parents even get close to the point where they'd give up on such an…investment.

"How do you know?" Mrs. Lane dropped her gaze to the table. "You know when you stop talking. When there's nothing left to say because everything has already been said. And said. About eleven thousand times. I'm tired."

"So it sounds like you need him to do some of the heavy lifting for a change." They'd finally gotten to the heart of the matter. Now all they needed was a solution.

"That pretty much sums it up, doesn't it?"

"Don't worry, Mrs. Lane. I've got this."

"I see you're an eternal optimist. Just like your mother."

She nodded, though that was far from the truth. Pessimism had clouded most of her life. It was just always easier to handle someone else's problems. "I'll talk to him."

"If you can work your magic with that stubborn man, then more power to you. Twenty years *is* a long time. Don't get me wrong. I wasn't looking forward to the dating. I looked into a seniors online matchmaking site, but I won't put up my profile just yet."

Crisis averted!

Now for the next bit of news. Carly hoped that Mrs. Lane would understand and forgive this last part. Because Carly was a bit nervous about it. Sometimes good things did come to an end, and so it was with RockYourBaby.

"I also wanted to tell you something about RockYourBaby. It's being sold. But don't worry, it's going to a good home." She took a breath. "I just couldn't do it anymore."

Mrs. Lane nodded. "I saw the strain it's taking on your relationship with Levi. And, honey, please. You've got to let him help more. Don't kill yourself every night doing all the cooking and cleaning."

"That's… Yeah."

"Maybe now you'll be able to put all your efforts toward raising Grace."

"I'm still going to work." She'd never thought of herself as the stay-at-home-mom type. Her mother had worked. Her grandmother had worked.

"What are you going to do?"

Well, that was the fifty-thousand-dollar question, wasn't it? She still had no idea. She wanted to continue to design and sew, because that was her heart. Or at least, it always had been. And even if she never went back to New York City, she'd find a way to make it work.

"I'm still looking at all my options."

"I'm sure it will still be something having to do with babies, right?"

"Um, sure. I wouldn't rule that out."

"You are your mother's daughter."

But that wasn't true, and never had been. She'd always marched to the beat of her own drummer, as her father said. The entire family had been left-brain thinkers, and she'd been the odd one out. She'd been the one with dyslexia, which at times was her curse and at other times the one thing that made her unique. Because she'd been drawn to creative pursuits and found her success there. For the most part, anyway.

"Actually," Carly said, "I adored my mother, but we were nothing alike. This baby business was her thing, and I never understood it. When she died, I tried my best, but I'm a poor substitute. And that's okay."

It felt freeing to say the truth. She'd been selling and pretending to be someone she wasn't for so long that she'd almost forgotten who she was. Now so plainly stated and simple, the truth sat between them, clearing the air. Mrs. Lane didn't look shocked or at all surprised. But then again, if she was a mother and a grandmother a few times over, she'd probably already seen and heard it all.

"You're good with Grace." Mrs. Lane glanced at her granddaughter with clear adoration in her eyes. "And that's all I care about."

Grace cooed from her stroller, where she sat

swinging and kicking her chubby legs. Carly didn't know how it had happened, or when, exactly, but she did understand Grace. She was in tune with her mood swings and her needs. The way she liked to be held when outside, so that she got a clear view of the whole world in front of her. The way she seemed to understand Carly's words, and the sound of her voice talking to her through the day. Levi had been right. Carly might not be the most informed nanny around, but she was an encyclopedia when it came to Grace Lambert.

CHAPTER THIRTY-ONE

LATE IN THE AFTERNOON, Irene pulled back the lacy white eyelet curtains of her room at the Whispering Rose Bed and Breakfast on the outskirts of Fortune. Away from town, it was so quiet the only sounds she heard were crickets. The B and B was on several acres of a beautiful working vineyard. Just the kind of place where she'd wanted to stay with her husband. Said husband could be in here right now enjoying the beautiful ambience of the soft lighting and the wine tastings every evening, but instead he sat outside in the rental sedan spying on her.

Yep. Still there. She had her own stalker. Her husband.

He'd called and texted since she'd left their room at the Budget Inn. She hadn't responded. But the next day, she'd noticed him parked in the small visitors' lot of the B and B for hours. It hadn't taken a genius to find her, as she'd used his credit card to book the place.

"Frank," she muttered. "What are you doing?"

He wouldn't come to the door and knock. She told herself he was simply respecting her space. If

nothing else, she'd distracted him from his machi-
nations with the California family court system.

After spending most of the afternoon with
Grace at Happy Hollow, the local petting zoo,
Irene had come away firmly convinced that her
granddaughter was well cared for. Clean. Healthy
and alert. Levi and Carly had done a wonderful
job, and Frank should be happy with this knowledge. But Irene now worried that nothing on this
earth would be good enough for him.

At four o'clock, she walked to the tasting room
for happy hour. Frank sat in the sedan, hunched
over, as though he thought she might not see him
there. Afterward, she came back, trying to ignore
the sedan. Pretending and playing along that she
didn't see him there. She'd always said that Frank
was far more stubborn than any of the children.
This time she was going to wait him out. Two
could play this game.

But after sitting inside alone for another hour,
checking in with the kids via email and updat-
ing them on Grace, confirming her flight home,
Irene couldn't take it another minute. She flung
open the door of the small cottage, then marched
across the courtyard to the small side lot.

Frank slid down in the driver's seat and covered
his face with the bill of his Giants baseball cap.

She rapped her knuckles on the driver's-side door.

He rolled down the window, then straightened
the bill of his hat.

"Why are you here?" Irene asked, hands on hips.

"I had to make sure you were okay."

Irene sucked in a breath. The sad truth was it was quite possibly the most loving thing he'd said to her in months.

"Oh, Frank."

"I'm sorry to bother you." He leaned forward and turned the key in the ignition.

"Don't you want to see the room you're paying for?"

Frank blinked as if he couldn't believe he'd heard right. "Yeah."

She led the way to her room in the small cottage to the right of the main building. Due to its exorbitant price, it had been the only vacancy, so she'd splurged. The honeymoon suite had lots of privacy, which she didn't need. Truth be told, she'd be helping Frank pay the bill off when they returned home, even if it meant substitute teaching again.

"This is very nice," Frank said, nodding as he glanced around the room, his gaze lingering on the fireplace that took up half a wall. "You were right. This is much better than the Budget Inn."

Her gaze stayed riveted to the man she'd been married to for over twenty years. He'd gotten older when she wasn't looking. When they'd been busy with daily life, but not *noticing* each other. He had gray hairs, many of which she'd probably given him. Wrinkles around his eyes, laugh lines around his mouth. A deep worry groove between his eyebrows, which had surely formed when she'd been rushed to an emergency C-section with Meg.

In that moment she realized she'd never find anyone else who could take his place. She'd been so stupid to think she could walk away from him. From their shared history.

"I miss you," she blurted out.

How long had she held that in, afraid to say it out loud? Afraid it would seem…selfish.

"I'm right here."

She rolled her eyes. "I think you know what I mean."

He met her eyes. "I understand. And I'm sorry. It's just I… Things haven't been…"

"I know."

"Honey, you have to know—I didn't mean—" His voice shook.

Her big and strong man who'd been knocked to his knees by life. She went into his arms. "Frank, I miss her, too. Sometimes it feels like I'll never be the same again. I have good days and bad days, too. But you haven't allowed yourself to have any good days. I can't stand watching you hurt like this. Let's just start over. Can we?"

"At our age?" He chuckled, holding her tight.

"I love you, Frank. We've both got a lot of living left to do, and I don't know about you, but I want to do that together."

"That's all I want, too." He stroked her back.

"I've lost so much in my life, but the one thing I can't stand to lose is you."

She glanced at the California king–size bed that she'd slept in alone. "What do you say we start by breaking in that monster bed?"

Frank grinned. "Yeah?"

They held each other all night long, which turned out to be a good beginning.

As RESIDENT NFG, Levi understood he got the grunt work. He'd occasionally be tasked with a morning coffee run to the Drip, a lunch run and all the difficult passengers. Even the nonhuman ones. But he would only be NFG until Stone hired someone new. He'd been talking about that a lot recently, in addition to buying another plane. Hell, he'd been planning to buy a whole fleet of planes, according to the latest word. Things were moving right along at Mcallister Charters in a forward trajectory, and Levi liked the way it looked for him. Because pretty soon he wouldn't be NFG anymore.

"What are you smiling about?" Matt walked up to the Snack Shack, where Levi sat nursing a cup of coffee between flights.

Pick one. For the first time in a while, he had a list of things to smile about. Grace was sleeping through the night—mostly—and any lack of sleep on his part was for all the *right* reasons. Those reasons being Carly and the kind of chemistry and connection he hadn't experienced with anyone in a while. Or ever, if he was being honest. To top it off, he had no concern that he'd lose Grace or be stuck paying legal fees for years. And he had Carly to thank for that, too.

"I've got my reasons."

"Two of those reasons are named Carly and Grace, I take it."

"We've been spending some time together, yeah."

"Drove by the other night and saw you three at the Lick 'n' Spoon."

"Yeah?" It had been his idea to go out for ice cream even though the October nights were getting chillier. And when he'd given Grace a taste, he'd loved seeing her eyes grow wide at the cold and sweet taste. She was definitely Daddy's girl. "Why didn't you say hi?"

"I was on my way home with a pizza. And anyway, it looked pretty cozy there. Didn't want to interrupt."

It had felt cozy. Like a real family. The kind that didn't drive you nuts. Carly didn't try to control him or seem to have many preconceived notions about what he should or shouldn't do for her. Ironically, this had the reverse effect of giving him a desire to take care of *her*. Something he didn't want to analyze too closely. Point being, everything felt right with her. Simple.

Now that she'd been honest with him, he understood what she'd been dealing with and why she sometimes had that troubled look in her eyes. Sure, she might still have some stuff to work out in her life, but the important thing was she wasn't going anywhere.

He'd help her through it if she'd let him—the PT issues with her father, her mother's baby business. What Carly would do next with her life. He would do his part and be the supportive boyfriend. Not rush a damn thing or overthink the situation. "Aw," Sarah said as she came by and refilled Levi's cup with more coffee. "Look at you. Your woman problem is all fixed."

Levi didn't say a word but merely took another gulp of his coffee and set the cup down.

"Babe, have I told you I don't like it when you read other men?" Matt said.

Levi almost snorted coffee through his nose. "Dude."

Sarah had been a forensic artist in Colorado before she'd moved to Fortune, and Levi wasn't crazy about the way she read him, either. "That's so sweet and annoyingly possessive." Sarah leaned across the counter and made out with Matt for several minutes.

These two were oblivious to anyone else. He cleared his throat to remind them he was still here. "Anyway."

Sarah managed to pull herself away, not that Matt made it easy, hanging on to her the way he did. She finally laughed and slapped his hands away. "So. Today it's all in your shoulders, Ice Man."

"My shoulders. What the hell?" Levi swiveled his head.

"They're unkinked. For the first time in weeks." She gave him a cocky grin and threw a dish towel over her shoulder, then sashayed over to tend to another customer.

Matt leaned back on his stool and gave Levi a good appraisal. "Hey. Yeah, she's right. I'm not crazy about the fact that she noticed it, but yeah. Unkinked."

Levi lifted one of those unkinked shoulders. He was not surprised, since nearly every part of him was relaxed. For the first time in his life, he couldn't chalk it up to good sex, though that certainly hadn't hurt anything. He was relaxed because…he cared deeply about someone. And that someone happened to be a woman he could trust with the single most important gift he'd ever been given. Carly had his back. He trusted her, and he hadn't trusted easily in years.

"So what? I'm unkinked. That's a good thing."

"I'm glad you think so," Matt said with a smirk. "About time you settled down."

"Who said I'm settling down?"

"Apparently, your shoulders." Matt got up, glanced at his watch, then walked toward the tarmac.

Levi finished his coffee and considered the fact that he had officially settled in Fortune. While he'd had wanderlust for most of his life, this felt right. He would have expected being grounded to make him feel trapped. Had been ready to feel it, and to have to talk himself out of the itchy feeling. But thanks to Stone and Matt he was still a flyboy. Always would be. That was in his DNA.

Later that afternoon, Levi left the airport and caught himself anticipating seeing Carly. Pulling her into the circle of his arms and feeling her warm breath as she buried her face in his neck. She'd drawn him in at some point along the way. He didn't know when or how, but Cute Stuck-Up Girl had morphed into this woman he craved every day. It was in her smile, and in the way she gazed at him with such hope that it kicked him in the gut every time.

He was so wrapped in his thoughts that he almost didn't notice the man standing beside the rental sedan in the airport parking lot.

"Levi," the man called out.

Well, Mr. Lane had finally stepped up and decided to have it out. And Levi was more than ready for this meeting. He continued walking toward his truck, opened the driver's-side door and threw his laptop inside.

Mr. Lane strode up to him, hands stuffed in his pants pockets. "We need to talk."

Up close and under the lights illuminating the

now-dark lot, he appeared much older than he had a few weeks ago when Levi had taken custody of Grace. His close-cropped hair was whiter, and the furrow between his eyebrows deeper. Levi could admit that he hadn't spent much time worrying about Mr. Lane's state of mind. He'd had an entire new life to adjust to and his own problems. But now, knowing what Carly had been through with her father, he had a different perspective. The relationship between fathers and daughters could be a minefield of complications. A lot of expectations thrown in with all the love. He'd never had a sibling, but he now had a daughter and a new attitude.

"Thought you were leaving," Levi said, shutting the door.

"Not yet." Mr. Lane studied the asphalt and tipped back on his heels. "My wife threw a wrench in my plans."

"I heard."

"Of course, she was right. She usually is." He shook his head and looked up to meet Levi's eyes. "I've been an idiot. I need to apologize."

At this point, he didn't care if Mr. Lane was apologizing under duress and in order to reconcile with his wife. He'd take it. "Apology accepted."

"I can explain, not that it's any excuse."

"You don't have to. I realize how hard this has been for you. I didn't want to hurt you."

"No, I'm sure you didn't. Grace is your daughter, and you have a right to raise her. Wherever you'd like."

"A good job brought me out here, or I wouldn't have taken her so far away."

"It was meant to be, I'd say. Carly has a heart of gold. So did Sandy, despite what anyone else thought of her. I need to tell you something about her. I'm not trying to excuse what she did in any way. As fathers, we have it tough. We don't always have a say in what happens. But even though you two weren't together, she *should* have told you about Grace. You shouldn't have found out the way you did."

Levi nodded, but he wasn't blameless, either, he could now admit. He hadn't given Sandy his phone number or the slightest indication that he'd ever want to see her again. And the temporary nature of their relationship had come back to bite him in the ass in a most significant way. Would it have been different if he'd treated Sandy with more respect and consideration? Maybe she would have at least tried to contact him. Now he'd never know.

"Sandy was a handful for most of her life. Her mother died, too, when Sandy was ten. Irene did her best, but Sandy remembered her mother too well and Irene was no substitute in her book." He dragged a hand through his short hair. "We were too strict with her during the teenage years. When she went away to college, she went wild. And because she probably knew we wouldn't approve, she didn't keep in touch after she graduated. I thought maybe I could right my wrongs with her through Grace, which was a dickhead move. You don't get to do this over again. Remember that if you don't remember anything else."

Levi didn't speak, but he'd always remember those words. *You don't get to do this over again.*

"My wife and I are going back home in a couple days."

"Both of you?"

"Yeah." Mr. Lane gave a half smile. "I'm finally listening to her. Truth is, I know I need help. It's not going to be easy, but I'm going to talk to someone about all this…crap that's swirling around in my head making it hard to think straight."

Grief. Levi understood a little bit about that, too. "Smart."

He pointed. "Women are smart. Remember that, too."

"Yes, sir."

"Irene assured me that Grace is a wonderful baby girl, smart and well cared for, and that you have everything to do with that."

Not just him. "And Carly."

Interesting that after three failed attempts he'd wound up with a nanny who didn't know babies but had managed to school them all. And it wasn't because of her baby business; it was because of her heart.

"Right. She's something. She called me, too. After getting off the phone with her, I won't lie—I wanted to talk to my daughter. But I won't get that chance." His voice cracked. "Don't you be an ass, son. Make sure you tell the people you love how you feel every day."

Levi drove home. Carly now usually met him at his place at the end of the day. One other thing she'd done for him without being asked was become Digger's official dog walker. When he opened the door, Digger greeted him, wagging not just his tail but essentially his entire backside. Levi squatted, always feeling like a giant next to his dog. "Hey, Digger. What's up?"

Digger ran to the sliding glass door and scratched on it to be let outside. He guessed that he was now officially stuck with his adopted mutt. According to Emily, he'd joined the club of flyers who'd wound up with a dog of their own through the program. Levi followed the sounds of splashing water and Grace's squeals to the bathroom. Carly was probably giving Grace a bath in that new contraption someone had sent her to review. He heard her voice before he opened the bathroom door.

"Should we wash your hair now? This little plastic hat will keep the water out of your eyes. Why didn't I think of this invention? I know the water is a shock to the eyes, but it's not going to hurt you." More splashing and squeals from Grace. "For dinner, you can have mashed carrots. I have no idea what I'm having for dinner. Or what your daddy is having. Do you think he wants to have dinner with me again tonight?"

"I know he does."

Carly startled and turned. "Levi! You scared me."

He stared for a moment, because damn, she was so beautiful. Her always wild, wavy blond hair fell partially over her right eye. She knelt beside the tub, slightly disheveled and wet from all of Grace's splashing. Cheeks flushed. A breathtaking mess. His mess. So here he was, taking ownership. Staking his claim.

Make sure you tell the people you love how you feel every day.

She had his heart. The words, which were right on the tip of his tongue, caught in his throat. No wonder, since his own parents had never been too keen on the words. Love was all in the actions, and the way Levi had been taught.

While he'd once thought Carly held back from him, the tough-to-face truth was that he was the one with issues here. He'd been the one to hold himself in check for years, his heart locked up tight, an ice man to the core. As long as he didn't feel anything too deeply, he couldn't be hurt. But first Grace, then Carly, had changed everything for him. Try as he might—and he had tried, at least with Carly—they'd both single-handedly wormed into his heart. With an ice pick.

Smart.

CHAPTER THIRTY-TWO

AFTER CARLY FINISHED bathing Grace and dressed her in pajamas, she went home to change. Levi offered to heat up cans of soup and wanted her to have dinner with him, but she'd be damned if she would stay with her hair looking as though it had been through a category-three hurricane. She took her first shower of the day—if one didn't count the spit bath with Grace—blow-dried her hair into submission, then dressed in jeans, a black sweater and black ankle boots. Levi might look good in only a towel, but she had to work at it.

At least, she wanted to work at it—not that he'd given her any indication he wouldn't just as soon strip her down where she stood and have her on any available surface. She was a girl, damn it, and she cared about these little things. She didn't want to look like a hot mess to her... Jeez, what was Levi to her? Her boyfriend? Employer? Neighbor? Fake fiancé? All of the above? It had always been her nature to push for a commitment, for a clear definition of who, what and where a relationship was headed. *Where do I stand? Where is this thing going?* But now, she didn't have many doubts left. Whatever they had going on here, it was rare and special. She didn't need to hear his words to confirm it because this time her heart knew.

Showed maybe she'd grown up at last.

She checked her email one last time for the day and answered a few customer questions about her latest blog post on the molded baby chair. Her mind went briefly to that place of fear and doubt whenever she contemplated what could have happened to Grace that day.

The good news was that she'd accomplished her main goal today. Mrs. Lane had dropped Grace off the previous afternoon with nothing but compliments on what a great baby she'd been. Carly had phoned Mr. Lane to talk to him, only to find out that Mrs. Lane had beaten her to it. And, yes! They were going to try to make their marriage work. Poor Mr. Lane had agreed to get help for his depression, and Mrs. Lane was determined to hang in there now that he'd come to that realization.

Now all I have to do is figure out what I'm going to do with the rest of my life.

"I guess I'll start by having dinner."

Baby steps, one at a time, and she'd figure it out sooner rather than later. She was already on her way with her new designs.

She had her hand on the doorknob when her phone rang. Kirk again.

"Hey, how's Dad? Is everything okay?"

"Great. PT efforts are looking up big-time since he talked to your friend."

"My friend?"

"You know, Eric, the guy with the titanium hip. I don't have to tell you how patriotic our father is. One word out of this guy is PT gold. The fact that he has the same titanium hip? I haven't seen Dad this fired up in months."

"I don't know what you're talking about."

"He said Levi asked him to call."

Levi. She'd told him about her father's hip, and he'd mentioned someone who'd been through a difficult recovery. This had to be the guy. "Let me talk to Dad."

"Hang on." She could hear sounds in the background as Kirk told their father she was on the line and handed him the phone.

"Hello, sweetheart," Dad said. "Listen, the doctor says I'm doing better. Finally manned up and I'm getting this hip in shape."

"Did Levi call you?"

"His friend did, but thank Levi for me. Calls me every day, the persistent guy. It's the shot to the ass that I needed. Eric was right. I've worked hard all my life for other people. I'm doing this one for me. As soon as I reach the next milestone, I'll come back home to Fortune."

"That's good news! I knew you could do this."

"I'm sorry I put you through it, honey. You shouldn't have been worrying about me after your mother died. And trying to sell the baby business. Now that you sold the business, and I'm no longer a worry, there's only one thing left for you to do."

Carly knew the next words were coming.

"You need to go back to New York and finish. I want you to do it for me."

"Dad—"

"Look, until you go back there and figure out what went wrong, you won't be able to move on."

But I know what went wrong, and it wasn't my fault.

"Go try again. You were almost done, and it's a crime not to finish. I don't want you to give up. That's what I did. Maybe we were both stuck for a while. But I'm coming out with my big guns today—your mother would have wanted this for you."

Too bad Carly had never told either of her parents the truth about why she'd come home with her tail between her legs, but it didn't matter anymore. Alec couldn't hurt, intimidate or stop her. Only her doubts could stop her now. And she was so ready to be done with her past determining her future.

Dad continued, "I'm sorry you had to run the baby business for Mom, when it should have been me. You should have been doing your own thing.

But now that you're free, I think we both know where your heart is."

"I've already decided. I just haven't officially told anyone yet. I'm going back."

Ironically, Levi had given her the strength to face her fears. Her body now thrummed with excitement and not anxiety about the future.

But if she thought her life was complicated before, she'd now fallen head over heels for a man who had a big and open heart. He'd tried to help not only her, but her father, too. He cared more than he'd ever let on. More than he'd ever let her see. It might not have been spoken in words, but it was certainly in his actions. And he, of all people, would understand if she had to do this. She had to be honest with him, and soon.

Carly swallowed hard. Her heart rate had kicked up, her legs felt numb and she bit at the quick of her fingernail. She'd tell Levi tonight, and he'd understand. They could work it out—it didn't mean that this…thing between them had to end.

She didn't want it to end.

She'd find Grace the best babysitter she could from the most reputable agency in the state. Just temporarily, of course. Levi could visit her in New York. He was a pilot and would probably love the idea. It would be hardest on her. She'd miss both of them, but she wouldn't be gone forever. She'd be able to renew some of her contacts in the industry, work on her portfolio of baby clothing designs, meet with Jenny and the Cutting Edge in person, and figure out her next career moves.

Carly hung up, then ran across her shared lawn with Levi. She let herself in the front door and found him standing in the kitchen.

He held up two soup cans. "She's asleep, but the bad news is that all I have is chicken noodle soup. I'm thinking we need options."

She didn't speak, just stared at him in all his gorgeous male glory. He'd changed into jeans and a long-sleeved gray T-shirt. His hair was now officially on the wrong side of a haircut, his eyes deep and so blue. And she loved him so much her pulse kicked up just being in his presence.

"What?" He set down the cans and slid her a slow grin.

She launched her body into his arms, and he easily caught her, his hands dropping to grip her hips. Her legs wrapped around his back and pressed into the warm strength of him.

"Thank you," she whispered into the strong curve of his neck.

He smelled so good. Ten percent soap, one percent baby powder and one hundred percent man. Okay, so she couldn't do math when it came to him. Maybe because he was larger than the sum of his parts.

"I don't know what I did, but you're welcome.

Tell me what it was and I'll do it again." One hand tightened on her hip and the other wrapped around the nape of her neck.

She kissed his neck, then moved to draw his earlobe into her mouth and felt his entire body tighten like a cord. "Your friend talked to my father because you asked him to."

"It was nothing. The least I could do."

"It isn't," she said fiercely. "It isn't the *least* of anything."

His hand tugged on a handful of her hair and pulled her back enough for him to gaze into her eyes. "I'd do anything for you."

Those words filled her soul. She'd never had a man like him. Never had a man who had her back like Levi did, who looked out for her. Who selflessly cared for her needs. Her wants. Her desires.

"Anything?" she teased him, her fingers circling his tight biceps.

His piercing gaze never left hers. "You heard me."

"You don't know. I could go crazy with that kind of power."

"Long as you go crazy on me."

His eyes softened from the earlier hot gaze and were smiling, too, and right there and then, she caught it. Something in his eyes other than pure and unbridled heat and lust. A tenderness that had her slipping and falling even deeper into him. It was going to be even tougher to leave him now, even for just a little while. And it wasn't fair because she probably still felt a whole lot more than he did.

But life wasn't always fair. She'd learned to live with that.

"I want you to kiss me. Hard. Did I ever mention you're the world's best kisser?"

"Don't make it too easy for me. Make me prove it every night."

Her lips parted, and his tongue caressed hers, first tenderly, then not so tenderly. The kiss went hot and wild. Her fingers threaded through his hair, then her hands were everywhere she could manage to reach on him. He walked them to the couch and plopped down with her straddling his lap.

"Levi." She broke off the kiss, wondering whether or not this would be a good time to mention her other news.

"Yeah." His lips got busy teasing her earlobe; his talented hands were busy under her sweater, softly caressing her stomach and settling at the small of her back.

No, she'd tell him tomorrow. Tomorrow she'd think of the perfect way to explain. And he'd understand. She knew he would. He'd have her back, no matter what.

"We can eat dinner later."

"Much later." His fingers drifted up and down

her back and skimmed her skin. She shivered at his touch.

She pulled off her top, enjoying the way his eyes took in her shiny new demi bra. A good investment, judging by the approving glint in his gaze.

But there was one thing she would tell him tonight, and not hold back. He needed to know, and it might make it easier for him to understand all the rest. The strength she'd gained in the past few weeks had come partly from loving him. From allowing herself to fully open up her heart. From taking a risk simply because only he made that so…safe.

Hands on her ass, he lifted her and settled her on the couch. He pulled his shirt off, never taking his eyes off her. Then he knelt beside her and kissed from the throbbing pulse at her throat down to her shoulders, pulling the bra strap off with his teeth. His warm, wet openmouthed kisses continued in a line down her chest to her belly button. He licked there, making her moan and grind against him.

Words had never come easily for her. She'd fought for most of her life to understand the words on a page, to memorize them, to carry them in her heart. So when she wrote words down, when she said them out loud, they were particularly meaningful for her.

"I love you, Levi," she said, knowing she meant it for the first time in her life with a man.

He glanced up at her with a smile that told her she'd just given him the world, then proceeded to drive her clear out of her ever-loving mind.

It was hours before either one of them thought about dinner, and by then all the take-out places were closed.

CHAPTER THIRTY-THREE

When Levi woke early the next morning, it was with a hope for the future he hadn't thought he'd ever have again. Next to him, Carly's legs and arms were a tangled mess with his. He no longer had any feeling in his left arm, but he didn't much care. Grace was awake in her crib but, by a small miracle, not crying. The monitor showed her simply babbling, grabbing on to the rails of her crib and attempting to pull herself to a standing position. Well, crap, *that* was going to happen any day now.

This had happened, too. Love.

He'd fallen stinking in love. Like a silly teenager. That was the way Carly made him feel, too, like he'd do anything to have her. Steal a car, rob a liquor store, drive a minivan. He gently removed his numb arm from under a sound-asleep Carly. With his other hand, he let his fingers glide down her bare back. She didn't move.

He let her sleep, knowing she'd get up when she smelled the coffee brewing and closer to the time he had to leave for the airport. Grace squealed in

excitement when he opened the door to her bedroom and lifted her out of the crib.

"Hey, baby girl." He changed her diaper and
dressed her.

"Dada," she said, and he felt sure this time she
meant him.

He carried Grace into the laundry room to say
good morning to Digger. The dog was still stuck
on the idea that this little spot was his home.
Once, Levi had put Digger's dog pillow in the
living room, thinking he should join the family
and stop being a hermit. With his small teeth,
Digger had tugged it back into the laundry room.

"Arf!" Digger rolled over, showing off his soft
underbelly, shameless when he wanted to be fed.

Levi fed Digger, let him outside to do his business, then headed to the kitchen with Grace. He
was due at the airport a little later than normal
this morning, so he planned to make Carly a big
breakfast. After settling Grace in her high chair,
he started the coffee brewing and found the bacon
and eggs in the fridge. Once the bacon starting
sizzling in the pan, he knew Carly would come
staggering out of his bedroom seconds later, hair
sticking up in four directions.

Personally, he'd grown to love that look on her.

His phone buzzed with a text, and he reached for
it. It didn't take him long to realize he'd reached for
Carly's phone. Or maybe it took too long, because

the text message from her father scrolled across the screen before he recognized his mistake.

Let me know the exact date you're heading back to New York City. I'll buy your airline ticket. I'm excited for you.

Levi stared at the words, not computing. When had she decided to leave for New York? Why hadn't she told him? One more thing she'd kept from him, just as good as a lie. Last night she'd said she loved him, and unless she liked to throw that phrase around, she'd lied to his face. She couldn't love him if she planned to leave.

She walked into the kitchen then, and he handed her the phone without a word. He went back to breakfast.

"Oh," Carly said. "Did you read this? Because I can explain..."

He let her voice trail off and didn't fill the silence with words. He cracked an egg instead. Two eggs. Three eggs.

"I was going to tell you this morning."

"No need." Four eggs. Should he crack a fifth? Oh, to hell with it. Crack. Five eggs. Six eggs.

"Babe, really. Please look at me."

He should probably go for an even dozen. Seven eggs. Eight eggs. Well, he was better off cracking eggs than cracking heads. Anyone in their right mind could see that. Nine eggs. Ten.

"You do what you have to do."

"Levi," she pleaded with him. "Don't do this. Don't freeze me out."

"Seems like you're the one who did that. You're leaving. And you didn't tell me." Good. He was talking. That meant he wasn't too pissed for words. But he was pretty damned close, and yeah, it had been a long-ass time since he'd felt so much of...freaking *everything*.

How great for him

"Only for a little while."

"How long? A week? Two?" He knew the answer.

She ran her hand along the counter edge. "No. A few months. That's it."

"Yeah. Long distance doesn't work, babe. You're looking at someone who knows this like I know the back of my hand. It doesn't. Work."

"But you and I—"

"It's fine. You should go back and finish school. Makes sense. I get it." He looked at the dozen eggs in the mixing bowl and remembered he had to take a shower. Get to work.

"You're a pilot! I'm sure you can visit me." She followed him out of the kitchen. "Are you saying I don't even mean that much to you? You won't take a plane ride to see me? I'm the one who said I love you first. Don't think this is going to be easy for me."

"Listen, you probably said you love me in the heat of the moment. You didn't mean it."

"But I do mean it!"

"Too bad, then. Relationships are hard enough without putting distance into the equation."

"Are we talking physical distance or emotional distance?" She put her hands on her hips. "Because I know how I feel. I know I will be faithful to you no matter how far away I am. Is that what you're worried about? I'll hook up with someone else?"

He didn't answer, because damned if he'd let her know she'd hit the nail on the head. It had happened before, time and again. Even his parents had left him for the greater good. Which meant that he was still apparently not enough for the people he loved to stick around. No, he wasn't going to go there and open up his stupid heart any more than he already had so she could throw her poison-tipped darts at it.

When her eyes filled with pain, he almost knew what she'd say before she did. "Oh, I get it. You're the one who will find someone else."

"I need to get to work. I'll be late."

Forget the damn shower. He'd shower at the freaking gym he'd joined but never went to. He dressed in his uniform, shoving pants, socks and boots on viciously. He'd just stepped out into the cold October morning when Carly called out to him. He turned back, and she stood in the doorway holding Grace in one arm. She held up his white Mcallister Charters shirt in the other.

He glanced down, shocked to find he was outside with no shirt on. No wonder he was so damned cold. He walked a few steps back and took the shirt from her, tugging his arms through the sleeves quickly.

"Thanks."

"I want to talk." The words squeaked out. The misery in her eyes reflected the feeling in his heart and kicked him in the gut hard enough to make him wince.

"Later," he said. "I need a minute."

Or two.

Twenty minutes later he arrived at the gym, bench-pressed until his eyes crossed, and ran a mile in six minutes. He hit the shower, still angry, and hoped that by the time he arrived at the airport he would have cooled off. Carly had already texted him once, which he'd ignored. She didn't text him again, which was wise. Maybe she'd come to her senses and give him some time.

He dropped by the Drip for a coffee to go and on his way out saw Lily.

She grabbed on to his elbow. "I'm glad I ran into you. I've decided to forgive you. I know the engagement with you and your nanny is just a ruse for the sake of the grandparents. So if you're still thinking you want to revisit that second date…"

"No. I can't. Sorry."

"Aw, did she break your little heart?" She licked her lips. "Because I can fix that for you."

"That's a nice offer, but I'm going to pass."

"Let me know if you change your mind," she called out as he left the shop.

He couldn't talk. Couldn't be civil. Because, truthfully, he felt dangerous right now. Like a caged animal let loose on an unsuspecting public. Carly had lied to him. Again. He didn't know why he'd been surprised. She'd lied about being a baby expert. Lied about their engagement. Lied about leaving. She'd also lied about loving him. This time the lie went deeper and had caused far more damage. He wished he could say what he felt for her was a lie as well, but most unfortunately for him, it was real and alive. Consuming him.

The person he was most pissed with? *The honor goes to me, myself and I.* But Carly followed a close second. She'd made him care, damn it. Drawn him in, hooked him, and for what?

CHAPTER THIRTY-FOUR

FIRST, SHE CRIED. A lot.

Then, realizing that Grace was deeply affected by her emotional state, fussing and weepy, too, Carly got her act together and stopped sniveling. Smiled and laughed and put on a show. Played peekaboo with Grace until she giggled in a beautiful belly laugh. Carly faked it well. Even after Levi still hadn't answered her one text from hours ago. She was beginning to fear that maybe Levi didn't have any use for her if she couldn't be his nanny friend with benefits. Simply put, he didn't love her. And oh, yeah, he hadn't told her that he did, so he got points for honesty. That smile on his face when she'd told him she loved him was to be expected, because who didn't like to be told someone loved them? No one.

In the end, she'd called Jill and Zoey and told them she needed an intervention. Because what she wanted to do was drive to the airport and force Levi to listen to her. Force him to listen to her explanation. If he was going to walk away, it would be for the right reasons. Not because he had some mistaken impression of how difficult it had been for her to come to this decision. How hard it would be to leave him and Grace, even for a couple of months.

"You just told him you loved him? Just like that?" Zoey snapped her fingers. "First the engagement and now this. Girl, you've got a serious set of cojones."

"Where were you and exactly what were you doing when you told him?" Jill said.

"I'd rather not say." Carly's face heated.

Now she had to admit it wasn't the world's greatest timing. She could see why Levi might think she'd been…er, unduly influenced. Caught up in the moment. Not true, but she saw his point. Given that she'd followed her confession of love by getting caught in a lie, he might not fully appreciate the honesty of her words. Nope. Instead, he might think she'd lied to him. Again.

"Uh-huh," Jill said. "I thought so."

"So what do you want to do?" Zoey asked, holding Digger.

Carly had brought him next door with her, too, and he seemed out of sorts, since her laundry room just wasn't the same as Levi's.

"I want to go over to the airport and make him listen to me!"

"Won't he be busy in an airplane?" Zoey said.

"The point is—" Jill thrust her index finger toward Carly "—you called us here for a reason.

This meeting is to stop you from doing anything stupid."

"It is?" Zoey wrinkled her nose.

"Of course! We're here to prevent any more of this foolery. I don't know who ever told you to let a man know what you're thinking, but you should take away their friend card."

"No one told me that," Carly said miserably. "It was all me. I thought I'd be honest for a change."

"Bad move." Jill shook her head. "Bad."

"No. Maybe it isn't what I told him but what I *didn't* tell him. It looked like I was lying, but all I wanted was to find the right time to tell him. And I waited too long."

"You *should* be honest," Zoey said. "Always. Because men are like dogs."

"This is what I'm saying," Jill said.

"They're loyal and loving. Fiercely protective of the ones they love. And like Digger here—" Zoey patted his smooth head "—they want to know they're not going to be abandoned."

Jill narrowed her eyes. "Seriously?"

"Yes," Zoey said, chin up. "I know you all think I'm just an animal nut, but I pay attention to other things, too."

"Of course you do," Carly said.

"I noticed a kindred spirit when Levi first came into the shop with Digger. He didn't just buy what he needed, but also some of the stuff he thought Digger would like, too. I think I knew before he did that this was no temporary adoption. Digger's always going to be with him. Huh, Digger? See, I think Levi's a rescuer. Maybe not an animal rescuer, like I am, but a people rescuer. And who knows? Maybe he's hurt because he thinks you're abandoning him, Carly."

"But…but I told him I wanted him to come see me in New York."

"Those are just words. Don't you think Digger heard them once, too? 'Oh, you're so cute. You're coming home with me. It'll be fun. Oh, wait, I changed my mind.' Do you know how many times that happens?"

"You're getting sidetracked, Z." Jill nudged Zoey. "I don't think she's going to leave him at the pound."

"Well, you know what I mean," Zoey said. "You need to put your words into action."

"I know exactly what you mean," Carly said, near tears again. "Levi's my dog."

"Exactly!"

"What are you two fools talking about?" Jill said.

"He needs to understand that I didn't lie to him. There's such a thing as changing your mind. And I'm not going to abandon him when I go to New York. He needs to know that. More than words. I need more than words."

Actions, more so than words, could never lie.

"Uh-oh," Jill said, turning to Zoey. "What have you done?"

Zoey just smiled.

"Would you two watch Grace for me?" Carly said. "I've got to go to the airport."

TODAY HAD BEEN the day from hell.

His day had gone as if all the forces in the universe had gotten together and decided *this* was the day Levi Lambert would be tortured to within an inch of his sanity. *This* was the day he'd have difficult, entitled passengers. *This* was the day he'd have mechanical failures and have to change planes. *This* was the day every damn delay possible would present itself. *This* was the day a woman would make her way onto the tarmac and wave her arms around like ground control.

Wait. What?

Okay, that was not possible. Yet right before him, his twenty-twenty vision did not lie. He saw Carly arguing with Jedd, who was trying to pull her into the hangar. Levi removed his aviator glasses. She was still there, the crazy woman.

Good thing this wasn't yet a regional airport or she'd probably be under arrest by now.

"Dude, who the hell is that?" entitled passenger number ten of the day asked.

He was taking a skateboarding pro and his entourage to some kind of exhibition in Reno. "Another delay."

"Dude, she's hot. Maybe we can take her with us. As long as she's not nuts."

Levi ignored that and stopped his preflight safety check. Now he'd have to start all over again. Man, this day. Somebody shoot him. He climbed out of the plane and walked toward Carly, unable to hear anything but the blood coursing through his veins. There had better be nothing wrong with Grace. But he'd checked his phone right before boarding and there'd been no new messages. And if there was something wrong with Grace, Carly wouldn't waste time coming here when she could be on her way to the hospital to have a skinned knee checked by an orthopedist.

"Sorry, Levi," Jedd said.

"It's fine." Levi waved him off. He turned to Carly. "Is Grace okay?"

"Yes! She's fine. Zoey and Jill are watching her. That's not what this is about."

"Then…what?"

She squinted at him in the bright sun. "Why didn't you answer my text?"

He nodded toward the plane. "I'm a little busy here."

"That was hours ago." She wrung her hands together.

He stared at her, his heart shifting painfully at her obvious discomfort. She knew the answer. He was too pissed to talk. Or text. He was being a child, in other words. Not wanting to deal with the fact that she'd hurt him because he'd opened himself up to the opportunity. Not wanting to face the fact that he was a grown-ass man with a few abandonment issues. Not wanting to deal, period. Give him his bird and the safety of the open skies and he'd be all right. Eventually.

"I have to explain." She looked past him, and Levi followed her gaze to his passengers plastered up against the windows, watching them.

"Ignore them."

"Okay." She took a breath and closed her eyes. And kept them closed. "I know we promised not to keep anything from each other. I was going to tell you about New York as soon as I decided, but I didn't have a chance before you saw the text. And I do love you, Levi. That's the truth. I wanted to tell you in a place where you had to know that I meant it. There's no other reason I'd say this right here and now. This is terrifying. I might be arrested at any moment and, even if I'm not, I'm pretty sure Stone is going to be royally pissed at me. There's no other really good feeling that could be influencing me right now. If you know what I mean." She opened one eye to peek at him. "These aren't just words to me."

His heart pinched, because she looked so small and vulnerable out here under the bright sky. He loved her so much it physically hurt. She'd taken a risk coming out here now, knowing he was angry.

Also taken a risk being the first to say *I love you*. And so far, she was still all alone in that. Her courage slayed him.

Just like clockwork, Stone marched toward them looking like a pissed-off warden. This might not be a regional airport yet or have TSA, but Stone did not suffer fools. Even fools in love.

"I've got to go now," Carly said and walked toward Stone.

Levi watched them both walk to the hangar, Carly leading the way, Stone following her like he wanted to make sure she wouldn't turn back. The door opened and shut.

Never miss a chance to tell the people you love how you feel.

He had a flight and passengers waiting. But you know what? To hell with it. He turned, gave them a hold-on sign, then jogged to the hangar. Opened the door and there stood Carly, clearly being lectured by Stone while surrounded by Cassie, Jedd, Sarah, Matt and Emily. They all turned to him expectantly when he strode in.

Yeah, he didn't know what he was doing because, for the first time in years, his emotions were calling the shots for him. This was strange, the feverish pounding of his pulse in his eardrums. His sweaty palms. So odd, it almost didn't feel like his body as he moved toward Carly and everyone stepped out of his way. But then he picked her up in his arms and it felt very much like him. Like a part of him he'd forgotten. The best part.

She smiled, and everyone smiled now. Even Stone, though it was a reluctant pull of his lips.

"I love you, Carly." And the words weren't hard to say at all.

"I'm sorry?" Matt cupped a hand to his ear. "I don't think I heard that."

"Say it louder, flyboy," Stone said. "So those in the back can hear."

"He said he loves her," Cassie said. Loudly. "Are you all hard of hearing? I'm sixty-seven and I heard him clear as a bell."

"I love you." Levi set Carly down. He turned to his audience. "I said I love her. But the rest of this is private."

Emily folded her arms. "There is no such thing as private at Mcallister Charters and Magnum Aviation. We're family here."

A loud, obnoxious, intrusive family. The kind he'd grown up without. He loved them, too, and what's more, he needed them. They were all going to help him and Carly raise Grace. He didn't need to do this alone. Didn't want to.

"I still need a minute alone with my girl." With that, he took her by the hand and pulled her into Stone's inner office.

Of course, they all followed and stopped just outside the door. "You're all extremely annoying." He shut the door.

"We know," Matt said from behind the now-closed door.

"Am I your girl?" Carly said.

He tipped her quivering chin up. "You don't think you can back out now, do you?"

"Never."

"Let's get one thing clear. I don't want anyone else. While you're gone, I'm going to be some kind of monk. There's no one else for me. I said I wouldn't share you, and it goes both ways."

She met his gaze, her hazel eyes piercing into his. "I don't have to go if you want me to stay. Maybe I can find some other way to finish. An online pro—"

"No. You need to go back. I'm not going to be the one who keeps you from finishing what you started."

"But I don't want to abandon you. Or Grace."

"You won't. I'll make sure of that."

"Do you mean it?"

"But if that human piece of excrement is still there, you tell me, because I'll need to pay him a visit."

"You always have my back."

"I always will."

"I'm going to miss you like crazy. Will you promise to come see me?"

"As often as my hard-ass boss lets me." He directed this comment, loudly, in the direction of the door.

"Well, excuse me for living," Stone said from the other side.

"Speaking of living." Levi grinned and traced the curve of her lips. "I have to go make one."

She gave him a watery smile full of her heart. "I love you. Did I say that already?"

He pressed his forehead to hers. "You did. And I'm never going to get tired of hearing it."

He kissed her, long, warm and deep. A kiss full of the love he'd kept wrapped up in his cold heart until he'd met the one woman in the world perfectly right for him.

EPILOGUE

December 31

IT WAS NEARLY midnight and beautifully quiet on the evening of Emily and Stone's wedding. The red barn on Emily's ranch was lit by soft candle-light, the rows of seats decorated with white rib-bon and baby's breath.

Levi winked at her from the altar, where he stood next to Matt and Stone. In a black tux, Levi looked drop-dead gorgeous. And he also looked a little like her heart walking around outside her chest. She'd become a little more used to that feel-ing in the past two months, the sensation where she forgot to breathe when he walked in the room. She was so gobsmacked, so head over heels in love with her fiancé that it was a little humbling.

She twisted her engagement ring around her finger, not quite used to its presence there. Her new lucky ring. She'd have to get her mother's ring resized now. She hadn't expected for it all to happen so fast, but the past two months in New York City meant she and Levi had spent more time alone together than they had since they'd first met. And it was still easy. Perfect. He'd sometimes bring Grace along, because Carly missed her desperately, but usually he would leave Grace with Cassie, Emily and Stone, or Matt and Sarah for the weekend. Rather than hang out with her roommates, he'd rent a hotel room in the city, where they'd spend long, lazy mornings in bed. They'd walk in Central Park and eat hot dogs from the street vendors.

It was in Central Park where, last month, Levi had dropped to one knee.

"I've never been this sure about anything in my life. We fit together. Will you marry me?"

Carly had stood, wrapped in her wool winter jacket and scarf, the cold winter air swirling all around them, utterly speechless. Her heart had hammered out of her chest and she'd smiled until it felt like her face would freeze that way permanently.

"Yes or no?" Levi had said with his easy smile. "Don't leave me hanging."

It was only then that she realized she hadn't said her answer out loud. She'd said the words in her heart, where they always seemed to go first.

"Yes!" she'd shouted. "Oh my God, yes!"

"So I can get up now?" He'd winked. "Because it's freaking cold out here. Remember, I'm from Texas."

She'd tugged him up and into her arms. "I love you."

"I'm glad to hear it, because I love you, too."

Then he'd slipped on the ring, and there hadn't been a day since that she'd wanted to take it off.

The wedding party tonight was small and intimate. Too late for the children, so Levi and Carly had left Grace with the new babysitter—a wonderful woman who lived down the street and watched only Grace and her own grandchildren.

The wedding march began, and Rachel, the matron of honor, then Molly and Sarah, Emily's bridesmaids, started down the aisle. When it was Emily's turn to walk down with her father, there was a stillness in the night air that felt almost sacred. The vows were exchanged exactly as the midnight hour began the first day of a new year. Beginnings. Emily had said she would always make Stone observe two wedding anniversaries. The thirty-first and the first. Then he'd never forget.

Carly caught Levi's gaze, and as the vows were spoken, neither broke away from the other's gaze. *To love, honor and cherish. As long as we both shall live. For better or for worse.*

Later, when it was time to dance until the wee hours of the morning, Levi grabbed Carly and pulled her onto the floor. "Are you ready to say those words to me?"

"More than any other words I've ever said. How about you?"

"Never more ready."

He'd proved that to her in the past two months they'd been apart. There had never been a single day without a phone call, usually twice a day. While apart, they'd talk far into the night about their hopes and dreams and plans for the future. A future together.

In New York City, Carly had reconnected with her classmate Jenny and produced a portfolio that had impressed both her and her director. At the moment, Carly and the Cutting Edge were negotiating terms for an offer. Carly would work from Fortune, with two trips a year to the city.

Someday, she might even have her own label. RockYourBaby had a nice ring to it, and she thought Mom would like it, too.

"We have a lot of planning to do," Carly said. "Bring it on."

Oh, she would. She had a surprise for him. He didn't know it, but she'd be coming home sooner than planned. She'd done what she had to do. Finished school. She'd worked hard and had more credits than even she'd realized. And even though Levi had been more than patient, and as loyal to her as she'd been to him, she was ready to come home to Fortune. By spring, her father would be home from Maine, and soon after that there would be a wedding.

She'd done the tough work. Worked out her fears, and gained all her confidence back and then some. Now she wanted easy again, just for a little while.

Easy and perfect, like the rest of her life with Levi and Grace.

* * * * *

If you enjoyed this story,
you won't want to miss
other titles in Heatherly Bell's
HEROES OF FORTUNE VALLEY *series:*

BREAKING EMILY'S RULES
AIRMAN TO THE RESCUE

Available now!

Get 2 Free Books,

Plus 2 Free Gifts—

just for trying the Reader Service!

YES! Please send me 2 FREE Harlequin Presents® novels and my 2 FREE gifts (gifts are worth about $10 retail). After receiving them, if I don't wish to receive any more books, I can return the shipping statement marked "cancel." If I don't cancel, I will receive 6 brand-new novels every month and be billed just $4.55 each for the regular-print edition or $5.55 each for the larger-print edition in the U.S., or $5.49 each for the regular-print edition or $5.99 each for the larger-print edition in Canada. That's a saving of at least 11% off the cover price! It's quite a bargain! Shipping and handling is just 50¢ per book in the U.S. and 75¢ per book in Canada.* I understand that accepting the 2 free books and gifts places me under no obligation to buy anything. I can always return a shipment and cancel at any time. The free books and gifts are mine to keep no matter what I decide.

Please check one: ☐ Harlequin Presents® Regular-Print   ☐ Harlequin Presents® Larger-Print
(106/306 HDN GLWL)   (176/376 HDN GLWL)

Name _____ (PLEASE PRINT) _____

Address _____ Apt. # _____

City _____ State/Prov. _____ Zip/Postal Code _____

Signature (if under 18, a parent or guardian must sign)

Mail to the Reader Service:
IN U.S.A.: P.O. Box 1341, Buffalo, NY 14240-8531
IN CANADA: P.O. Box 603, Fort Erie, Ontario L2A 5X3

Want to try two free books from another series?
Call 1-800-873-8635 or visit www.ReaderService.com.

* Terms and prices subject to change without notice. Prices do not include applicable taxes. Sales tax applicable in N.Y. Canadian residents will be charged applicable taxes. Offer not valid in Quebec. This offer is limited to one order per household. Books received may not be as shown. Not valid for current subscribers to Harlequin Presents books. All orders subject to approval. Credit or debit balances in a customer's account(s) may be offset by any other outstanding balance owed by or to the customer. Please allow 4 to 6 weeks for delivery. Offer available while quantities last.

Your Privacy—The Reader Service is committed to protecting your privacy. Our Privacy Policy is available online at www.ReaderService.com or upon request from the Reader Service.

We make a portion of our mailing list available to reputable third parties that offer products we believe may interest you. If you prefer that we not exchange your name with third parties, or if you wish to clarify or modify your communication preferences, please visit us at www.ReaderService.com/consumerchoice or write to us at Reader Service Preference Service, P.O. Box 9062, Buffalo, NY 14240-9062. Include your complete name and address.

HP17R2

Get 2 Free Books,
Plus 2 Free Gifts—
just for trying the Reader Service!

HARLEQUIN
HEARTWARMING™

HOMETOWN HEARTS ♥

YES! Please send me **The Hometown Hearts Collection** in Larger Print. This collection begins with 3 FREE books and 2 FREE gifts in the first shipment. Along with my 3 free books, I'll also get the next 4 books from the Hometown Hearts Collection, in LARGER PRINT, which I may either return and owe nothing, or keep for the low price of $4.99 U.S./ $5.89 CDN each plus $2.99 for shipping and handling per shipment*. If I decide to continue, about once a month for 8 months I will get 6 or 7 more books, but will only need to pay for 4. That means 2 or 3 books in every shipment will be FREE! If I decide to keep the entire collection, I'll have paid for only 32 books because 19 books are FREE! I understand that accepting the 3 free books and gifts places me under no obligation to buy anything. I can always return a shipment and cancel at any time. My free books and gifts are mine to keep no matter what I decide.

262 HCN 3432 462 HCN 3432

Name	(PLEASE PRINT)	
Address		Apt. #
City	State/Prov.	Zip/Postal Code

Signature (if under 18, a parent or guardian must sign)

Mail to the **Reader Service:**
IN U.S.A.: P.O. Box 1867, Buffalo, NY. 14240-1867
IN CANADA: P.O. Box 609, Fort Erie, Ontario L2A 5X3

READERSERVICE.COM

Manage your account online!

- Review your order history
- Manage your payments
- Update your address

We've designed the Reader Service website just for you.

Enjoy all the features!

- Discover new series available to you, and read excerpts from any series.
- Respond to mailings and special monthly offers.
- Browse the Bonus Bucks catalog and online-only exculsives.
- Share your feedback.

Visit us at:
ReaderService.com

RS16R